Arise The Dead I:
The Great War

MIROLAND IMPRINT 14

Canada Council Conseil des Arts
for the Arts du Canada

ONTARIO ARTS COUNCIL
CONSEIL DES ARTS DE L'ONTARIO

an Ontario government agency
un organisme du gouvernement de l'Ontario

Canadä

Guernica Editions Inc. acknowledges the support of the Canada Council
for the Arts and the Ontario Arts Council. The Ontario Arts Council
is an agency of the Government of Ontario.

We acknowledge the financial support of the Government of Canada.

A family memoir

Arise The Dead I: The Great War

Elizabeth Langridge

MiroLand
publishers

MIROLAND (GUERNICA)
TORONTO • BUFFALO • LANCASTER (U.K.)
2018

Map of the battlefield at Loos
(Crown copyright, the Imperial War Museum, London—with permission)

Connie McParland, series editor
Michael Mirolla, editor
David Moratto, cover and interior book design
Cover Images provided by Elizabeth Langridge
Guernica Editions Inc.
1569 Heritage Way, Oakville, ON L6M 2Z7
2250 Military Road, Tonawanda, N.Y. 14150-6000 U.S.A.
www.guernicaeditions.com

Distributors:
University of Toronto Press Distribution,
5201 Dufferin Street, Toronto (ON), Canada M3H 5T8
Gazelle Book Services, White Cross Mills
High Town, Lancaster LA1 4XS U.K.

First edition.
Printed in Canada.

Legal Deposit—First Quarter
Library of Congress Catalog Card Number: 2017955483
Library and Archives Canada Cataloguing in Publication
Langridge, Elizabeth, author
Arise the dead / Elizabeth Langridge.

(MiroLand imprint ; 14-15)
Contents: Book one. The Great War -- Book two. World War Two.
Issued in print and electronic formats.
ISBN 978-1-77183-281-6 (book 1 : softcover). --ISBN 978-1-77183-284-7
(book 2 : softcover). -- ISBN 978-1-77183-282-3 (book 1 : EPUB).
--ISBN 978-1-7183-283-0 (book 1 : Kindle). --ISBN 978-1-77183-284-7
(book 2 : EPUB) .--ISBN 978-1-77183-286-1 (book 2 : Kindle).

1. World War, 1914-1918--Personal narratives. 2. World War,
1939-1945--Personal narratives. 3. Creative nonfiction. I. Title.
I. Series: MiroLand imprint ; 14-15

D640.A2L32 2018   940.3   C2017-906410-X   C2017-906411-8

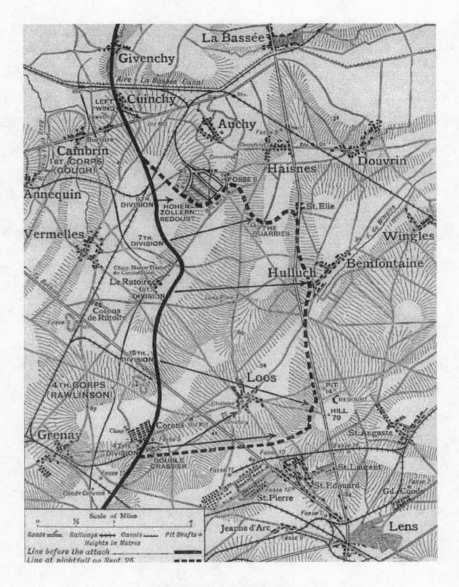

Map of the battlefield at Loos,
late September, 1915, just north of the
coal-mining towns of Lens and Loos,
Pas de Calais, France.

On April 6, 1915, in the face
of an imminent attack by the enemy,
a young French adjutant, Jacques Pericard,
seeing that his comrades in the trench
were either dead or wounded,
cried out: ARISE THE DEAD!

For James Langridge and May Wigley
and all the other 'ordinary' men, women and children
who suffered and endured through the two World Wars,
whose stories are seldom told.

❧ Chapter 1

Lizzie got out of the tour van in front of Le Rutoire Farm from where they could look across the vast, flat plain of the former no-man's-land towards the Lens-La Bassée road to the east, near Loos, Pas de Calais, in north-eastern France.

A dog barked at them from the farm house garden, showing its teeth. The house was new, of course; the old one had been nearly at the Front. From there the communication trenches would have started. The day was sunny, pleasant, although not warm enough for July, tempered by a stiff breeze.

She saw a small brick barn with a steep-pitched roof that looked very old; it would have been sheltered from shells by the original house. Perhaps his eyes had rested on it. There were the remnants of something else, a brick pillar, festooned with ivy; it held the suggestion of a house.

There was no one about, other than the dog and themselves — she and Bob Goode, their guide, and her husband James, along with the few who were remaining behind in the van.

"This way," Bob said, walking ahead along the dirt lane from the farm towards the Hulluch road, a little to the north. "We shall be walking in your father's footsteps, more or less, Lizzie."

She looked about her, scanning the wide open country landscape, flat as far as she could see, with few trees, planted with crops. Going east on the Hulluch road they could see, far to the right, the tall, conical slag heaps, unchanged for decades, from the coal mines at Lens and Loos, and the two towns south of where they were now. Some way ahead and to their left, behind a clump of trees, was the village of Hulluch, which had been held by the Germans. This was the landscape that her father would have seen in 1915, the beauty of it littered with the excrescence of war. All was tidied up now. Yet, as she looked out over the windswept crops, she imagined that she could see, hear and smell something of that vulgarity.

That day she and James, with the five other people on the tour, the two guides, and the van driver, had come from Paris. Later that day they would go on to Ypres in Belgium, where the war had started in the summer of 1914. They had two weeks. Later still, they would go to Passchendaele, then southward along the old Western Front, through Ploegsteert and Neuve Chapelle, back into France. They would continue south, in a wavy line, back past Loos to Vimy Ridge, to Beaumont Hamel where the Newfoundlanders had been wiped out, on to Arras, the Somme, Reims, then all the way down to the Verdun sector and to the St. Mihiel Salient, where the Americans had been in the last two years of the war.

"Between these two landmarks, north and south — the village of Hulluch over there at the north end," Bob said, pointing east towards Germany, "— and the slag heaps that you see on our right at the south end, close to the town of Loos, was the plain of Loos that we're starting to walk across now. This is where the battle took place. The Germans called it 'the corpse field of Loos' and they were referring to our men, not their own. This is the no-man's-land, where there was almost no cover from enemy fire, as you can see. It hasn't changed much."

"I don't know why my father came into this war," Lizzie said. "I wish I knew."

"I expect he was wondering that when he got here," James said.

"There was one tree near the British lines, the Lone Tree on trench maps," Bob said. "It was a flowering cherry. There had been a first-aid dugout near it, for the Queen's Own Royal West Kent Regiment."

"Yes, I read about it in a regimental history," she said. Perhaps her wounded father had gone there first. For over ten years she had read about the war, looked at maps, pondered. "The tree was destroyed by a shell on the night of the 25th September, 1915. That was the night that my father came up to the Front, into the firing line."

"Yes. That was a great loss, because the tree was a landmark," Bob said. "I expect it was blasted in front of his eyes on that night."

Beyond the Lens-La Bassée road — the road that they could see now in the distance to the east, running north and south — beyond the deep banks of German barbed wire and the lines of enemy trenches, there had been Stutzpunkt IV, a gun emplacement. That was their impossible objective then. Few had got beyond the Lens-La Bassée road.

Now all was quiet, save for a wind blowing and murmuring among the stalks of wheat that stretched before them as far as the horizon and the line of the blue summer sky.

"This is the St. Mary's Cemetery, looked after by the Commonwealth War Graves Commission," Bob Goode said, as they stopped on the Vermelles to Hulluch road. "It's the site of the St. Mary's Advanced Dressing Station, the first place that the wounded could go to, or be taken to, nearest to the battle, apart from any first-aid posts. The aid posts were vulnerable to being shelled and knocked out. Your father would have come here, Lizzie, for sure."

The place was rural and beautiful, planted with a few trees whose branches shifted in the wind.

It was a small, walled cemetery by the road and on the edge of crops. There was a substantial wrought iron gate that one walked through, by a tall white cross of remembrance that bore the words: "Their name liveth for evermore." On the cross, etched out of the stone and painted gold, was a sword. There was no sound other than the creaking of the gate hinges as they went through it, no traffic on the road.

Did a sword and a cross go together? Lizzie wondered, as they let themselves through the gate into the enclosed space. For did not Jesus Christ say, "Let he who is without sin cast the first stone"?

Her hiking boots crunched on the gravel path as they crossed it to get to the lawn where the grass was very green and neatly trimmed, with no weeds. Birds were twittering in the few trees. Rows of white stones, each one with a rose bush and clump of lavender in front, filled the walled space. Tiny wooden crosses, with poppies of remembrance pinned to them, had been left here and there, stuck in the ground by visitors. In other places Lizzie had read epitaphs that had brought her to tears. "We mourn in silence, unseen" had been one of them. Now she looked for those few words penned by families who had lived over eight decades ago. Time had halted here, she thought; this place held the grief that was timeless.

"The St. Mary's Advanced Dressing Station on this site would have been underground, dug out," Bob said. "This was the burial ground then too, of course."

"Very convenient," James said.

Were you here, Dad? Lizzie asked the question silently.

The three of them walked along the rows of grave stones, looking at the names and the ages. Most had been between nineteen and twenty-two. In the normal course of events, these young men would have been the fathers and grandfathers of her generation. Now she was old enough to be a mother, or a grandmother, to most of them, petrified in time as they were. Here in this time that was out of joint, she felt something of the maternal mourning that surrounded them.

Those graves that housed the unidentified stated: "A Soldier of the Great War: Known unto God." Lizzie's eyes ached with tears as the three of them walked quietly and stood about, feeling like trespassers. At the same time their presence, the living, somehow affirmed that these young men had indeed lived. Here we are; we have come to see you, to bring you something of home. We have crossed an ocean. Here we are; we carry on. We mourn you and miss you; but nonetheless, somehow, we are here, we have found our way to you.

As a still-born baby, named, is affirmed as having lived once, outside the private love and mourning of its mother, so these young men were affirmed again, briefly. They had passed out of living memory. Even the unidentified could be conjured up in the wholeness of their youth. How much better if they had lived out their full span, Lizzie thought as she stood on the pristine grass, looking down at their names, at the roses and the lavender. The gardens were obviously tended carefully by professional gardeners. Here they were, these young men, far from home, in this alien soil, sacrificed by those to whom they had been instrumental and nothing more.

She stood in the wind, in the dappled sunlight, seeing above the low cemetery wall the slag heaps to the south, where there had been coal mines, and the vast plain to the east. It was easy here to believe in ghosts, in unquiet spirits. In the iron-fronted cupboard in the stone gatepost there was a tattered copy of a list of soldiers who were buried there, their names and addresses and the names of their parents, as though the parents were in those places waiting still for their sons to come home.

From there, Bob Goode, James, and Lizzie left the Hulluch road and took a dirt track directly across no-man's-land, a path made for farm machinery now. A few wild flowers grew beside the track, cornflowers, red poppies, clover, daisies, buttercups, and vetch.

"Look there," Bob said, pointing. Beside the track was a small pile of rusted shells. "Those are the big ones, full of shrapnel. You can see that most of them are unexploded. These come up with the farm machinery. The farmers pile them there, then the Army comes to pick them up now and then. They blow them up." On close inspection, they could see two rusty hand grenades among the shells.

"The farmers were brave to farm this land afterwards," James said.

"Yes. The land was cheap," Bob said.

Why have I come here? The question again presented itself to Lizzie, daughter of a soldier. Was it to try to make sense of what had happened here, even if that meant to acknowledge that there was no sense to be found? Was it to find a renewed sense of her father? Coming here was an act of respect, an act of remembrance. Her father and those others had come to right a wrong, so they had believed, not knowing what they were getting into. She had come, too, to be close to the spirit of the man she had not known when he was young. For surely something of that young man whose senses had taken in this landscape still lingered here. It lingered in her, if nowhere else.

Yes, I have an affinity with this soil, she thought; the blood of my people was shed here. Their names are on the memorials and on the graves, my family names and the names of my countrymen. Thirty-seven young men with my name were killed here on the Western Front. It is not a common name. They are there, etched in stone, on memorials and in cemeteries.

They walked on, along the rutted track, the three of them, in the footsteps of many men, thinking, asking. They could not yet see the roofs of the houses of Hulluch through the trees that shrouded the village. *The landscape speaks to us if we know how to hear it,* Lizzie thought.

There is an urge, an obsession, to undo events, as though it were possible to do so — events of such an unnatural and implacable nature, ending in the fait accompli of death, that the one contemplating them is brought to the edge of madness, or into the abyss itself. How far back in human history does one have to go to find the original meaning of the word 'justice', that which is right?

"Thou shalt not kill." Is that far back enough? Is that right?

Bob Goode walked among the crops, picking up little balls of shrapnel, made of lead, brought up by the plough. He knew what to look for, where to look. "There is so much weaponry that it will never come to an end," he said, as they passed another small pile of rusted shells placed at the roadside by a farmer.

"Here," he said, tipping ten or so of the heavy, small spheres into Lizzie's hand. "These are for you, from the Battle of Loos. When the big shells exploded, these things sprayed out. You wouldn't credit the damage they could do, by just looking at them."

"Oh, I would, I would. Thank you."

It had rained in the night and puddles of water lay in the ruts of the track, on the clay soil. Here and there were piles of chalk, dug up by farmers, left by the sides of the tracks.

The Lens-La Bassée road had been covered by the fire of enemy machine guns. Then beyond that road, beyond the old German first line, had been the banks of barbed wire. White clouds now moved with the wind from Hulluch to Loos. Then there had been smoke and chlorine gas.

The men had said then that the machine guns sounded like giant sewing machines. They had said that from a distance the mounds of men who had fallen looked like sleeping sheep in a field at home. She had read those descriptions in anthologies, in the brief outpourings of men of the infantry who had been there, the survivors whose words had seen the light of day decades later. No doubt those few had thought they would be forever silenced.

The wheat gave way to crops of peas and beans, here and there. As the three of them approached the road, larks were singing in the sky, hovering, tiny black dots. Lizzie had not seen larks since she was a child in Sussex. It was surprising that there were any left here because, she thought, larks nested on the ground. Didn't they?

"The 8ᵗʰ Battalion of the Royal West Kents would have crossed about here," Bob said, pointing. "Those that got this far."

A single cyclist moved from left to right, north to south, coming from the direction of La Bassée, then was lost to view, swallowed up by the road.

Lizzie, with Bob and James, walked across the newly surfaced road. There was no other traffic. "The Germans were dug in along that small ridge, so they could look down at the advance," Bob said. "They had every advantage. They cut the boys down as they came over this road. Way over there was Stutzpunkt 1V, the enemy dug-in heavy artillery, and the final objective for them. Taking that was an impossible task."

"Yes."

"The British heavy artillery on the day before, the 25ᵗʰ, which was the bombardment before the first advance, was supposed to breach the wire," Bob said. "But when the few survivors made it to the wire, on the 26ᵗʰ, they found no holes in it, so of course they couldn't get through. They tried, God knows they tried. The Germans had come out in the night and repaired any holes."

"I read about it in a history of the 8ᵗʰ Battalion. The Colonel of the 8ᵗʰ was wounded out here, in front of the wire, on the 26ᵗʰ September," Lizzie said, looking about her. "He was lying on the battlefield for a long time, because no one could bring him in. The Germans picked him up eventually, when it was safe. Because he was an officer, I suppose."

"They picked up others as well, treated their wounds."

They walked on, up a slight incline. "When the reserves came over here, on September 26, my Dad with them, the fields were littered with the dead and dying of the day before," she said. "My Dad's lot had been told not to stop to give water to anyone, not to help anyone, just to keep going."

"Yes, that's more or less standard," Bob said.

"I feel sick to think of it."

"The old German trench was somewhere here, their first line," Bob said. "The men coming over here on the 25th, the first day of the battle, found it full of German dead, presumably killed by our heavy artillery. There was fierce fighting. A few Germans reoccupied it during the night of the 25th, but most were in another trench behind the barbed wire."

They climbed slowly up the incline towards the low ridge, a slight elevation scarcely worthy of the name. Where there was now peace and silence, there had once been the screams and cries of the wounded as they waited to die, the crack of rifle fire and the tac-tac of machine guns, then the roar and crash of shells as the advancing men came under enfilading fire. During the night there would have been the unholy commotion of the heavy artillery, the clouds of earth rising up into the air, the craters forming in the earth that a short time before had brought forth crops.

Somewhere here, Lizzie thought, he was hit by shrapnel. He must have walked, or crawled, in agony, to the St. Mary's Advanced Dressing Station, dripping blood from the clumsily applied first field dressing, getting into whatever cover he could find on the way, the shell holes, the abandoned trenches, listening posts, tunnels for saps. Once in the dubious sanctuary of the dressing station, the medical officer would have dug out the shrapnel, probing through sensitive flesh without anaesthetic, Lizzie imagined. With each jab of the instruments he must have welcomed again the gift of life, even as he cursed in order to bear the pain. With luck, there might have been a tot of rum for him. Luck was in short supply that day.

"What does it all mean?" Lizzie said to Bob, an American who had walked the battlefields for decades, from his teen years, to search out the isolated places where no one else went, where trenches still remained in lonely woods, where no birds sang. That was his passion. *Lest we forget.*

"There is no meaning, other than what you can see and imagine," he said. "The extent of your imagination is the extent of its meaning, the extent of the madness of mankind. If your imagination, your intuition, tell you that its only purpose is to kill, to murder, then that is its meaning. It does not have to do with politics or economics; it has to do with the dark pathology of the human mind. The intent is there in the brains of man. One must assume such madness, or go mad oneself."

Old men killing young men in their millions, she thought. Old men far behind the lines. Old men who rode out on sleek horses, who moved pins about on maps, drank the best wine in chateaux, slept in proper, clean beds, removed from their decisions.

Names of some of those old men came to her: French, Haig, Joffre, Foch, Falkenhayn, Ludendorf, Asquith, the Kaiser, Lloyd George, Kitchener, men who would order the deaths of hundreds of thousands, who now stood as bronze statues in prominent places in cities. Lizzie, steeped in readings and lectures on war, saw the young men killed before they had a chance to mate, to bring forth young. Was that the intention?

They climbed up to where the land met the sky. "Over there, Stutz-punkt 1V," Bob said. "All this has to do also with the uses and abuses of power. It's not normal to crave power over others. Power can be perverted, and generally is."

Lizzie turned to look back over no-man's-land, over softly waving barley, where shell-holes, craters from saps, trenches, had long ago been filled in. Here the secret soil still cradled bones of young men, those rusting shells, some never exploded as she knew now, the detritus of murder. Once in a while the earth gave up her treasures, as she had seen.

"Your father never saw this view exactly, not from this distance."

"No."

They could see over to where the British trenches had been, in front of Le Rutoire Farm to the west. The farm looked tiny now from this distance, as did the small, walled cemetery, with its few trees inside and the tall white cross at its entrance.

So this was where the four regiments, the Royal West Kents, the 'Buffs', the East Surreys, the 'Queens', came out of the trenches in front of Le Rutoire Farm and the Lone Tree ridge on the 26th September, 1915, at 11a.m.

"Quo fas et gloria ducunt." That was their motto: "Where duty and glory lead." Did any man believe it? Duty, perhaps, but not glory. They were there to help the Belgians and the French against tyranny. That must have been why they had joined up, those volunteers of the reserves, who had been cut down like so many stalks of wheat at harvest.

This was where they had come out, up out of the earth, on command, had walked as though on parade, following orders, steadily and in perfect order and discipline. Ten thousand had come out on that morning. Of those, seven thousand and five hundred, thereabouts, had died, been maimed or otherwise wounded, in the space of a few hours. They had achieved nothing of a military nature.

What bitterness.

Lizzie understood the mind of the working man, of the infantry, bearing the weight of his own history upon his shoulders, out of serfdom, bowed down by the ascription of his inferiority by his self-appointed superiors.

In private she would weep.

This was where they had swarmed out, each man of common sense, Lizzie speculated, knowing that their task was impossible and asking: "Why?" Defence, she thought, was one thing, offence quite another. In offence you lose your defence; you lose your men.

∽ Facing the wide plain of Loos from higher up, beyond where the thick coils of enemy barbed wire would have been, Lizzie looked out from where he would not have been able to look, taking it in with all her senses. Seed of his seed, bone of his bone, blood of his blood, flesh of his flesh. Against all odds she was here.

Was she here to finish something for him? There had been a compulsion and a longing to come.

For a long time she looked.

It was July, 2004.

❧ Chapter 2

October 1914

Afterwards, James Langridge could not have said with any precision why he had gone to the army recruiting office that day in Tunbridge Wells, Kent, on the 26th October, 1914, and joined up. He had been sent a notice, but he could have declined even then.

Perhaps it had more to do with the sense that he did not want to lose face with his foreman and the others on the farm where he worked, having mentioned to the man that he was thinking of joining up and had given a tentative two weeks' notice. Normally he would have had to give at least one month's notice. These were not normal times. A strange, feverish, excitable fear and indignation seemed to have gripped most people and caused normal common sense to be suspended.

Sometimes one made life-altering decisions for the wrong reasons — he was well aware of all that, decisions that one could not easily get out of, if at all. Yet on he went, as though compelled by a fate that was out of his hands.

Another explanation was that he had been thinking it over during the month of October because several men he knew from the village had joined up. Increasingly it seemed like a good idea: to do his duty by his country's pact to help Belgium in her hour of need, on the side of right against wrong.

Perhaps it had something to do with the beer that was sloshing about in his stomach when he came out of the Duke of York pub in the town, that it was a half-day off after a period of heavy, back breaking work. Then he felt a familiar discontent, wished fervently for a change in his life, for an adventure. Here was one, staring him in the face, presented to him.

That he could be killed was, of course, a possibility, one that seemed far outweighed by the chances that he would live and the probability that the war would be a mere skirmish, over in three months. If that were the case, he might never actually leave England.

The final impetus came from a poster that was stuck up on a wall near the pub. On the way out it seemed more compelling. "Gallant Little Belgium," it said, showing a drawing of Belgium personified as a beautiful young woman with flowing garments being picked up with one arm by a demonic looking Hun, on whose lascivious face was the clear intent of ravishment. Implied in this illustration, Jim thought, was the message that the Hun would also ravish English women if only he could get across the channel in sufficient numbers.

Not that Jim believed that; it was clearly propaganda. Yet the truth of the matter was that the Germans were indeed in Belgium, intent on getting through into France, that, as it was now, the small British Army could not hold out in helping the Belgian forces. Even with the realism, tempered with cynicism, that came with his twenty-nine years of maturity, he was moved in some way by the poster. It seemed to appeal to him directly and privately as an individual. That, too, he knew was vanity.

When he left the vicinity of the public house, he walked towards the High Street. If he kept walking he would come to the railway station, near where he had seen the army recruiting office, where he had been instructed in the Notice to report if he intended to go through with it.

A drizzle of rain was coming down, depressing and cold. He turned up the collar of his jacket and pulled his cloth cap down closer to the tips of his ears.

For army purposes he supposed that the work he did on the farm would be considered labouring work; he would be classed by them as a labourer. There was much skill in what he did. It took time to learn about the ways of horses that he had worked with since the age of fourteen: how to care for them, groom them, and treat their illnesses, to harness and drive them, with the plough, the reaper, the hay wagon. It took knowledge and skill to sow and reap, to tend crops while they were growing, to milk cows and to care for them.

As he walked up the slight incline of the High Street, his tread slow while he was thinking, he understood that if he did not have an adventure soon it was likely that he might never have one. Was that a good enough reason? Back and forth his mind went, taking in possibilities and probabilities. No certainties came to mind then. How could one ever be certain about anything like that? It was because people were certain in specific issues, such as whether to fight or not, he suspected, that they went over into madness.

He was short and stocky, strong and muscular, with no excess weight on his frame. His fine dark hair was plastered to his forehead by rain below the cap; his skin was pale, his eyes a clear blue. Aware of himself as outwardly a type, of his rough hands that were the hallmark of a working man, which also helped to define him on the social scale, he knew in himself that no man or woman was ever the same as another. Each one occupied a space that could never be encroached upon by another, the hidden self. Only in deep love could another know that place, partially.

Occasionally, another person looked at you as though they saw you as you really were, as you saw yourself at your best, as they acknowledged your humanity. As a soldier he would be even more of a type, a machine of flesh and blood that could be used as a means to an end.

That week he had mustered up the courage to ask for a pay rise from the foreman, up from the thirteen shillings a week that he was paid for the dawn to dusk work, to be told by the foreman that if he were to be given a rise, someone else would have to be sacked. Usually a fair man, the foreman was not the one who finally decided on the rate.

How could a man marry on that money? Anne Jefferson, training to be a cook in private service, was waiting for him, he sensed, to ask her, but they would live close to starvation if she had a child. They had something of a silent agreement between them, which would be brought out into the open when there was a possibility that it could come to fruition. Anne, fragile looking, fair and sweet, worked in her way as hard as he did. After he had paid his landlady, a widow, for his lodging and his food, he had little left. Always he gave something to his mother, who lived in Penshurst, nearby.

Slowly he walked, head down, mulling it over. The clop clop of horses' hooves and the trundle of wheels of the delivery vans and carts going by on the High Street served to draw him into the normality of everyday living, divorced from the life that would be his if he joined up. The tedium of much of that life, slow moving and predictable, for the most part, weighed him down. He moved around from job to job among the villages, trying to better his prospects by a shilling or two here and there, keeping his ears open all the time for something better.

Now he gave part of his mind to how he was going to get back to the village of Fernden. To get to the town he had walked part of the way, then got a lift with a carter with his two-horse van. With luck, he would do the same on the way back.

∾ At the recruiting office there were a few other young men milling about, mooching up and down in the street, with their hands in their trouser pockets, their caps pulled down, feigning nonchalance. One of them approached Jim as he stood, indecisive, looking up at the building. "They say that, once you've taken the 'King's shilling,' you can't get out of the army. They shoot you for desertion if you try to get out."

"Is that so?" Jim looked at the other fellow, who was fair haired, thin of face, and intelligent looking, a little taller than himself, strong and weathered.

"Are you going to join up?"

"I'm thinking about it," Jim said.

"I'll go in, if you will," the other said. "They might not take me, since I had TB when I was a kid. You have to have a medical, they do it on the spot."

"Right you are, mate," Jim said, dwelling on the depressing words of the farm foreman. Perhaps if he left his job, the ones who were left would get more money, and have to work twice as hard. "What's your name?"

"Roy Carter." The other man Jim judged to be younger than he looked, perhaps twenty-five, although there was a hardness about him. Jim took his extended hand. "I'm training to be a gamekeeper, with my father."

Roy, Jim noted, was carefully dressed in grey wool trousers and a neat black jacket, waistcoat, with a narrow tie and a tie-pin, and a nicely ironed white shirt with a thin blue stripe. A gamekeeper was, after all, a cut above a common labourer, and had to keep up appearances in his Sunday best.

Together they went into a cavernous hall that had once been a ballroom. Jim's legs felt as though they had a life of their own, divorced from the directives of his brain, as they carried him forward. Several other young men followed along behind them. Recruiting officers in uniform were sitting at tables.

A motley crew of men, mostly in their Sunday best, which was not saying much, stood about in some semblance of queuing in front of the tables. As Jim looked about him he saw that some of the 'men' were maybe fourteen or fifteen, while some others looked far too old and tired, as though they had not eaten a square meal for a long time. The majority of them appeared to be between sixteen and twenty-three.

Curiosity drew him in, together with Roy Carter, while he was still nagged by the common sense thought that he ought to get out. It was as though his body had developed a stubbornness of its own. Behind the tables there were screens of wood and fabric, behind which naked men, inadequately screened for privacy, could be glimpsed. There was a smell of damp wool and old sweat.

In due course Jim found himself standing behind a wooden chair that was in front of a table with a recruiting officer at it. Now was the time to flee, yet the presence of the other men in waiting had an inhibiting influence on him. The insignia of the regiment for which the officers were recruiting was displayed on a poster behind the table: "The Queen's Own Royal West Kent Regiment."

"I'll meet you outside, mate," Roy Carter said to Jim, "if we get through this. We'll go for a drink."

Jim fingered the pennies inside his trouser pocket, thinking that perhaps he had just enough money for a half pint of beer. "Right you are, mate."

"Sit down, man," the officer said. "Name, please."

"James Langridge."

"Did you receive a Notice?"

"Yes, Sir." He fumbled in his pocket and handed over the piece of paper.

In short order he found himself behind the screens being asked to strip off in front of a medical officer, who fired questions at him. The man measured his chest.

"Thirty eight inches," he said. "Breathe in as much as you can and hold your breath." Jim's chest was measured again. "Forty one inches. Do you have fits, Langridge?"

"No, Sir."

"You're A1. Take this form and go back to the Attesting Officer."

On the table in front of him was a form that would be filled in by the officer, which Jim could read upside down. He saw Short Service (Three years with the Colours) at the head of it. The sick excitement and apprehension that he felt informed him that he could still get up and walk out, yet he remained as though glued to the chair. After giving his name again, his age and address — and noting that the form stated "apparent age" and that he was not asked for a birth certificate, he answered most of the other questions with a 'yes' or a 'no'. His religion was duly noted.

"Can you read and write?"

"Yes, sir."

"Are you willing to serve for a term of three years, unless war lasts longer than three years?"

"Yes."

"You are required to swear an oath," the Attesting Officer informed him. "Please repeat after me: 'I, James Langridge, swear by Almighty God, that I will be faithful and bear true Allegiance to His Majesty King George the Fifth, his Heirs and Successors, and that I will, as in duty bound, honestly and faithfully defend His Majesty, His Heirs, and Successors, in Person, Crown, and Dignity, against all enemies, and will observe and obey all orders of His Majesty, His Heirs and Successors, and of the Generals and Officers set over me. So help me God.'"

Stumbling a little over the words, his mouth dry as though he had never drunk the beer a short while ago, Jim repeated those put to him. Even with the cynicism that he thought had come to him in his relative maturity, he felt the import of the moment and was moved by it, against his will, as he finally signed his name to the form of Attestation that would commit him to the oath that he had made.

"You will report to Maidstone barracks tomorrow, the 27th October, Langridge, where you will be approved and appointed finally to the Royal West Kent Regiment by the Approving Officer responsible for recruitment there, Captain J. Walter. Is everything clear to you?"

"Yes, Sir. Thank you, Sir."

"Goodbye, and good luck."

∽ Stiffly he walked out into the fresh air and drizzle. A sense of shock held him, something like panic, for he was no longer a free man. With undue haste, it seemed to him, the attestation had been achieved, with hardly time to think before he had to report to Maidstone barracks. It sounded grand, in a way.

"What a lark, mate!" another young man, who had followed him out, said to him. Jim made no reply as he looked around for Roy Carter. Roy was there behind him.

"What about a pint at the Dog and Duck?" Roy asked. "Well, we've done it. For good or for evil, as they say."

"I've only got enough coppers for a half," Jim said. "So they took you on? Even with the TB?"

"I didn't tell them about it, and they didn't ask."

They moved off, up Mount Pleasant, away from the milling men who were undecided about going in to the recruiting office.

"Were you approached by a recruiter?" Roy asked.

"Yes ... about two weeks ago, here. They're very persistent. I suppose now I've joined, he'll get his two shillings and six pence fee, or anything up to five bob."

"I'm beginning to think they're a slimy lot of bastards, those recruiters," Roy said. "They go after young boys. Don't give a damn. Encourage them to lie."

At the pub they sat with their beer and contemplated the deed that they had done, suspecting that it was more momentous than it at first glance appeared. There was comfort in company.

"Perhaps if we're at the barracks at the same time tomorrow they'll put us into the same section," Roy said. "I reckon they're starting a new battalion with us, the volunteers, at the regiment."

"I don't know much about the army," Jim said, nursing the half pint of beer. "I reckon I'll be there by about ten."

"We'll meet there, then, mate."

∽ When he got to the barracks the next day, in another town, he found the regiment overwhelmed by the numbers of new recruits there, with not enough food, cutlery, or plates to feed them, no uniforms, nowhere for them to sleep, very little essential equipment. Some of the new men had been forced to go into the town and buy their own food, young working men who scarcely had two pennies to rub together, and find lodgings.

Early on, he met up with Roy, and they managed to stay together. They searched out a place to sleep, a way to get food from the barracks kitchen.

Then in the following days they found that they had to march and drill in their own clothes at first. The Army had called for men without being ready to receive them. It was a real eye-opener for Jim, the first intimations of a monumental cock-up, a hint of things to come, which brought with it tinges of apprehension.

Weeks went by. He found himself in a section of twelve men, which included Roy, part of a platoon of fifty men. The men quickly formed friendships, held together by a certain amount of bewilderment and apprehensive excitement, and the shared, close life that each young man had hitherto only experienced with his family. When they eventually had their own places to sleep, Jim found himself next to Frank Boakes in the hut, a pale, thin young man, of common sense and sincerity, with a gentle sense of humour that appealed to him and formed a bond between them. When he was with Frank and Roy, although they were all uncertain, Jim had a sense that he had perhaps done the right thing in joining up.

Still they clung to the idea that this was an adventure, perhaps the greatest adventure of their lives. Very soon they found out that there were no real rifles available then; they were issued with wooden rifles for drilling purposes. Even when they had started musketry training, and the sergeant of his section had introduced then to real rifles, with the words, "This here's a Lee-Enfield," the private soldiers had not been issued with their own guns. Jim's apprehension deepened as he learned to march, to wheel, to turn, to fall-in, to fall-out, to present arms, to slope arms, to run at the double, to dig trenches, to stand-to, to stand down, to stand at ease, to march in battle formation, and to march easy. What became apparent was that his country was nowhere near ready for a war with a country like Germany.

The saving grace was those friendships that he built up with his mates, who were with him night and day, in very close quarters. In a hurry you got to know them in all their facets, and they you.

🙠 Chapter 3

It dawned on him more clearly that he would be required to kill, not necessarily cleanly with a bullet at a distance, but perhaps close up with a bayonet. Country boys, used to tending the soil and feeding animals, were being turned into murderers. The shouted order "Fix bayonets!" produced a peculiar withdrawal of one's mental faculties, as all that one had considered civilized was held in abeyance. As he was ordered to run, with rifle and fixed bayonet, at a large sack filled with straw to represent a man, he was required to repeat to himself: "Thrust, twist, pull out; thrust, twist, pull out." They were required to yell as they approached the enemy, whether to distract themselves from the fact of murder, or to try to frighten the enemy, he was not sure. In any event, he felt stupid doing it.

Yet in a perverse way, as time went on, he also felt proud of having come through so far.

🙠 He had had about eight months training with the 8th battalion of the Royal West Kents before they were all shipped over to France on the 30th August, 1915. The troop ship, with others, slipped out quietly from the port of Southampton under cover of darkness, to sail to Le Havre. They were escorted by destroyers that had moved into place beside them in the intense dark of the choppy, open sea of the English Channel.

There were the twelve men of his section, under the section sergeant Jack Dawson, men he had come to know and like. There were now forty-eight men in his platoon, under Lieutenant S. Barton, about twenty-eight years old, a quiet, efficient man, whom they all respected. Then there was the section corporal and the lance corporal, of the NCOs. Some of the officers were aloof, walking around with their swagger sticks and their highly polished Sam Browne gun belts.

Not far out of dock, the ship began to roll in the swells, and he and his best mate, Frank Boakes, were soon spewing over the side of the ship, as were others, trying not to be down-wind of one another.

"Want a fag, Jim?" Frank said, the panacea, as they eased themselves down against the railing of the deck, with their kit around them, to rest after a particularly wretched bout of vomiting. The ship was packed, with scarcely any room to lie down, if it were possible to rest. They all wore life jackets, in case the ship was sunk.

"Yeah," he said. They had difficulty in lighting up, with the wind blowing around them. "Thanks, mate." The other men packed tightly around them gave them courage as they went into the unknown, with strange smells in their nostrils, the need to sleep, and a sick fear and excitement inside them that had nothing to do with the motion of the ship.

Only a month before their departure had they been issued with real rifles of their own.

The sergeant, a good bloke, moved among them in the darkness like a mother hen rounding up her brood. They could not show any lights. "All right, lads?" he said as he went. What could one say to that? If you were not all right, he was not going to do anything; he was not going to put you off the bloody ship. "Be careful to hide those fags. We don't want this to look like a bloody light ship."

The weather was reasonably mild, a warm breeze blowing over the sea, although now and then a small squall of rain would sweep over them.

"When do you reckon we'll be at the front, Jim?" Frank said, their heads close together. Frank was short and wiry, thin, although muscular and strong, as he was himself. Frank had worked on a farm before joining up. Nonetheless, he always looked pale, as though he had never had enough to eat before he joined up. The sun did nothing to change his colour. Like him, Frank had dark hair and blue eyes, his hair cut in the preferred way, longish on top, with the back and sides very short, with a bit of hair that flopped over the forehead.

"Search me," Jim said. "They don't tell us anything, do they? We haven't had what you could call any proper training yet, have we?" What he meant was that they had not been under fire, did not know what real trench warfare was like. Surely they would not be sent into the front line without any such training. Pretending at home, in pristine trenches, that you were under fire was not the same, when you could even see it as a joke.

"No, we haven't," Frank said.

They had drilled and marched, been taught to shoot, been moved from place to place in Kent and Sussex, in billets, in tents, in barracks, to Worthing, Shoreham, Shorncliffe, Blackdown, where others had passed through before them. Now here they were, spewing their guts out, not knowing what was to happen to them. They were told nothing, other than the very next small move.

They disembarked at Le Havre as dawn was coming up. At last, on the dry land of the dock they mustered, hundreds of men, loaded down with kit and rifles, while sergeants and corporals hurried about yelling "Fall in!"

Parties of men were detailed to help unload certain equipment. Every regiment had its own horses and mules, its own artillery, its own field kitchens and supplies. Dog tired, they heaved and shifted things like automatons.

Later, army guides came to show them sheds where they could sleep and the regimental field kitchen cooks got their fires going in their mobile units. "Quick march! March at ease!" Accompanied by the sound of many boots mashing down on tarmac, concrete and cobblestones, they moved back from the immediate vicinity of the docks to an area called Honkville.

Tomorrow they would get on trains. That was the rumour.

Sergeant Jack Dawson, who kept a forbidden diary, wrote in it later, by the light of a candle as he lay on his side in the corner of a dark shed: "We are here on French soil, 31 August, 1915."

∞ Jim and the rest of the 8th battalion, one thousand men in all, following breakfast served from their field kitchens, were marched down the next morning from the sheds and tents to a railway station. "Quick march!"

Their progress was followed by local people, waving and shouting a welcome. At the station there was even a small band playing. For the first time in his life he heard the *Marseillaise*. A small child ran up to him and handed him a peach. In spite of his efforts to maintain a certain cynicism, which he felt might help in some way to preserve his life in a pinch, he felt a pride in his country and what he and the others had come through so far.

Forever he would remember the name of that station, the Gare des Marchandises. Once there, they discovered that they were to travel in cattle cars, each wagon suitable, so the signs said, for forty men. The smell of muck clung to them, prompting expressions of disgust from some of the men. He had never seen such a long train. There were a few proper carriages for the officers.

As they climbed into the wagons at about eleven o'clock, from the platforms that were swarming with men from his own and other battalions, Jim's disquiet grew. Some of the wagons were open at the top, some enclosed, with big sliding doors that could be left open to let in air. It could not escape them that they, like cattle, were being moved closer to the place of slaughter.

For a few shillings the powers-that-be of the British Isles had bought their lives, and were now preparing to take those lives away from them. He had, of course, colluded in that. Each man took his chances, and each man hoped and prayed that the bullet or the shell would not get him. If it was over by Christmas, they had a chance.

There were three army sections in his wagon, together with the NCOs. In unison, they lit up their fags.

"Be careful with those fags," Sergeant Dawson said. "We don't want to set this thing alight."

"That's just what we do want to do," Frank, next to Jim, said. "Then perhaps they would give us a proper train."

"Not likely," he said.

The journey was slow. The train stopped here and there so that they could get out to relieve themselves and have their meals. The weather was warm and sunny. Out of the train, the men flung themselves down in the long grass of the fields beside the tracks, drawing into their lungs the sweet air, which contrasted with the smell of cow muck.

From these stops, as well as from the train, Jim could see that French farming did not seem as advanced as it was at home. The implements lying around seemed like things out of another age. Yet perhaps these French peasants owned their land, which was much more than he could say.

It was a beautiful country, burgeoning with verdant life. An old farmhouse, made of stone, thick with climbing roses and ivy, drew his eyes. Grape vines grew in gardens. When the men stared into the distance, squinting against the light of the golden summer sun, away from the accoutrements of war, they could almost imagine for a few seconds that they were there on holiday. Most of them had never had what could be called a holiday, of more than a day or two, and then never away from home.

They lifted their faces up to the sun, took off their army caps so that the breeze, smelling of hay and flowers, could ruffle their hair. They joked and laughed, sometimes sang, wrote letters home.

Sometimes they got out at stations. They passed through Rouen and a place called Abbeville. After a journey of seventeen hours they arrived at Montreuil, in darkness. It was 4 a.m.

Stiffly they jumped down onto a platform or onto a track, sober from lack of proper sleep. "Number one platoon, fall in!" Sergeant Patterson, the platoon sergeant, yelled. The section sergeants identified their men in the near darkness. Their platoon officer, Lieutenant Barton, conferred with the platoon sergeant.

He, Jim, was in number one platoon and, along with three other platoons, in "A" Company, under Major Rathburn. There were two hundred men in their Company. All seemed chaotic as they milled about, as they jostled to stay close to their section NCOs, their mates of the section, and the platoon sergeant who was rounding them up.

"'A' Company, fall in!"

They shouldered kit and rifles, automatically going through the motions that they had been taught. Mess tins clanked, equipment rattled.

They could hear the snorting and stamping of the horses and mules that had come on the train with them, animals destined to be hitched up to the transport and the gun limbers of the heavy artillery.

Weighed down, each man moved into position.

"'A' Company, right turn! Quick march!"

They moved forward, four abreast, to leave the station from the end of the platform that dipped down and gave way to grass. Before long they found themselves on a road. "Left wheel! Quick march!"

The breeze that played over them was cool and fresh, bringing with it the scent of new hay. The country boys could almost imagine, in the darkness, that they were home.

The sound of marching boots on the road kept Jim connected to the many men in front and behind him, a sound that drew him in to the comradeship of his regiment and those of others around them. Nonetheless, the fear that was a strange knot in his chest did not go away.

"I wonder where the hell we're going," Private Roy Carter, next to him, said.

"I heard Lieutenant Barton tell Jackdaw that we were going to a place called Huck-villers, or near enough."

"I hope there's food before we get there," Roy said, grumbling. "I'm just about ready to drop."

Before long, birds began to chirp and sing.

As the light of dawn, grey and pink, started to manifest itself in the sky, showing the dark shapes of marching men with rifles, an order came down, from the rear, moving up to the front. "Battalion, halt! 'A' Company, halt!"

"Stand at ease! Left turn! March easy!"

They moved into an open field, men pouring in from the road. "Fall out!" the command came, the signal for men to fling themselves down on grass moist with dew. They could see their field kitchens, pulled by mules, coming in with them. In no time, the fires in them would be started up and they would have breakfast.

Eventually, they received bread, a hunk of cheese, two rashers of bacon, and a cup of hot, very sweet tea. As well, they received biscuits for later, iron rations.

Men ate and drank quickly, and a few were soon snoring.

Sergeant Dawson moved round his twelve men, talking to them quietly. "All right, lads? We're going to a place called Huck-villers, into billets, where we can rest for a while and get some kip."

After dawn had come up completely, they marched on. Before long, Jim saw a roadside sign saying Hucqueliers, at what looked like a large village. They marched through the main street and out the other side to farms and brick barns, where they halted. 'A' Company would stay together. Major Rathburn, on horseback, addressed his Company.

Sergeant Jack Dawson announced a roll-call for his section. "Stand at ease!"

What a relief it was to unshoulder the rifle, to sag a little under the heavy pack.

"Private Boakes!"

"Present!"

As the names were read out once again, they seemed to Jim already the names of dead men, out of place in this burgeoning life around them, passing through, as they were, temporarily on the landscape that was not the place of their birth. All around them others were doing the same, shouting out orders, names of the infantry, while their field kitchens, horses and mules, artillery on limbers milled about in organized chaos. There was a moving sea of khaki uniforms. They spread out over the summer meadows.

"Baker! Carter! Church! Hewitt! King! Langridge! Mitchell! Os-borne! Penfold! Tomsitt! Wheeler!"

"All present and correct, Sir," Sergeant Dawson informed his platoon sergeant, who passed the information on to Lieutenant Barton.

"Number one platoon, fall out!"

An orderly came to show them their billets. Special mates stayed close together, hoping to be billeted in the same quarters. Jim moved in with Frank Boakes, Roy Carter, Bert Tomsitt, and Bill King. They went into one of the brick barns that was in good condition and clean, directed up a narrow staircase into a spacious loft that had been swept and cleared of hay and straw.

"Stay out of the lower parts of the barn, if you can," the orderly advised. "There are fleas and lice in the straw. You'll be seeing plenty of those later on. This is where you'll sleep and leave your kit. Be careful with fags here. Better to smoke outside. There are wells where you can get drinking water and water for shaving."

There were windows in the loft and it was light and airy, yet cool enough that they would sleep. Nearby there was a large farmhouse and other barns and out-houses. The officers would no doubt get proper bedrooms in the farmhouse. There was a collective sigh as men divested themselves of their packs, knapsacks and rifles.

Some had already unwound their puttees and eased off their boots when Sergeant Dawson came in. There was an odour of unwashed feet, coupled with the smell of cow muck that had clung to their clothing in the cattle cars.

"I want five volunteers to dig latrines," he said.

No one spoke.

"Well, you enthusiastic lot," he said, looking round, his eyes lighting on Jim and his four mates who had found sleeping places for themselves on the floor near the top of the stairs. "Right, you lot! Carter, Boakes, Langridge, Tomsitt, and King. Follow me."

They rattled down the wooden stairs. They were not displeased, although they longed to sleep. If they were not digging latrines, they would no doubt be detailed for other fatigues before they could sleep.

When this job was over, Jim would shave and wash, sort through his kit, write a letter to his mother, then sleep.

It was Thursday, the 2nd of September, 1915.

∞ His battalion, and others, stayed on at Hucqueliers, waiting for orders. No one of the infantry knew what the next move would be, except that they would move up to the Front eventually, go up the line. Surely they would not go into the front line without having had any experience of being under fire, of real warfare? As the days went by, they grew thoughtful.

There were fatigues on most mornings, trench digging, mock raids, musketry. After one such morning, exhausted, they had a time of rest. Jim's Company had done field firing, wherever they could without endangering the lives of the local population; they had practiced target firing at the seven ranges that had been set up. There had been field exercises and surprise alarms in the night.

He lay on his back in the sun, looking up at the blue sky that had clouds in it like the fleece of sheep. As he lay smoking, his other hand was spread out on the stubble from where wheat had been harvested. In between the stubble were tiny pink flowers here and there, which he identified as scarlet pimpernel.

So much was familiar about this land, so like England, like the green fields and the woods of Sussex and Kent. Yet it was an alien sky, an alien soil that he could feel beneath his outstretched fingers, as was the wind that shifted the tall weeds at the edge of the field. Was this to be his place of death?

An old soldier he had met told him, months back, that it was surprising how quickly a dead man could become a skeleton when exposed to the elements, lying out in no-man's-land. The flesh would retreat from the bony angles of the face. The flesh of the nose and lips would disappear. Bones would poke forth where there had once been fingers. Clothes and boots would hang on bones, reminding any observer that there had once been life.

There was something especially poignant about a man's hands, quiescent in death, he thought, although he had not seen many. Those hands that might have touched, gently, a woman's hair, the velvety ears of a dog, held the hand of a child, dug hopefully in a kitchen garden, grubbed up new potatoes, plucked purple plums from a tree, held a fag as he was doing now.

He felt himself fully in his flesh then, warmed by the late summer sun, by the blood running through him, by the even beating of his heart, impersonal and out of his control, to be sure.

Life was a tenuous thing; he had never felt it so before. How thin was the line between life and death.

"What ch'er, Jim." Frank Boakes stood above him. "I saw you come out here, then you disappeared, and I thought you might have copped it from one of them firing ranges. Some of them blokes can't shoot straight."

"Nah. Just having a little lie down."

"I can make myself scarce if you want to have a kip."

"No. Just thinking."

"You don't want to do too much of that, mate. Not good for your health," Frank said, squatting down beside him. "Here, have another fag." He extended a flattened packet of Woodbines, from which bits of tobacco were dropping out.

"Much obliged, mate." Jim sat up, easing his painful body into the cross-legged position. Over the past few days he had done more than his fair share of fatigues, as well as the obligatory exercises, the night alarms.

They sat side by side, smoking and coughing, the little puffs of white smoke rising upwards and dissipating in the breeze. They both took off their khaki caps, wishing they could take off their puttees and boots as well, which were irksome in the warm weather.

"This is a nice country," Frank remarked, gazing out over the summer fields.

"Yeah. Pity there's a war on."

Frank cleared his throat and spat. "When do you reckon all this will be over, Jim?" Frank's face was pale, as always, now an unnatural pale it seemed to Jim, exhausted, and his hand shook as he held the fag up to his lips.

"Buggered if I know," Jim said, feeling old at twenty-nine as he looked at Frank, five years younger, little more than a boy. "It isn't exactly winding down, is it? Won't be home for Christmas."

"I'm worried about killing a man. I don't know if I can do it."

"I expect when the time comes that you have to defend yourself, or your mates, you'll do it automatically," Jim said. "You won't have to think, because if you take time to think, you'll be dead. That's what I reckon, anyway. Can't say that I've done it." Who was he to talk? When the time came, if he didn't get killed first, he would be in a funk.

"I'm getting a bit sick of that Roy," Frank stated. "Although I like him all right. He never volunteers for fatigues if he can help it. When he sees the corp or the sarge coming, he just happens to be going to the latrines, or something. He's so bloody lazy, he'd let you shit for him if you could."

Jim laughed, considering Private Roy Carter of their section. "Roy's all right. He wouldn't let you down in a fix. I think he's bored a lot of the time. He knows a lot about guns already, his Dad being a game-keeper."

"It's a luxury to be bored in this place. When we get up to the front, we've got to watch out."

"Roy told me about some poachers, back in Kent, who fired a shot-gun at his Dad. There were four or five of them. They picked him up and shoved his head and shoulders down a fox hole, then put a stake between his legs. He had the devil's own job getting out of there, with-out bringing the earth down on him and getting suffocated."

Frank laughed. "I can picture it," he said.

"Well, when his Dad got home, he took Roy out to the woods, put a gun into his hands and taught him how to shoot. They did it every day, until he could more or less do it with his eyes closed. Then when-ever his Dad had to go out at night, he took Roy with him, to cover his back, so to speak. Roy was eleven years old at the time."

"I'll remember that," Frank said. "Might come in useful."

"Come on," Jim said, getting up, "must be time for tea."

They walked back over the peaceful field. Jim felt strangely disem-bodied, wondering what he was doing there. As they neared the centre of the camp, with its tents, wooden huts, barns and outhouses, and the commandeered farmhouse, they could hear men singing, "Take me back to dear old Blighty." Men in khaki swarmed about.

In one of the older, dilapidated barns there were horses that be-longed to the 8th battalion, strong horses for pulling limbers with artil-lery and ammunition, and the field kitchens, then sleeker horses for the officers to ride. Sometimes Jim went in there to stroke and pat them, to inhale the familiar scent of horse. He had an affinity with horses, and now a pity.

A light haze hung over the flat landscape, behind and around them, giving it a surreal air. Grass and shrubs were so bright that they almost hurt the eyes. All around was sweet air, and a scent of smoke from the farmhouse chimney and the field kitchens. Some cooks and orderlies went by them with dixies of tea.

"Tea's up!"

"This is our night off," Frank reminded Jim. "Might as well go into the village and see if we can get drunk."

They had been to the village several times, mainly to a café, an estaminet, where they had drunk wine for the first time in their lives. There, a know-it-all in another section had said to them: "All you need to know of the language for now, you blokes, is 'wee,' 'non,' 'tray bon,' 'sill-voo-play,' and 'mercy'."

"What's wine and beer?"

"Beer is beer and wine is 'van'."

"Tastes like vinegar to me," someone had said.

They found the other men of their section, stood about and drank the sweet, hot tea and ate the chunks of bread that were handed out, smeared with plum jam.

"I'd give anything for a bit of raspberry jam," someone said.

"There are more plums about than raspberries."

"Gooseberry for me," another man chipped in.

Food occupied their thoughts as much as the girls they had left behind, those that had girls. Jim thought of Anne Jefferson, who was not really his girl, but he thought he would like her to be. After he joined up, he asked her to write to him. Already he had received two letters in France.

Later that evening they walked along the road to the village. Left, left — left, right, left, swinging their arms, freely, without packs or rifles.

At the café they did their best to get at least partially drunk on the little money they had in their pockets. It was a small place, packed with men, standing room only, replete with noisy speech and laughter, with a tinge of desperation in it.

Someone found a piano-accordion and began to play.

"Harry! Harry!" someone yelled. "Sing for us!"

Harry Baker, of Jim's section, had a tenor voice that could move a listener to tears and silence, especially when he sang "Bread of he-a-ven, bread of he-a-ven, feed me till I want no more! Feed me till I want no more!"

Harry, shy and blushing, was pushed forward to the front of the room, away from the door and near a fireplace. "Can you play 'Sweet Sixteen'?" he asked the accordion player.

A silence fell as the sentimental and poignant notes of the love song, from the piano-accordion, dominated the room. Even Madame, who ran the café, paused in waiting. Harry, an ordinary sort of a bloke otherwise, took on a quiet authority when he sang, as though he entered another world, as though his talent were a gift of God.

> *When first I saw the love-light in your eye,*
> *I dreamt the world had naught but joy for me,*
>
> *And even though we drifted far apart.*
> *I never dream but what I dream of thee,*
>
> *I love you as I've never loved before,*
> *Since first I met you on the village green,*
> *Come to me, or my dream of love is o'er,*
> *I love you as I loved you*
> *When you were sweet,*
> *When you were sweet sixteen.*
>
> *Last night I dreamt I held your hand in mine,*
> *And once again you were my happy bride,*
> *I kissed you as I did in old lang syne,*
> *As to the church we wandered side by side.*
>
> *I love you as I've never loved before ...'*

Harry made a motion with his hand that they should join in the chorus.

Their voices roared and rose up, as from one man. For a few seconds all was blotted out other than the private image that each man had of a girl who might one day be his, if he were lucky.

> *When you were sweet,*
> *When you were sweet sixteen!*

The next morning after reveille, after the bugle had sounded and they had performed their ablutions and eaten breakfast, they were required to fall-in for drill and told that Major Rathburn, their Company Commander, would address them.

"Something's up," Private Roy Carter said. Men listened to Roy, for he was invariably correct in his observations.

There was the usual feeling of sick excitement as the members of his section agreed with him. Those who had not bothered to write a letter to their mother the night before regretted the lapse.

They gathered, 'A' Company, of two hundred men, or thereabouts, standing to attention, presenting arms. The other companies of their battalion were doing the same. In all, there were about a thousand men in the 8th battalion.

Major Rathburn stood before them on horseback.

"Stand at ease!" Sergeant Patterson, the platoon sergeant, yelled.

"This evening, at six o'clock, we shall leave Hucqueliers," the Major said, "to march to Dennebroeucq, which is directly east. We shall arrive there in the middle of the night. There will be no camp or billets available to us, so we must bivouac in fields. The following day will be spent in preparation and rest, then at night we shall march on to Isbergues. We march at night because it is vital that as we go up the line and approach the Front we are not obviously visible to the enemy. The Colonel will now address you."

The Colonel, the Commanding Officer of the 8th Battalion of the Royal West Kents, addressed all four Companies. It was a pep talk. He ended it with. "Good luck, and God bless you all." No doubt he would say that a few more times.

Jim felt ill at ease. Forced to stare straight ahead, he wanted to exchange glances with Frank, Roy, Bert, and Bill who were standing near him. There was the feeling of lambs to the slaughter, a certain sense of finality, as though they were indeed going up to the firing line, even though they were innocents who had had no experience of being under fire. A feeling of incredulity was added to the usual emotions when an announcement of change was made. Perhaps they might yet be spared.

"Attention! Present arms!" They went through the motions while their Colonel rode off the field.

"Stand at ease!" There was a crashing of equipment as they stood easy, man-handling their rifles.

Lieutenant Barton addressed them then, saying there would be a kit inspection, and that they must be ready to muster and depart at least an hour prior to the actual departure.

Platoon sergeants addressed their platoons. "You heard what the major said. We're going to Dennebroeucq. That's Donneybrook to us."

They were marched off the temporary parade ground and dismissed. Jim's section clattered up the wooden steps to the cosy loft, where they had already spent their last night. They were literally going into the unknown. They all lit up, crowding close together to share a match flame.

"Well, that's it," Bill King said. "We've got our marching orders."

Some were talkative, some were silent as they squatted in their sleeping spaces to get out their kit for the inspection, to clean and oil rifles, to make sure nothing was missing — the entrenching tool that they would need if they had to dig a makeshift sleeping or sheltering hollow for themselves, the first field dressing that might save their life by staunching blood, the iron rations.

"Where do you reckon we'll end up?"

"Surely, they aren't going to put us in the front line now?"

"We're going due east. That looks like the firing line to me."

They polished buttons and boots, laid pieces of their kit neatly on the floor for Sergeant Dawson to inspect. They opened the windows of their temporary home as it filled with smoke. To a man, they would be sorry to leave it. They liked the way the sunlight slanted through the small windows morning and evening, the angled ceiling under the roof.

Silently, they took out notebooks and indelible pencils. Jim licked his pencil. Should he put, "My Dear Mother"? Or just "Dear Mother"? To call her "My Dear Mother" seemed a little pretentious and might make her wonder, as he had not done it before. Of course, he hadn't been away very long ...

With his hand hesitating over the paper, very mindful that his Company Major, or the Lieutenant, would read the letter before it was sealed, he decided to put "Dear Mother," as he always had done. "I hope this finds you well," he wrote. "I am all right myself. We are moving on." Would that be taken out, he wondered. "There is not much else to report. So far, we have had good weather. Look after yourself. I will write every day, if I am able." Did that make sense? As always, he signed himself "Your Loving Son, Jim." What he wanted to say was deep inside, not for the eyes of any Lieutenant.

He looked again at his pay-book, where he had been required to write, on a separate piece of paper, his Last Will and Testament, as had all the others in theirs. It had seemed almost a joke at the time. He had written: "I, James Langridge, of Fernden, Sussex, England, leave all that I own to my mother, Fanny Langridge, nee Osborne." He had printed and signed his name, with his Army identification number and the date.

It was a joke from the point of view that he would have next to nothing to leave. Those brief words now depressed him.

∽ At six o'clock in the evening they moved out onto the road, in full kit — packs, mess tins, "housewife," ammunition, greatcoats, waterproof sheet — and rifles, weighing then down.

"Number one platoon, left turn! Quick march!"

Their field kitchens, their limbers and artillery, their horses and mules, their supply wagons, lumbered out of the farm fields behind them.

They had been at Hucqueliers, which they called Huck-villers among themselves, Jim calculated, for almost three weeks. It was the 21st of September.

℞ Chapter 4

As the major had said, they reached Dennebroeucq—Donneybrook, to them—in the middle of the night, slogging under their heavy packs. The senior officers were on horseback.

At first, on the march, they had sung some of the old, familiar songs, the sound moving back and forth in waves over the marching men. As exhaustion set in, they fell silent. They had rested at the sides of roads and in fields, waited for their cooks to produce food, usually a stew of unidentifiable meat, with vegetables, and globules of fat floating on the top. If you soaked a bit of bread in it, it wasn't too bad, Jim had found.

"Halt! Left turn! March easy and fall out!"

They swarmed through gates into fields of stubble. Platoon sergeants were yelling, then the section sergeants rounding up their ten or twelve men.

"'A' Company, platoon one, right turn!" Darker shapes stumbled about in the darkness. It was not one of those pitch black nights where you could see nothing.

"If I don't get these bloody boots off," Stan Penfold mumbled to Jim, who stood next to him waiting for the roll-call, "I'm going to bloody collapse."

Jim grunted. His feet burned, replete with bleeding blisters, the raw flesh stuck to his socks. Legs and back hurt. As soon as roll-call was over, they would find a sleeping place for themselves and take off the pack, boots and puttees.

Names were called out, then as they waited, bowed down, they heard: "All present and correct, Sir!"

Down on the ground with kit lifted from the shoulders, they eased off boots. The cool night air played over the flesh of raw, heated, swollen feet.

Most of the water bottles were empty. Tomorrow at dawn they would refill them at the nearby farm.

The men of Jim's section bivouacked close together, for warmth in the early hours, and for security of mind. "You there, Jim?" Frank said.

"Yeah, here." They lit up, sharing a match with four others. They lay back, staring up into the star-lit sky.

"I'm that tired, I could bawl like a baby."

"You all right, lads?" Sergeant Dawson, the Jackdaw, was doing his rounds.

"Yeah," they muttered.

"In case you're envying those officers in the barn, I've had word that there are fleas." He chuckled. "You're better off out here."

They were inclined to agree with him as they rolled themselves in their greatcoats and the waterproof sheets. Some of the men were already breathing heavily in sleep.

Jim remained awake, thinking. As they approached the Front, or what he assumed was to be the front for them, they were being very gradually induced, by circumstances or design, he did not know, to give up their humanity. They could all do with a good wash; the smell of dirty feet and rank sweat, even in the open field, wafted over them, together with the smell of cigarette smoke. That was not to be for now. With luck, there would be a stream nearby where they could shave and wash in the morning. Very insidiously, Jim felt a mental change coming over him, a shift, a holding of himself in readiness for something. It was a gathering together of an indefinable thing, in silence, in the depths of himself.

He could not say that he was not frightened. Deep in that silence was a stirring of what he took to be terror.

"Where do you think we're going, Jim?" Frank asked quietly.

"I reckon," he said, "they're going to put us into the firing line. It's what they haven't told us that gives me that idea. If we were going behind the lines, to a safe place, for more training and to get a taste of being in real trenches under fire, they would have said." The thing inside him stirred, as he made his thoughts manifest in speech.

Pictures of Sir John French that he had seen in newspapers came to mind: an old boy in a top hat and frock coat in London, the commander of the expeditionary force in France. No doubt he would be far behind the lines, a man to whom this war was largely theoretical, he thought. He would most likely never see the mud of Wipers, or anywhere else.

Others lying near them, their heads close, agreed with Jim. "Food's getting worse," Bert Tomsitt said.

"That stands to reason," Bill King said. "It ain't easy to get supplies in, the closer you get to the Front."

"We're still quite a way from the Front," Roy Carter said, in his quick, cynical way. "If we were close, we'd hear the guns, the heavy artillery. The French have got railways, and we've got those light railways, single gauge."

"Perhaps there isn't one anywhere near us."

"How close do we have to be before we can hear the guns?" Private Harry Baker said.

"About twelve miles, or so," Roy said, "depending on the lay of the land. If it's flat, you hear them sooner. If there are a few hills, they deaden the sound. Then there's the direction of the wind, and the type of gun."

"How do you know all that?"

"I read about it," Roy said.

'They don't tell us much.'

Jim considered Roy, who sat near him. Although Roy looked deceptively boyish, there was a hard maturity and cynicism about him, a certain wisdom that one usually found only in older men. There was a stubbornness about him too, especially when he was confronted with tasks that he thought had no useful purpose, were simply make-work projects to keep men occupied when they might otherwise be questioning what was happening to them. Jim respected and liked Roy, knew that he would not let you down in a pinch, as he had told Frank. When he spoke, people listened.

Exhaustion overcame them. They rolled on their sides, under the coats and the waterproof sheets, bare feet curled up, in the close company of their mates. The Jackdaw was close by. Oblivion came, like the shutting of a door.

∞ "Tonight we leave here and march to a place called Isbergues. While there, we'll be billeted in a brewery," Sergeant Dawson said to his section of men who squatted in a circle in the field where their rifles were stacked in stooks and their kit piled neatly. There was a general laugh, covering up uneasiness.

"There won't be any beer, I'm afraid," he said. "At least, not in the brewery. We'll be more comfortable there than we were last night. Now, I want each man to look at this map I've got here. This is where we are now. This is where we're going. It's a long way, a much longer march than the last one. You've got to look after your feet. Lieutenant Barton will be round to do a foot inspection."

"Where are we making for, Sarge?"

"I haven't been told yet. We're going to the Front, as far as I know. I haven't received my orders yet. To tell you the truth, I don't think they've made up their minds, the generals behind the lines, but don't repeat that."

Each man looked at the map, as he thought of the generals fifty kilometres or so behind the lines, most likely moving pins around on maps while they lived in chateaux, ate the best food, drank good wine. Twelve thousand men here, fifty thousand there, moved about, sent into the fire, with the certainty that they would not come out of it.

"I'm telling you this," Sergeant Dawson said, "in case you get lost. Of course, as we get up close to the front, in darkness, all will be chaotic, and we shall be under fire, I expect. There will be guides, if we don't miss them, to show us the communication trenches. As you can see, Isbergues is near a forest, Forêt de Nieppe. It's northwest of the town of Béthune, a place where a lot of army divisions meet. We'll be going there, I expect. We're gradually moving east and south. Memorize that."

They were subdued after that, going about their business, sorting through kit again, finding clean socks. Having found a stream, they paddled into it, washed their hair, shaved. Some stripped off and waded in. After that, they wrote letters. Jim wrote to his mother again and to Anne Jefferson, as well as sending two "quick firers," those printed letters where you could cross out what you did not want to say, the most pertinent line crossed out being "I am well." It was, he thought as he did it, a feeble attempt at rebellion.

There were the inevitable fatigues, the waiting for food, filling up water bottles, getting ready, hanging washed socks over hedges to dry, securing their iron rations.

They set out, under cover of darkness, to march to Isbergues. Left, right, left, right, left, left, left, right, left.

"March at ease! March easy!" They marched four abreast, the officers beside them on horseback. The clip-clop of the horses' hooves blended in with the sound of hundreds of marching feet.

When it was time to rest, the order to halt went along the line. "Fall out!" They collapsed onto the grass verges, in fields beside the road, in cool woods. Now and then, tea came from the field kitchens. Water was sometimes scarce, nothing drinkable being available. Fags were becoming scarce for some.

At a crossroads, other marching divisions joined them on the country roads, causing confusion and congestion. Shouted orders moved back and forth. Transport was going the other way, horses and mules, empty ammunition limbers. The whinnying of more horses added to the sounds of approaching war. Jim and Frank moved closer together.

"All right, mate?"

"I hesitate to say I'm all right."

The brewery in the town was a welcome sight as they marched towards it, a large brick building of several storeys, as they were detailed to their specific billets.

The small town, in the grey dawn light, was milling with men in uniform of the British Army, together with horses, mules, transport, and heavy artillery pulled on limbers. It was a sobering and fearful sight.

Jim, weary beyond endurance, felt like the proverbial cog in a very big machine, far from home and insignificant. He wondered whether the nausea that he felt now was from lack of adequate sleep and food, from physical exhaustion, or was entirely from nerves, that sick fear that events were inexorably moving along at great speed and had long since escaped from personal control. His control had ended the moment he had joined up in Tunbridge Wells, Kent. That seemed like years ago rather than months. There was no way of knowing whether he would live out the year.

"Ironical, ain't it?" Bill King said. "Going to a bloody brewery. What I would give to walk into an English pub and order a pint of beer."

"Best not to think about it, mate."

There were still some civilians living in the town, whom the soldiers stared at in disbelief, even as the local people stared at them, these foreign soldiers, in strange uniforms, who did not speak their language. Mostly, they were generous, offering food.

There were ambulances about, some horse-drawn and some motor, which the men looked at furtively and away again, uneasy that they might themselves be in one of those, if they were lucky perhaps, to be carried away with a chance to live.

Men collapsed onto the brick floor inside the brewery, welcoming the smell of old beer. Here and there were wooden barrels, empty. They let down their rifles and eased off their packs, drank the last of their water from their water-bottles.

Jim and Frank found sleeping places for themselves and put down their kit. Roy joined them, as well as Bert Tomsitt and Bill King.

"Pay attention," Sergeant Jack Dawson said to his section. Short, stocky and muscular, as most of them were, he came up to them without very obvious signs of fatigue. "We're going to get breakfast very shortly. We'll get some sleep here during daylight hours. Tonight, after dark, we're going to move out, will march about three miles into the country, will billet in barns. The following night, we'll march to a place called Chocques ... as far as I'm concerned, that's Chokes. That's near Béthune, which I've mentioned before. That will be south and a bit east of where we are now. Any questions?"

They were silent, digesting the information. They would ask their questions of Corporal Jackson of their section, who was squatting among them, when the Jackdaw had departed.

"I'll be talking to you later," Sergeant Dawson informed them as he departed to his own business. In a snatched, quiet moment, in the latrine area behind the brewery, he wrote in his diary: "We are now at Isbergues, not far from the Front. Tonight we march on, a short distance to barns, mainly south. The officers have received some orders. Nothing has been told to me yet. It is the 23rd September."

In the brewery, Corporal Jackson was being questioned by the men. "Are we going directly into the firing line?"

"Wish I knew," he said. "But I don't get told much more than you. In my opinion, it looks like it. Sarge told me that the officers have received some orders, but he hasn't been told what they are. If you ask me, they don't know what they're doing yet. Something's up, something big, I reckon, and it looks as though we're to be in the thick of it. That's all of the blokes of the 21st and 24th Divisions, all of Kitchener's Army, the volunteers."

They squatted in a tight knot around their section corporal, smoking. Tea was being brought up in the large cans, dixies, and they reached for their mess kit. The orderlies with the tea moved around the groups of men. They also promised tots of rum.

"When is it going to happen?" one of the lads asked.

"Search me, but I reckon it's soon, seeing as we're almost up to the front line," Corporal Jackson said, drawing deeply on his own fag.

Jackson was twenty-five, although he looked younger, thinner than some, and boyish. "My advice to you is make sure your kit is in good order, your water bottle full, and your iron rations safe. Keep your rifles cleaned and oiled. As we get closer up the line, you'll be issued with extra ammunition. We'll march in darkness, so we won't come under a lot of fire, God willing. I reckon Fritz knows where we are all right — he can see us from the air, but we don't want him to know how many of us there are."

Now that Jim had sweet tea in his stomach, he knew that the nausea was not from lack of food. Where was God in all this? He did not see any evidence of God.

As darkness fell, on the night of the 23rd, they moved out onto streets and then roads that were crowded with the traffic of war, going in both directions. It was difficult to march four abreast; their formations were constantly disrupted, as they were forced to the sides of the narrow country roads.

They lost sight and touch of each other in the chaotic movements of men, animals and machines, in the clatter of horse-drawn wagons and motor vehicles. They strained their ears for the bawled commands of their own sergeants and corporals, for a familiar hail.

Frank, Roy, and Jim stayed close, their arms touching, their rifles, with the straps over their shoulders, clanking together from time to time as they came into contact. There was the fear of losing touch with one's platoon and section, of getting lost.

In the next stopping place, with apparently no name identifiable to the Army, they moved into barns that had straw and hay in them. It was about three miles, Jim reckoned, from the place they had left. At least they would be able to sleep for part of a night.

"Bloody hell!" someone said before too long. "This straw is lousy."

"That's nothing," someone else volunteered information. "Some of us have got the trots from the bloody awful food."

"Go outside to smoke," Sergeant Dawson ordered. "It wouldn't take much to set this place alight."

Lying back on straw, with his greatcoat wrapped round him, Jim tried to sleep, to ignore his throbbing feet and back. Near him were Frank and Roy and the other men of his section.

Softly someone began to sing:

Just a song at twilight, when the lights are low,
And the flick'rin' shadows softly come and go,
Though the heart be weary, sad the day and long,
Still to us at twilight comes love's old song,
Comes love's old sweet song.

As he felt himself on the edge of sleep, Jim heard someone crying quietly, the sound muffled as though the man had his head under his greatcoat. Then from out of the distance, from the east, came a sound like rumbling thunder, or a freight train far away.

The silent terror that was in him began to uncoil itself like a sleeping serpent disturbed. Although he had not heard the sound before, close up, he knew it to be the guns of the heavy artillery, the guns of their own side, opening up for a night bombardment.

The next morning, the 24th September, Lieutenant Barton spoke to the whole platoon. "Tonight, in darkness, we'll march closer to the Front, we'll be going up the line, first to Chocques, just passing through, which is very congested, so we have heard, then on to the town of Béthune. In Béthune we shall go into billets at a tobacco factory. Your officers will be in an empty house on the other side of the road. The 21st and 24th divisions, in the 72nd brigade, of which we are a part, will move on to Beuvry, then to the village of Vermelles."

Lieutenant Barton paused, looking around at the men of his platoon, of 'A' Company, silent and intent on what he was saying. From them he drew a kind of comfort. They were good men, honest, brave and disciplined. He wondered if they drew much, or any, comfort from him when considering the ordeal ahead.

"From Vermelles, which is close to our front line, we shall go through a farm, Le Rutoire Farm. Near there are communication trenches, which we shall enter to move up to reserve trenches and then into the front line, when ordered to do so."

There was complete silence from the listening men, as the reality of what was to happen to them was sinking in to their consciousness.

Lieutenant Barton again looked around him, not liking what he had to say. With them, he would be in the thick of it. Orders had come up, been modified, cut back.

At that moment he did not know when they would be required to attack. All he knew was that they had to be ready. The officers had been told that they were to take part in a battle bigger than the world had ever known. Why these untried soldiers should be required to be a part of that, he had no idea, and he was one of them, as inexperienced as they.

"Tonight there will be a bombardment by our artillery of the enemy lines; then there is to be an attack on the morning of the 25th by other divisions. When we know the outcome of that battle, we shall receive our final orders and our objectives, as we are the reserves. We must, however, be ready and in position. We shall go into the front lines, as you know, with other regiments — the East Surreys; the East Kents, the "Buffs"; the West Surreys, the "Queens." That is all I have to say to you for now. Major Rathburn will address you as soon as we have further news, and your commanding officer of the regiment, Colonel Brookes."

There was nothing left of lightness now; they seemed to meld into a single unit, the men of the section, and the men of the platoon to which it belonged, held together by a new-found fear. This was what their inadequate training had tried to prepare them for. The lack came home to them now as they waited once again for the cover of darkness so that they could move out of their shelters and up the line.

The black humour of being billeted in a brewery and then a tobacco factory, with no beer or fags for them, did not escape their notice.

The platoon sergeant showed them maps of where they were and where they were going. "To our right will be the town of Loos," he said. "It's a coal-mining town, and Fritz will be hanging about near there. It's being shelled by them. To our left and east is the village of Hulluch, very close to the enemy lines. As far as we know now, they are in the village. Our boys are not too far away."

❧ Chapter 5

That night, the 24th, they moved out of the shelter of the barns, to pass through Chocques to get to Béthune. Chocques was full of ambulances, guns, and other equipment. Roads, inadequate to begin with, were clogged with traffic. Relentlessly, weighed down by weariness and their heavy kit, they moved behind their own lines. During that night, their heavy artillery opened up.

In the town of Bethune they tramped to the tobacco factory where they were to rest, if that were possible. In the town they were able to buy cigarettes. Jim, Frank, Roy, Bert and Bill stuck close together, keeping that closeness by calling out: "Jim, you there, mate? Frank, that you?"

"Over here."

Among the swarming multitudes, there was a sense now of chaos, a sense deepened by the darkness in which they were forced to move.

Sergeant Patterson, the platoon sergeant, did the rounds. "We rest here," he said. "We most likely have had the last proper sleep we're going to get. From now on, there will be a lot of noise, as we move up to the front line. Tomorrow morning, we shall be forced to march out of here in daylight, to a place called Beuvry. It's just beyond the eastern edge of this town. Tomorrow morning, a battle will start in front of us, with other divisions."

The men looked at each other, furtively. Their questions, silent and spoken alike, had been answered. Beyond a shadow of a doubt, they would be going into the firing line.

"We shall muster at Beuvry," Sergeant Patterson went on. "Then we shall march east and south to a point behind the village of Vermelles."

Lieutenant Barton, who had been standing silently, took over. "As we move through Vermelles and beyond, later, the roads will be very congested and we shall soon be under fire from the enemy's heavy artillery. We shall stay behind Vermelles until nightfall; then we shall move up to take our positions in the trenches. As I've said, the exits to the village will be shelled. The Boche know very well that we are there. However, we are not going to make it easy for them."

Lieutenant Barton, very pale and tired, looked around the men of number one platoon, good soldiers, who were intently listening. A few of those men were older than he himself was. Sometimes, the incongruity of his leadership came home to him. Even though he put on an impartial face, he had the wind up now, before they had even been under fire. Yet he was supposed to demonstrate leadership, inspire confidence.

He wondered if he would be in a funk as they came under fire, no more qualified to lead than they. Would he lead them into unnecessary danger? Would his voice crack when he gave orders? Like them, in the broad term, he must follow orders, whatever he might think of the wisdom or stupidity of those orders. Only in certain circumstances, such as when his senior officers were dead or wounded, could he take it upon himself to give direct orders, to order a retreat, to fall back.

What he wanted to do now was go outside, behind the building, and vomit up the whisky that he had drunk from his flask not long before. It lay in his stomach in a disagreeable mass, not bringing with it the expected distancing of his perceptions that he wanted.

"From Vermelles" — he forced himself to go on — "we shall move up the line, go through a farm, Le Rutoire Farm, as you've already been told, then into the communication trenches, then on to the reserve trenches until further orders, depending on the outcome of the battle which will start in the morning. I shall speak to you again in the morning, when I shall have new orders to impart. Goodnight."

Jim felt that he had lost himself, and all the other men with him had lost themselves now, more or less completely, lost their individuality. That was what the army had been trying for all along, he knew that. You do not think for yourself; you do not think about your personal safety; you set no store by your own life. Yet he, and they, as far as he could see, clung to the little bit of humanity that they had left. As long as they drew breath, it would be there. I am my mother's son. My name is Jim.

"Fall in for fatigues," Sergeant Dawson said. "You ... Wheeler, Baker, Langridge, Hewitt, Osborne, and Mitchell, get outside and bring in our breakfast. Our kitchens are behind the building. We've been told that our regimental field kitchens are to stop operations after today, and we're going to get our grub from the divisional kitchens, the 24th division."

"That means we won't get any bloody grub," someone ventured.

"Fill your water bottles before we leave here," Sergeant Dawson said. "We've identified the water that's drinkable."

Weary beyond description, the six men of the section went out again to find their field kitchens. It was still dark, with only a weak suggestion of dawn in the sky. This time they were in no mood to joke with the cooks, or even complain about the food. The cooks themselves were in no light mood either, having slogged through muddy roads with recalcitrant mules pulling their equipment. It was a wonder that they had got through at all. It was not easy to find fuel for their fires.

A light rain began to fall, a cool wind with it. The summer was becoming a memory.

The food they were going to eat now passed as breakfast for the coming day; there had been no meal that they could have called dinner. The cooks were handing out what food they had on hand. There were hunks of bread, some cheese, raw onions, some bits of bacon, and tea. With this, the six men slogged up the stairs in the factory to their section, where the men queued up for their rations.

The tea was smoky and the bread stale, but they did not complain. They even bit into the raw onions with an appreciation, and the knowledge that this could be the last meal they would ever eat.

They lay down after, or propped themselves against a wall.

"I'm bloody lousy," Private John Hewitt remarked, scratching under his armpits.

"I reckon we all are."

Before long, their heavy artillery started up in the near distance, the sheer power of it shocking them, a steady crashing. The taste of the onion and the smoky tea reappeared in Jim's mouth. That would be the bombardment before the attack, he knew, the heavy shells that were supposed to breach the barbed wire in front of the enemy trenches, so that the advancing infantry, their infantry, could get through to capture the enemy trenches and to take prisoners.

At least, that was the way it should be in theory. He felt sick, wishing he had not eaten the bloody onion. At home he liked a fresh onion, eaten with bites of Cheddar cheese to counter the sharpness of it.

He twisted this way and that, restlessly on the floor, feeling the lice crawling on him. Scratching seemed to make it worse, for it inflamed the skin. Trying not to scratch was hard. The marches over the last days blended in his mind to a blur of weariness, one road much like another. "Fall in!" then "Fall out!" they had been instructed, over and over again.

They had collapsed onto the sides of dusty roads, had gone down into ditches to let oncoming traffic pass. There seemed to be little order or sense to it. From their perches on horseback, the senior officers had tried to rally the men. Sense of direction, if they had had any when they set out, was lost. Each man had concentrated on putting one foot in front of the other, trying to forget the dryness and dust in his mouth and throat.

"I see what they mean about our last kip," someone remarked as the guns roared and crashed south-east of Béthune.

"Shut your eyes and pretend."

The building was solid, red brick, with a rough wood floor, that did something to muffle the distant din. Those who could not doze, smoked, careful to put the ash and the dog-ends into a tin.

Sergeant Dawson was outside to watch the dawn come up. It was not possible that he would sleep. His responsibilities weighed heavily on him, and his stomach was not behaving itself. Lousy, like all the others, he scratched.

Inside a small, lean-to shed, crouched down by the light of a well-shielded candle stub, he wrote in his diary. Mindful that it might be his last entry, he wrote: "We are in Béthune, a small town. There are still a few civilians here, which surprises me no end. The heavy artillery has started up. There is to be an attack today. It is not us yet. The dawn will be coming up soon. It is the 25th September, 1915."

If he were killed tomorrow, or in the next week or two, he hoped that whoever found his diary would not destroy it. On the first page he had written a note asking the finder to send the diary to his mother, and he had put her name and address. Some of his kit would be left behind the lines with the quartermaster before they went into the firing line. The diary would be with that. If he were lucky, he would perhaps meet up with it again.

He got out of the lean-to in a crouching position, to go back inside to his men in the section. They were a good lot and might be needing him. There were stars up in the black-purple sky, the same stars that looked down on Kent and Sussex, over home. It was difficult to grasp that at times, when home was so distant, like a dream. A funny old world, it was. What the hell were they doing here? It didn't do to think too much of the people you had left behind, because that was when questions came to you that could not be answered, when you felt that you had already gone mad.

↬ Lieutenant Barton, sharing a small bedroom with two other junior officers in the empty house opposite the tobacco factory, could not sleep either. Apart from the awful noise of shelling, there was everything else churning in his brain. They sat, the three of them, on their makeshift beds, leaning against walls, their pale faces shining like pallid moons in the shaded light of a candle. In spite of feeling sick, he sipped diluted whisky from a cup without a handle that he had found in the house, and the others did the same.

The owner of the house had departed and taken some of the furniture and belongings, yet had left enough that they could feel it had been someone's home, those people they did not know and would never know. In this parody of a home, he tried to conjure up in himself an idea of normalcy. It was to no avail. Terror gripped him. The presence of his two friends prevented him from sobbing. What little comfort they could give each other seemed to go round in a circle, ebbing and flowing. When you needed so much, what was there to give?

There was Anthony and there was Barnabus, Barny for short, good chaps both. They had been together from the beginning.

"How are you feeling, Seb, old chap?" Anthony said to him, passing cigarettes. Lieutenant Barton liked his name, Sebastian, and liked the diminutive, Seb, even better.

"Not good," he said. There was no point in not being honest. They had ceased to think of honour and glory. These terms were for old men who wanted to bully the young into going into the cannon's mouth. "I can't help thinking of my sisters, Margaret and Beatrice. They'll be absolutely devastated when they hear of my death. I love them so much."

"You've made up your mind to die, then?"

"I expect to die. It's out of our hands."

They went outside to look at the shelling, at the flashes of red in the still dark sky. The sound, deep and booming, held awe in it. Yet the prominent emotion was one of dread.

Men from the brewery had come out to look as well. They stood in small groups, at strategic points where they could get a view of the sky, low down.

Lieutenant Seb Barton smoked with his friends and watched their war unfolding. Soon, at dawn, or just after, the divisions that were now waiting in the front line trenches would receive the order to attack, to go over the top. What use was flesh and blood against all that?

∾ When morning came, the 25th, they moved out on a road to Beuvry, a road on which vast numbers of men from their brigade, the 72nd, marched. Gusts of rain came now and again. Water formed puddles in the shattered roads. The going was slow. All around them they heard the noise of war. Still there was the sweet air of the countryside, wildflowers on the road side, some dying now that autumn was coming, a transition that mirrored their own, the men of the 21st and the 24th divisions, of the 72nd brigade.

The 8th Battalion of the Royal West Kents, part of the 24th Division, kept together on the march, with their horses and equipment. Their Colonel rode at their head. The men of the infantry, looking at him, knew he would be going over the top with them. Not for him the sheltering behind the lines with the Brigadiers and the Generals.

Lieutenant Barton thought of 'Mort d'Arthur': *Now all day long the noise of battle rolled across the plain beside the wint'ry sea.*

They marched through Beuvry to the western outskirts of Vermelles, where they rested beside the road and in fields. Never had the men seen such a sight of massed soldiers.

From what they could see of Vermelles, it was in ruins, piles of rubble, with a wall or two standing here and there.

Men relieved themselves where they could. Scouts went out to look for drinkable water. Sergeant Dawson's section stayed close together and men got out their notebooks to write a last letter, which would be collected before they went farther up the line. This time, Jim wrote to his mother only, signing it "All my love." It would be something for her to keep if he was hit and snuffed out.

The sergeant spoke to his men. "Tonight, when it's dark, we go through this village here, which, as you've been told, will be under fire. We'll try to get through as quickly as we can, but that may be impossible. Over to our right is a place called Nœux-les-Mines, this area being a coal mining district. If we have to retire, we will most likely retreat to there, or we may assemble initially at the Lone Tree ridge, if our trench there still exists afterwards." He paused, clearing his throat and licking his dry lips, for his water bottle was empty and there had been no food since they had left Béthune.

'We have to take our chances going through here; there isn't anything else I can say. Once through here, we branch to the right to get to Le Rutoire Farm."

"Where are the communication trenches, Sarge?"

"There are some on the other side of Vermelles, but we will not take those. We'll get into ours after going through the farm. You know about the Lone Tree, just west of another village, Hulluch, which is a landmark, more or less straight in front of us on this road. The Boche are in Hulluch as I speak. Beyond the farm, we will take a compass bearing on the Lone Tree and go into trenches as close as we can to there. We'll be close to Fritz there, all right. Any questions?"

Nobody spoke. Their questions could not be answered.

"When we get through Vermelles," Sergeant Dawson said, "we'll spread out into artillery formation because of being under fire."

One of the regimental chaplains came round. They were from a breed of men, Jim thought, not often seen near danger. Those few rare exceptions were respected by the men. This one they liked, so they bowed their heads when he led them in prayer. "Into thy hands I commend my spirit, O Lord," he finished up, requiring them to repeat it after him.

There was no sight of their field kitchens, now not their own but of the 24th Division. They looked obsessively for a likely small, smoking chimney of a kitchen.

"No food, by the look of it," Harry Baker, the singer, sitting next to Jim, remarked. They sat on a dusty verge, where detritus of war shared the space — wagon wheels, broken axles.

"Looks like you're right there," Jim said.

Dead men don't need food, he thought. If they were lucky, they might get a tot of rum before they went into the firing line. News that had come to them from old soldiers was that men sometimes went into battle semi-drunk on rum. Well, perhaps you wouldn't know what hit you, could slip into death under the influence.

Sounds of battle went on, then lines of weary prisoners straggled up the line, guarded by two or three soldiers of the British army. A weak cheer went up at the sight of them, while some men scrambled to their feet.

"We must be getting somewhere," Private Frank Boakes remarked, looking at the prisoners.

"They've most likely got some of ours," Roy Carter said. "They're out of it."

The mood changed as ambulances began to appear, together with the walking wounded, bloodied bandages around heads, arms in slings, men with leg wounds leaning on wounded mates who could still walk.

One of the wounded men turned sourly on a bystander who was smiling. "You won't be smiling when you get up there, mate." Some of the wounded wore kilts, of a Highland regiment.

"What's going on up there?" someone from the section asked a wounded man, with a thick, bloodied bandage around his head and over one eye, and his left arm in a blood-stained sling.

The soldier shook his head, seeming on the verge of tears, filthy and utterly spent. "All a bloody cock-up," he said. "A bloody cock-up."

One of their men handed him a lighted cigarette, which he put between his lips with his good hand.

"Good luck," Jim called after him, as he moved off, towards Beuvry. With luck, the man would get a lift on a horse-drawn ambulance, or on a motor ambulance or limber, which would take him to the Casualty Clearing Station.

They had been told the whereabouts of Advanced Dressing Stations, the ones closest to the Front, and the clearing stations farther back. Each regiment, Jim knew, would have an Aid Post as part of the trench system, a dug-out, the first place of refuge for the wounded who were able to walk or crawl out of no-man's-land. Those Aid Posts were liable to be hit by shells.

"Good luck!" others called after the shuffling man, each wishing they had more to give him.

Other wounded men were more cheerful, glad, perhaps, to be out of it. "We've got them on the run," one said.

The men of number one platoon watched as the parade of wounded passed by them, ambulances following the walking wounded. As the wounded came down, ammunition for the heavy guns went up.

Chapter 6

Darkness came and still there was no food. Men were cursing and complaining. The officers and NCOs hurried about looking important, but nothing came. Uneasiness grew. They were hungry, thirsty and exhausted.

"'A' Company, attention! Fall in!" The order came for them to move on through Vermelles. Soon they would reach the line of their own heavy artillery, over to the right. Shouldering packs and rifles, they moved into formation.

They moved forward in a mass, into the ruined village. Their heavy artillery opened up, the screaming of the shells drowning out all else. Left, left, left, right, left. In the intermittent light from gun flashes, Jim, weary under his heavy pack, saw the jagged walls around him, the timbers, the piles of bricks that had once been a village. Here and there, a chimney still stood, with nothing of the house left around it. Such destruction was difficult to grasp, unreal in the garish light.

They moved aside into the rubble as ambulances passed. The going was slow, packed together as they were, shuffling rather than marching. Then at last they were through, and the order came to spread out. As they moved out of the village, Jim saw a sign that someone had nailed up on a post. "Suicide Corner," it read. "Don't Hang About."

Shortly after, enemy shells began to fall on the east side of Vermelles. "Number one platoon, right wheel!" The order was bellowed amid the noise. Somehow, Jim, Frank, and Roy stayed together, even though several paces apart in artillery formation. In the distance they could see the flashes of the enemy guns.

A horse screamed as a shell exploded near it. Never before had Jim heard that sound, and he knew that, for as long as he lived, he would never get it out of his mind. He did not look round. His body burned, muscles strained to near breaking point, stomach empty. A dizziness from lack of food distanced him from his surroundings, until a shell coming too close jerked him back as he stumbled on.

They took a dirt track to Le Rutoire Farm. All around were fields, visible in flashes. "Over that way," Sergeant Dawson bawled to his men, pointing. "The St Mary's Advanced Dressing Station!" They had been told to go there if wounded, if the First Aid Post had gone. Jim doubted that he would ever find it in this world of noise and chaos.

Rain that had been coming on and off all day began again. The ground on which they walked, churned up by marching men and horses, was sticky with mud.

Up ahead, a soldier carrying a muffled lantern appeared from out of the ground, a guide.

"Halt! Communication trench ahead! Pass it on!"

The men bunched up.

"Single file!"

"There's water in the trench," the guide said, going ahead. "Watch your step. Pass it on."

"Water in the trench!" The call went back, down the line of men.

As Jim stepped down into the trench, whose walls were scarcely high enough to cover his head, and he was short, he stepped into water up to mid calf. "Oh, sodding hell," he said, as water seeped into his boots and through his puttees. They were going more or less directly east again, he reckoned.

"Keep your bloody heads down!" Sergeant Dawson yelled from somewhere behind him. "Beware of snipers! Just in case they get behind our bloody lines."

They stumbled on, splashing and cursing, the walls of the trench crumbled here and there so that any sniper would have had a clear field, if he could see them. Even if he shot blind, he would hit someone, Jim speculated, trying to take his mind off his empty stomach. The smell of wet earth pervaded everything. Soon, his boots were sticking, sinking down into mud.

"Dip ahead!" The warning came back, followed by cursing and splashing as someone wallowed about in waist-deep water. "Pass it on."

There was just room to get around the dip in the trench bottom, a dry narrow ridge.

Before long they came across four wounded men crouched close together at the side of the trench, where there was a shelf of earth above the water. It was evident from the various bandages on their bodies that they had received cursory first aid and were now trying to get out of the trench to go behind the lines, had been cut off by deep water. In the light from shelling, Jim could see them. No doubt they did not want to get their dressings soaked with filthy water. They might have to wait a long time for the water level to drop.

Forward movement stalled. Level with the wounded men, Jim handed them two fags. "Sorry I haven't got any food."

"Thanks, mate."

They started up again, sloshing forward. "Corporal Jackson! Where the hell are you?" Sergeant Dawson's voice soared over them.

"Back here!"

Frank, Jim thought, was two back from him. The trench wound about so that soon all sense of direction was lost, apart from the roar of their own guns somewhere behind them, and the enemy guns ahead. They seemed to have turned very slightly north. He had also lost any sense of time. All he knew was that it was the night of the 25th September, 1915 and that tomorrow his battalion would go into battle, on a Sunday, for what it was worth. He wondered if a chaplain would be in evidence. It was possible that this time tomorrow he would be dead, perhaps lying out in no-man's-land. No prayers would be said over his body.

At last they came out into wider assembly trenches, having passed many more wounded men on the way, mostly from Highland regiments.

"That you, Jim?" Roy came up to him in the semi-darkness.

"It's me. Does anyone know what they're doing, the higher-ups, do you think?"

"Sometimes I wonder. If they did, we'd have some food."

"Seen Frank?"

"Yeah, he's just behind us."

Lousy, stinking, wet, hungry, and thirsty, they waited for orders, surrounded by the crashing, screaming, and whizzing of shells.

Corporal Jackson moved about among them. "We're waiting to make contact with other battalions of our brigade," he said. "You can smoke, but be careful about showing it. Assume there are snipers about."

Drawing smoke into your lungs when you have had no food brings on a dizziness, Jim found, as they squatted in the bottom of the muddy trench to make less of a target.

Lieutenant Barton loomed up in the darkness. "Attention, men. We shall advance soon to a trench near the Lone Tree, then will move on to take up our final positions in some old German trenches parallel to and about 1,000 yards west of the north-south Lens-La Bassée road. When we are in those trenches, we shall be about 1,700 to 2,000 yards from the enemy front line. The men yesterday already captured one of their lines, which we shall cross. Our objective will be to capture their other lines and to knock out a gun emplacement known as Stutzpunkt number four. The time of our attack has not been decided."

He did not mention food. There was no sign of any. Some of the men had pieces of stale cheese, or a crust of bread in their pockets, as well as iron rations of hard biscuit to be kept for emergencies.

As the night wore on, they moved up slowly to the old German trenches. It was a surprise to their officers and NCOs that there were no troops in the line on the way up, whom they were supposed to relieve, being the reserves, and no men in the captured trenches. A breech had been allowed to develop, which made them all uneasy.

All the way up they were under fire. Here and there, men were hit by shrapnel. If an officer were lightly wounded, he refused to go back behind the lines.

In the morning the men of the Royal West Kents were to advance due east, they were told, parallel to the Vermelles-Hulluch road, to their left. The Germans might or might not now occupy the village of Hulluch. The regimental scouts were out to take a look and give a situational report.

In the old German front line they settled in. The trench was deeper than their own, although damaged here and there by shell fire. Repairs were carried out, positions found, machine guns set up.

The men, hunched on the fire step, or on sentry duty, waited for dawn to come up, while they gnawed on any scraps of food they had in their pockets. Those who could, smoked.

"Stand to!" The order came for them to be alert against attack until it was light, when they would stand down. Normally, there would be breakfast, but it didn't look like it this time.

The men of the section stood restlessly waiting for something to happen, for last orders to be received. With his filthy hands holding his rifle, weighed down by the extra ammunition and packs, Jim peered through a slit in the sandbags of the parapet in front of them, looking around at the Very lights, the flares, going up in no-man's-land.

As he knelt on the firestep, looking out, the lights showed bodies of the day's dead, hunched in all sorts of positions, the bodies of those who could not be brought in. The bodies were beyond their own barbed wire, to where men had crawled and died. It made him feel sick to look at them. Fearfully, they waited. A man near him was praying, while another, a mere boy, cried quietly. Although Jim felt also that he could both pray and cry, he did neither; a peculiar detached calmness, almost like a mental paralysis, had come over him as he went through the motions of his duties.

The area was also lit up from burning villages and small towns around them, including Loos to their far right which had been bombarded and was in flames. Loos, a coal mining town, had huge colliery towers silhouetted against the flames. What was man against this?

As dawn came up on the 26th September they were ordered to stand down. With daylight, the shelling by the enemy intensified. Amid the screaming of the heavy shells, the churning up of vast amounts of earth around them, they stood waiting.

"Keep your heads down!" Corporal Jackson reminded them.

Their Colonel was summoned to see the Brigadier, behind the lines, for last orders. The scouts who had gone out in the night came back to say that the Germans were again in the village of Hulluch, over to their left, and that the Lens-La Bassée road, straight ahead of them to the east, was well covered by enemy machine-gun fire.

Corporal Jackson did the rounds once more, his uniform as filthy as theirs, his face paper-white, unshaven, as they all were. Mud clung to him up to the waist, signifying that he had fallen into one of the mud holes in a trench. "Attention, men," he said. "We've had news that our regimental Aid Post, the dug-out by Lone Tree, has received a direct hit by a shell and completely destroyed. If you are wounded and can get back, come to the trench if you can, then go on to the St. Mary's Advanced Dressing Station on the Hulluch to Vermelles road, that Sarge pointed out to you. If you can't get back, wait for the stretcher-bearers."

The men nodded, mumbling. Jim and Roy exchanged glances. Stretcher-bearers would not be able to get out very far. If you could not get back by yourself, you were as good as dead. Even if you could move, you risked being shot in the back.

"Jim," Frank said, "if I cop it, and you don't, would you get in touch with my mother? I would like her to hear from someone who knew me. Tell her that I died peacefully in the dressing station and didn't suffer."

"Of course, I will. But you have just as much chance of getting out of here as I do, Frank."

"What chance have we against this? Look at them poor buggers out there. From what I can see, nobody here seems to know what's really going on."

"It's too big, the whole damn thing's too big. It's got out of hand."

"If it was ever in hand."

"We're here, Frank. There's no way out."

By the time the Colonel came back, with orders to attack, to go over the top at eleven o'clock precisely, the men had only a few minutes to make final preparations.

Some men vomited onto the floor of the trench; all were quiet and strained as they saw death.

"Get your rifles!"

"Stand to!" the order came again.

"Fix bayonets!" There was a clattering as rifles were man-handled and bayonets fixed.

Sergeant Dawson moved among them. "Steady, lads, steady. Coming out with us, on our right, will be the 9th East Surreys."

All along the vast plain of that front, the men of the British Army would be coming out in waves, over ten thousand of the infantry in all. Knowing that brought no comfort to Jim as he waited.

Somewhere, out of sight, their Colonel prepared to go over the top with them, as did all the other officers below him.

Jim tried not to bring up the bile that was in his stomach. Now, the time had come. There was no more speculation. In the middle of his terror there was something in his mind that was still oddly calm, a core of coldness, as though everything that he had ever known in his life, all that he had done, was concentrated into a small, tight centre inside him. The past, with the people he loved, his unknown future, seemed to draw in together, into that tight knot that was the moment. So this was what it meant to face death.

Frank held out his hand to Jim, then to Roy, who were on either side of him. "Good luck," he said.

"Stand to, ready to advance!" The order moved down the trench, in the mouths of the NCOs.

Short ladders had been put up. A whistle blew.

"Over the top, lads!"

Stiff limbs moved, as though belonging to other bodies. Rifles were grasped tightly. Exhausted, lice-laden, stinking, mud-covered young men, faint with hunger, groped for the sides of ladders with their free hands as they heaved themselves up the side of the trench to face the vast flat plain of Loos that lay ahead of them as far as they could see, where there was no cover from enemy fire.

❧ Chapter 7

Once through the gaps in their own barbed wire, they spread out and walked in artillery formation, as they had been taught to do.

They walked steadily as though they were out on an exercise at home. There was grass growing out of the soil, quite high here and there, and there were shell holes. There were bodies of men strewn about, some hung up on their own barbed wire, as though they had had the strength to crawl back to their own trench but had been defeated by the wire, or had been killed by enemy shrapnel.

Though he was moved to pity by the sight of them, Jim found that he could not yet associate himself with them as his eyes skimmed over them. He walked on, with his rifle held in his right hand. Roy, next to him, a few paces away, held his gun easily, with no self-consciousness, as though it were part of himself.

Alert, tense, Jim scanned the ground ahead, to a few trees that were along the first road they would come to, the Loos to Hulluch road. It was possible that there would be snipers in those trees. Beyond that road was the Lens-La Bassée road, which was within easy range of the enemy machine guns, running straight north and south. Those who could get across this road would find a German trench that had been captured the day before by the Scottish and Middlesex regiments. This had been the German first line. They had been told that it was full of German dead, which they would have to cross somehow while under intense fire.

Beyond this abandoned trench was the German second line, behind thick barbed wire. The men of his battalion had been told that the wire

65

would be breached by their own artillery in places, where they could get through to attack the German second line. In Hulluch the Germans would be waiting to fire on them.

It was not a good situation, as any man who had any sense in his head could tell. They were walking into the closed end of a horseshoe, so to speak, where they could come under enfilading fire, from both sides, as well as the front, once they were over the Lens-La Bassée road. For not only did the Germans hold Hulluch, there were rumours that they had come up in the night and recaptured parts of a wood, Bois Hugo, which was on the right, negating some gains that the Scottish had made, at terrible cost, the day before. Something of this had been imparted to the section. The trouble was, nothing was very clear. Jim ruminated on this as he put one foot in front of the other.

As the line of men along the Front moved on at a steady pace, getting closer to the Loos to Hulluch road, the dead became more numerous, then in shell holes the wounded and dying from the day before, their own men, lifted up their arms and called for water and for help.

Their instructions had been to keep moving, not to stop to help anyone, not to give them water. "It will only give them false hope," they had been told. In other words, do nothing for them.

Delirious men called out. "Go back! Come down in here where it's safe!"

Going against all his own instincts, Jim was forced to ignore them, while his lips trembled and eyes filled. "Oh, God," he whispered repeatedly. "Bloody, flaming hell." Many of the dead were mutilated beyond description; heads blown off, legs gone.

He lifted up his head to look at the small ridge where the Germans were dug in, well beyond the Lens-La Bassée road. The task that had been set for him and his battalion was impossible to carry out. It did not matter how clever you were, how brave, how good a soldier, there were things that you could not do in the face of a well defended line, of arbitrary fate, the line of a shell or bullet. As he walked, sick in his heart, wanting to weep, he saw the situation clearly. As cattle are driven into a slaughter house, with no way of escape, so it had been intended that all at the front should die. It would not be an accident.

As he and his mates had been cautioned to leave the wounded to die, so he too would be abandoned in a shell hole, or out in the open, if such a fate were in store for him and he could not walk out.

Blood pounded through his body. He felt himself grimace like a wild animal baring its teeth when cornered, looking this way and that for a route of escape.

Crack! Crack! Crack! Rifle fire buzzed around them, like the sound of demented bees. Jim flung himself down, as he saw Lieutenant Barton fall to the ground a little ahead of him and to his left. Automatically he brought his rifle to his right shoulder, squinted down the barrel, moving his sights towards the few trees ahead.

"Snipers!" Roy called out, a few feet ahead of Jim. "In those trees by the road. Watch out!"

As Jim looked on, Roy, flat on his belly, brought his rifle to his shoulder and took aim at the nearest tree, which was still quite a way off. Again and again he fired, taking careful, unhurried aim. Bloody Fritz would be in the centre of the tree, near the trunk, high enough to see over the plain, but not so high that he could not scramble down quickly to make his getaway. As Roy fired, he swore. "Sodding buggers," he said. "Bloody, flaming shit-bags."

Likewise, Jim fired into the centre of a tree. Then with his rifle pushed ahead of him, he crawled over the uneven ground to where he had seen Lieutenant Barton drop, his body partially obscured by grass. It was easy for Fritz to pick off the officers, because they carried no rifles, only pistols. Bloody silly. Madness.

Lieutenant Barton had been hit in the neck, and the bullet had come out the other side. Blood had sprayed over the front of his uniform and pooled around his head and shoulders as he lay on his back, his blue eyes open, looking up at the sky. "Sir?" Jim said. He was older by one year than this man who lay dying.

Lieutenant Barton did not look at him. He whispered one word: "Margaret."

"Bloody bastards." Putting his head down in the grass, Jim wept. With a hand that shook, he closed the eyes of his lieutenant, the only thing he could do for him.

Up on his feet, he ran forward, bent double, catching up to the others who were ahead, running past heaped men, dead and dying, of his own battalion.

"Come on, Langridge," Sergeant Dawson chivvied him along. "Keep moving."

Some of their own men with machine guns, not enough of them, took aim to dislodge any snipers that might be in ditches fore and aft of the road.

Bullets zinged around them. Here the Loos to Hulluch road came in at an angle towards the village of Hulluch, and formed the apex of a triangle with the Lens-La Bassée road.

There ahead of them was the lesser road, with a shallow ditch beside it, which they fell into with relief.

"Forward, lads!" With a wave of his arm, Sergeant Dawson urged them out of the safety of the ditch, over the road and the dangerous open ground, towards the next road. More men were falling. Panting now and sweating under the weight of his ammunition and accoutrements, Jim ran forward, trying not to look too much to right or left, to concentrate his vision on the ground ahead.

In that short distance, for those men near the apex of the two roads, a sight met their eyes so terrible that Jim retched at the same time that he was forced to move forward, not make himself an easy target. "Oh, God, oh God, oh God. God help us."

Mutilated bodies from the day before lay all around them on the open ground, in unnatural positions, those bodies having been shelled by heavy artillery and hit repeatedly by machine-gun fire after they had died. At least, Jim hoped it was after they had died; he tried not to speculate as he ran past. Some were battered, flattened into the soil, while others were mere headless and limb-less trunks. Trying to avoid them was hopeless.

Some of the advancing men still walked as though on an exercise, while stragglers were running to catch up, bent down, as they neared the bigger Lens-La Bassée road. Burdened with ammo, they were slow, awkward.

Enemy machine guns opened up then, bullets spraying among them, back and forth along the road, and men began to fall all around, onto the road, so that men of the 8th battalion fell among the dead of the day before. "Tac, tac, tac, tac tac." The sound of the guns hammered in his ears.

Not knowing where Frank and Roy were, Jim felt lost as he was forced to move forward, to keep his eyes on the enemy lines and on the ground in front of him. He needed to find a pathway for his feet among the dead, to search out the deserted German trench that he knew was ahead of them on the other side of the road, up the slight incline. That would provide another temporary refuge. Grimacing and panting, he whispered again: "Oh God, oh God, oh God."

Some of the wounded were calling for their mothers; some started to crawl back the way they had come. Some ran forward, sobbing, the contortions of their features not accompanied by any sound as it was drowned out by the tac, tac, tac, tac of the machine gun fire, their own and that of the enemy. They were easy targets, swarming over the open plain and road, looked down upon from the ridge.

Jim dared not look behind him for Frank and Roy. From quick glances to the sides he could see that the numbers in his battalion were seriously depleted. Thoughts and emotions were jumbled together, disorganized, so that he felt himself moving by pure instinct, in this mad landscape that bore no resemblance to anything that could be called normal and sensible.

Tac, tac, tac, tac tac. Relentlessly they were mown down. Their own machine gunners took up positions every few yards as they advanced and fired back, not having obvious targets. Back and forth they sprayed, back and forth. The sound was like a giant sewing machine, demented, obscene.

Jim ran forward, bent down as far as he could without falling, his rifle gripped tightly. If he lost his grip on that he would be defenceless. His breath came, rasping, through his dry throat, reminding him that he lived. Men around him were discarding equipment, leaving it in shell holes. The day had turned hot, after a morning of mist. Wounded men were screaming in pain, crying, calling for help when there was none.

There was a shallow dip beside the Lens-La Bassée road, which he flung himself into, keeping his head down, fighting to draw enough air into his lungs through his parched throat. Other men flung themselves down near him, crouching between bodies of the dead. He saw Harry Baker and Stan Penfold. They looked as strained and fearful as he knew he did himself.

Tac, tac, tac, tac, tac, tac.

Bullets whistled over them.

"Shall we try to make a dash for it, across the bloody road?" Private Stan Penfold said to anyone who was listening.

"We'd better go one at a time," Jim said, his voice cracked. "Crawling." So littered was the road that they could shelter among the dead.

When his breath was steadier, he crawled out of the ditch, keeping his head down, slithering on his belly. It was slow going, his rifle pushed in front of him. Bullets smacked into the bodies of the dead and dying around him. Tense, he tried to brace himself for the impact that would get him. Every second seemed elongated. Behind him came the rasping breath of one of his mates.

At last they were through, rolling into the dip on the far side of the Lens-La Bassée road, on top of others who did not move.

"We're here, Jim," Stan Penfold said.

"Seen Frank?"

"Not for some time." Stan looked as though he wanted to bawl, his lips working. "What a bloody mess, what a bloody cock-up. I reckon most of our boys have been hit."

Jim nodded, unable to speak. He moved slightly sideways so that his head was sheltered by the head of a dead man who lay on the eastern lip of the makeshift ditch that barely covered them. Lying on his side, he risked a peep beyond the top of the head.

Before him he could see that some German soldiers, who had returned to their old front line trench, were coming out and swarming up the slight incline to the top of the ridge where they held the advantageous position. Some of these men had been snipers in the trees, Jim reckoned.

Men of the 8th battalion, the remnants, ran into the ditch beside Stan and Jim, as the enemy held their fire to allow their own soldiers to escape. They took aim with their rifles at the fleeing men.

Crack! Crack! Crack!

"That's for Lieutenant Barton," someone yelled out as one of the enemy fell. Awkwardly, on his side, Jim struggled to get his rifle into position for firing, without making himself a target. This was it, perhaps, the first time he would kill someone. The retreating line wavered as some fell. With sweat slicked hands he held his rifle steady, squinted down the barrel, took aim and fired.

A Captain from another company called out to the men: "While they're holding their fire, we should go forward! That's the old German front line ahead of us, where they came out. We get in there."

In twos and threes they moved out. There was longer grass now, brown, shielding the khaki and grey mounds of the dead.

"God help me, God help me, God help me." As Jim ran forward, repeating the words over and over again and waiting for the blow, suddenly ahead of him was the trench, its sides shattered by shell-fire. Bending further, he rolled into it, on top of bodies of men from British regiments, and dead Germans.

Retching, moaning, he slid off them. Already, with the warmth of the day, a smell of putrefaction arose from them. Remembering his training, he put his back to the side of the trench that faced the enemy and lifted his rifle, pointing it quickly first one way and then the other down the length of the fire-bay, ready to fire from the hip.

No one, it appeared, was alive in that section of the trench, although there was a damaged dug-out nearby. What use against all this was a rifle with a bayonet? At this rate, they would never get close enough to an enemy soldier to use a bayonet.

Not that he wanted to. It sickened him, the thought alone. Yet he would, to save his life. It was odd to be alone in a fire-bay, frightening, to be surrounded by the dead. He had lost sight of Stan and Harry. Desperately, he wanted a fag, almost as much as he wanted a drink of water. What little was left in his water bottle he was saving in case he was wounded and could crawl back.

Moans that he knew must be coming from him, for there was no one else alive near him, accompanied the mad beating of his heart. Someone jumped into the trench beside him, landing on the bodies, which moved and jerked as though alive. Quickly he brought up his rifle, trembling, then saw it was one of their own.

It was the company sergeant major, panting for breath. "Keep you head down," the CSM said, "if you don't want to get it blown off. There are snipers and machine guns to our left on the outskirts of Hulluch." He jerked his head in the direction of the village. "They have some heavy artillery there too, in the centre of the village, so when we get beyond this point we can expect some of that as well as the machine guns ahead of us."

"Yes, sir."

"We'll soon be getting it from our right too, from Bois Hugo. The Boche are in there again, came up in the night and took back some of the ground that our chaps took yesterday."

His chest was heaving and his eyes staring. Apart from that, he seemed calm, a strong, stocky fellow.

"Good man, for getting this far," he said.

"Thank you, sir." What bloody good had it done him, or anyone else?

"I'm afraid a lot of our platoon officers have been hit, I've personally seen some of them. The colonel, I believe, is still up ahead."

"Right, sir." What did he mean by that? Nothing was right. There would be no one left to give orders, in which case a decisive person would have to take over, whatever his rank. Private Roy Carter came to mind, if he were still alive.

"There's a dug-out over there," the CSM said, nodding to the point behind Jim's shoulder. "What say we look in there for some grub?"

"Yes, sir."

"I'll go first. There might be someone alive in there. Watch yourself."

The CSM, bent double, his rifle at the ready, walked over bodies that squelched and crunched, releasing odours. Close behind him, Jim moved, bent, with his rifle in the firing position at the hip, shutting his mind to all but staying alive.

The man ahead of him went down the shattered steps to the dugout. A shell had landed on the roof, leaving a hole in it which let in some light, by which they could see that the floor was littered with dead Germans and some of the British army. The CSM swept his rifle around him, into every corner, prepared to fire. Then he covered the entrance. "Look for food."

"Right, sir."

Over to one side was a makeshift table of two planks on ammunition boxes. Plates and tin cups stood on it, and what appeared to be remnants of food wrapped in cloths. There was a large square tin, which Jim reached for.

"Don't touch that!" the CSM yelled. "It could be booby-trapped, and we'll both be blown to Kingdom Come."

Jim unwrapped a cloth. Inside was a large mouldy loaf, which he broke open to find some good bread in the centre, still an off-white colour. "A bit of bread, sir. Looks all right." If it had been poisoned, he did not think it would also be mouldy.

With his filthy hands, he scooped out the centre of the loaf and handed a chunk to the CSM. It tasted stale, otherwise all right. Starving, they chomped and swallowed, while Jim continued to look under cloths. There was a hunk of cheese, alive with maggots on the top. He flicked them off with his fingers and, with a knife that was on the table, cut off the putrid surface. "A bit of cheese, Sir," he said, offering it to his superior.

Jim reached for an opened wine bottle. "I wouldn't drink that, if I were you," the CSM said. "Someone might have pissed in it."

There was a large German sausage on the table, thick with maggots and stinking. "Nothing else to eat, Sir." What he would give for several long swallows of good, cold spring water. As it was, he was so dry that he could barely speak.

"Right. We'll be on our way," the CSM said briskly. "We're directly opposite the southern reaches of Hulluch here. You can be sure that they'll have snipers and machine gunners training their weapons on this trench. They've got plenty of hiding places, some in trees. Some of our chaps are holding a bit of trench just a little west of Hulluch, the 2nd Welch, I believe, if they haven't been blown to smithereens by now. Remember that if you're wounded and trying to get back under your own steam."

"I will, sir. Thank you."

"I'll go over first. Watch my back, there's a good man. Wait a few minutes, then follow. We don't want to bunch up, we don't want to make it easy for the buggers. Any easier than it already is."

"Very good, sir." From outside he could hear again the rapid fire of the machine guns and cracks of rifles. Some were close by, signifying that a few of their men had survived, unless there was a counter-attack.

In case there were any enemy soldiers left alive in nearby fire-bays, he covered the advance of the CSM as best he could, as the man heaved himself up on to the fire-step and then over the parapet at a place where it was broken down, trying to keep as flat as he could.

Stumbling back over bodies, Jim quickly entered the dug-out again and went to a wall where he squatted down with his back to it, in darkness, keeping well away from the light that shone through the shell-hole in the roof. With his rifle across his knees, pointing towards the entrance to the dug-out, he brought out a packet of Woodbines from his tunic pocket and lit up. Ah, it was good to draw the smoke deep into his lungs, even though it made him dizzy. Quickly he got through it and ground the tiny stub into the soil.

As he mounted the steps from the dugout, his rifle at the ready and the barrel lathered with sweat from his hands, he said out loud to nothing in particular: "Have mercy."

As he came out, men from his battalion jumped down into the trench at the run, no one from his section.

"What's in the dug-out?" a captain, known to him only by sight, asked him. He was breathless, and there was a trickle of blood running down the side of his face.

"Only dead, sir. Mostly Germans. No food in there, Sir. There's a tin box which may be booby- trapped, so my CSM just said."

"Where is he now?"

"Just went over the top, Sir. Told me to follow in a few minutes."

"Right. Good man to have got this far. Ahead of us we have the barbed wire. We can only pray that it has been breached by our own artillery."

"Yes, Sir." Jim hoped that the Captain would not smell the smoke from his fag, otherwise he might think that he had been shirking. Thankfully, the Captain did not seem interested in the dug-out. There were stories and rumours that certain officers would shoot a man for showing any humanity, or for appearing to the officer that he would not obey orders under fire.

"I'm on my way, Sir."

❧ Chapter 8

As he and a few others farther along the trench emerged, a mad cacophony of fire broke out, from their left and directly in front. Although they had expected shelling from the direction of Hulluch, it still came as a shock as heavy shells screamed towards them and exploded around. Some fell short of where he was; others hit closer. Out of the corner of his eye, to his left, he saw two soldiers blown to pieces. Clouds of soil rose up high into the air, then rained down around him. His head bent, he did not turn to look. It was difficult to think, to decide what to do.

Looking ahead, he ran to get out of range of the shells. As soon as he could, he flung himself down among shell holes and long grass.

Just ahead of him, other men had done the same. As he lay, his head down, he felt a bullet slam into his haversack. Trembling, he lay with his face pressed into the earth, breathing in its scent and the smell of grass.

"What ch'er, cock," someone shouted near him. Roy Carter lay there about six feet away, his boyish face filthy and streaked with runnels of blood. Like Jim, he had his head pressed down to the earth.

"Glad to see you, mate." Jim managed to get the words out through cracked lips, shouting so that he could make himself heard above the mad screaming of shells, the tac tac of machine guns, and the intermittent crack of rifle fire. "What's up here?" The relief of seeing Roy made him feel for a moment that he had not been abandoned in hell by everyone he knew.

"I went up to take a look," Roy shouted back, his head pressed down sideways against the ground as he faced Jim. "There's ten feet of barbed wire in front of their trench, with no holes in it. I reckon they came out in the night and wired up any bloody holes, if there were any to begin with."

"What the hell are we going to do?" Jim shouted back, knowing that the trap was closing round them. It was a miracle that Roy had been able to get up to the barbed wire and back. This way and that he sought in the turmoil of his mind for answers, trying to dredge up logical thoughts against a paralyzing sense of panic.

In some ways he was glad there were no holes in the wire, because the next step, the prospect of hand to hand combat with bayonet, filled him with dread. They were nearly into the end of the horseshoe. In the last few minutes he had noticed firing from the right, as well as from the front and left. "I haven't seen any of our company officers."

"I think they've all been hit, mate," Roy yelled. "The colonel's up there, wounded, and there ain't a damn thing we can do for him. I saw him when I was up there near the wire. I'm going forward, Jim, to see if I can find a shell hole to get in. I reckon we'll have to fall back. There's nothing we can do from here. We might have to wait till dark."

"Yeah. No way forward."

"Don't hang about here too long, mate."

As Roy slithered away from him, Jim felt bereft, wanted to cry out to him not to go. Visions of how the two of them had stood in their civilian clothes outside the army recruiting office in Tunbridge Wells floated into his mind then as he saw Roy moving away into the enveloping grass and the shelter of the dead. That time seemed like another world, another age, a time of ignorance that would never come again. If only he knew where Frank was, and Bert Tomsitt, and Bill King, Stan and Harry. It wasn't that he could not make decisions on his own, it was more that they had a better chance if they could pool their resources, however meagre they might turn out to be in this trap that they found themselves in.

It was ironic that they were supposed to wait for orders; the men of the infantry were not supposed to think for themselves. Yet now, when the officers were not in evidence, perhaps dead, a man was thrown back on himself alone. There was a lesson there, if he lived to benefit from it.

Nauseated with fear, he tried to muster his initiative as shells crashed and banged around him. The thing to do would be to get into a shell hole until his nerves had settled and he could decide what to do next. Their original objective was not within human possibility, that was certain now. Just a little ahead of him, over to his right, he could see the lip of a shell hole. Perhaps if he could get into that, he would be all right for the next little while. It was a long time until dark.

Risking a semi-upright position, he ran towards it. The scream of a shell coming his way warned him, but it was there in the vicinity before he could take evasive action. The explosion knocked him sideways and he fell to the ground as shrapnel sprayed around him. Involuntarily he screamed as burning pain seared through his left lower arm and wrist, raised up in a feeble effort to shield his head and neck, an instinctive action. Near the lip of the old shell crater, he rolled into it, acting on instinct, registering as he did so that there was another man in there.

In the bottom of the hole he took stock of his injury, as dizziness wafted over him and the pain blocked out his surroundings from awareness. Blood was gushing from his wrist and lower arm, pumping in time to the pounding of his heart.

Knowing what he had to do, he fumbled in a pocket of his tunic to get out the first field dressing and the tourniquet, to get them on before he fainted. He got the tourniquet over his arm below the elbow, holding one end in his teeth, fumbling to get one end of it over the other, to pull as tight as he could and tie a knot. The gushing blood at his wrist eased. The pain was burning. By using his teeth and good hand he got the field dressing onto his wrist, tied on, where there was the worst of the bleeding.

Then, putting his head down, he fainted.

When he opened his eyes, he was surprised to find that he was still alive. Coming to awareness, sick and dizzy as he was, he noticed an odd silence. The guns had stopped.

The other man near him in the hole was dead, his face turned away, one of their own. By lying on his uninjured side, Jim was able to keep his head down and ease himself slowly over to the man, scrambling with his legs in the loose earth of the bomb crater to push himself forward. The pain in his arm was intense, bringing tears, even though he gritted his teeth and tried to stop them.

By turning the dead man's head towards him, Jim could see that it was Harry Baker who lay there, with several bullet holes in his chest. The colourless face was without expression, the eyes closed as though he were asleep, as though he had not suffered.

When you were sweet sixteen ... those words came into Jim's brain.

"Cheerio, Harry, old chap," he said. "Cheerio, boy. Sweet dreams."

Did he have the energy to move? To save his miserable life? He was crying now. Who was there to see him? It was not necessary to put on a brave face.

In the inexplicable silence of the guns he could hear the screams, cries and groans of the wounded. Risking a look over the edge of the hole, back towards his own lines, he did not have to wonder any longer why the German guns had fallen silent. There was no need for them to go on. All around him, as far as he could see, were the bodies of his comrades, mounds in the grass, like grazing sheep in a meadow in the countryside at home.

An extraordinary thing was happening before his eyes. The survivors of the battalions that had gone over the top that morning, the pathetic few out of the more than ten thousand, were straggling back slowly towards their own lines, the untouched even standing upright; the wounded who could move were hobbling and crawling. "Fall back! Fall back!" men were shouting all around him. As far as he could see, there were no officers left standing. The order to retreat had been decided by the men themselves, in their hopeless situation.

It was an obscene sight, one to break the heart. And the Germans, out of pity, he had to assume, were holding their fire. From where they perched safely on the ridge they could see the whole plain of no-man's-land laid out before them.

Yes, the pity of it, the terrible pity. Through tears he watched them go, those boys, set an impossible task, their duty to die. Soon he must join them, must risk standing up and moving back. A terrible anger and sense of betrayal against those who had sent them there gave him the impetus to scramble out of the hole, to stand upright and drag himself back the way he had come that morning. It was afternoon now, the autumn sun down from its zenith.

They had accomplished nothing for all this sacrifice. Expecting a bullet in the back, dizzy, he nonetheless held his head up and walked back west, inclining to his right a little and towards the Vermelles to Hulluch road where he knew he would eventually come to the Lone Tree ridge where there was a trench and some of his comrades would be, or perhaps the trenches of the 2nd Welch.

It was a long, stumbling walk, through mounds of the dead, the craters, and the dried grass, on numbed legs that seemed to move of their own volition.

They were waiting for him when he reached the parapet of a battered trench, a small gaggle of men, filthy and tattered, the survivors. They helped him down into it, onto the fire-step, arms reaching up, and when he fainted they caught him.

When he opened his eyes, he was lying full-length on the fire-step and someone had put a blanket over him, while another man, one of the stretcher bearers, was adding more dressing to his wound. "You'll be all right," he said.

Not one of those men was known to him.

Someone else thrust a tin of tea at him. "Sit up, mate, and get this inside you."

Sitting up, hunched over, his knees bent and his feet up on the fire-step, he cradled the hot tea. He could not say thank you because he knew he would bawl like a baby. Their solicitude touched him deeply, so that he simply nodded his thanks.

"When you've had your tea," the stretcher bearer said, "you can follow us to the dressing station, if you can still walk. It's not that far. We can stay in a trench for most of the way."

Again, Jim nodded.

The tea, which was sweet, tasted of smoke and onions. It was the best he had ever had in his life. The pain in his arm was intense, throbbing.

When he had regained the power of speech, he spoke to the stretcher-bearer who was kneeling in the bottom of the trench tending a man who lay full-length on a stretcher, who had wounds all over his body from shrapnel.

"Have you seen anything of a Private Frank Boakes?" he asked.

"Of 'A' Company, number one platoon? Or a bloke by the name of Roy Carter?"

"Can't say I have. But then, we don't always have time to get the names, and some of the blokes are unconscious. They look for the names in the dressing station, so you might find out something there."

"Thank you."

When he had drunk the tea, someone came out of a dug-out and handed him two chunks of bread with two rashers of bacon inside them. "Here's a bit of grub, mate."

"Much obliged. Haven't eaten properly for about three days." Leaning against the side of the trench, he ate. I'm alive. I'm out of it. Relief was so powerful that it made him tremulous and dizzy, more than the loss of blood and the pain would have made him feel. As he shook and trembled, the men around him did not remark on it, they were not there to judge him. In fact, as they watched over him kindly and cared for him as best they could, he thought they looked at him with a veiled admiration. As they passed him, they said: "All right, mate?"

When he had finished eating, one of them gave him a lighted fag, putting it between his lips so that he did not have to extend his unsteady hand.

What could he do but nod his gratitude, and go deep inside himself to find that small knot of something that was himself. I am my mother's son and I am here.

As Jim smoked and rested, a sergeant came along the fire bay. "We've received orders that there's a breach in our second line trench," he said, "and that all able-bodied men are to go forward to fill the gap."

"We're all wounded here, sergeant," a soldier said respectfully. "Or else we're stretcher bearers."

"The Irish Guards are supposed to be coming up to relieve us," the sergeant said, going on his way to the next fire-bay in the trench. "No sign of them."

Jim settled back into his former resting position, weak from loss of blood, having been fearful that he would be ordered back into the line, in spite of his wounds.

"Ready to move, mate?"

"I think so."

With the two stretcher bearers going in front of him, sleeves rolled up to reveal sinewy, muscular arms as they carried the stretcher with the badly wounded soldier on it, Jim shambled along the trench. Unsteady, he found himself hitting the sides of the trench as he moved. The going was slow. Everywhere there were wounded men, sitting or lying down, waiting for the bearers or trying to summon up the strength to walk on to the dressing station.

As he moved, Jim looked from right to left, searching faces. A deep sense of mourning accompanied his physical pain as he thought of Frank, his best friend, who might now be lying out there dead, or unable to get back. Perhaps it was a mistake to be too close to someone in this hell-hole, yet without that closeness one would not be able to hang on to a touch of something that one could call sanity.

They came up to the surface, like moles out of the earth, to cross a track briefly, then plunged down again, the stretcher-bearers grunting with their load. The two men, prematurely aged, as he was himself, in a torn and filthy condition, looked to be on the verge of collapse. Yet they never complained. "We're almost there, mate," one of then said, glancing over his shoulder.

Once again, crossing a road, Jim saw on the grass verges mounds of dead men whose bodies had been hit repeatedly by shells. There were not enough of the living to bury the dead.

Even looking down on the ground directly in front of his feet, to blot out the sight, his eyes found small puddles of water that had stayed on the surface of the clay, chalky soil. Those puddles were coloured with blood. With nowhere else to look, he fixed his eyes on the sweat-stained shirt of the stretcher–bearer in front of him.

"We're here."

A trench brought them to an opened-out area where the wounded lay on the ground, those who did not have life-threatening wounds or require quick surgery, Jim assumed, wearily looking around him. He still clung on to the hope of seeing someone he knew.

Steps that had been hacked out of the chalky soil went down into darkness. At the entrance was a small hand-painted sign which said

St Mary's Advanced Dressing Station. A medical orderly who was tending to someone above ground motioned Jim down the steps. It was a large dug-out, the top camouflaged with sand bags stacked on corrugated iron sheets. Over the sand bags was sod, that had kept green from the rain. The dug-out was reinforced with wood poles and beams. Hurricane lanterns, giving off dim light, showed them the way.

"Go left, mate." One of the stretcher bearers jerked his head to where there was a sign instructing the walking wounded to go left.

Another medical orderly came up to him. "Sit down over there," he said. "Where are you hit?"

"Left arm." He held up the arm, where blood had soaked through the dressings.

"We'll look at it as soon as we can. The MO will take a look. In the meantime, we have tea here. Give me your name, rank and number, regiment, company and platoon number, and the name of your commanding officer."

As he said his colonel's name, it seemed a life-time away that the man had sat on horseback in a farm field and addressed them. Would he be dead now? Or taken prisoner?

The orderly came back with a label which he attached to Jim's tunic through a button-hole. They gave him tea and a small measure of rum. All around him, men groaned in pain. Some were silent, perhaps dead; he did not know. There was a smell of blood, vomit, and human excreta. By shutting his eyes, turning his head sideways, he was able to draw into himself.

Someone was shaking his shoulder, the orderly. "The MO is going to take a look at you now."

In a smaller antechamber, which smelled worse than the outer one, the odour overlaid with the scent of carbolic acid, Jim saw the Medical Officer, a tall man wearing an oil-skin apron that came down to the tops of his boots. Over that, he wore a cloth apron with blood on it.

To Jim, he looked old. His hair was grey under a cloth surgeon's cap. "Where are you hit, son?" he said. His unshaven face was drawn with exhaustion and, in the light from four hurricane lanterns, Jim could see that his eyes were bloodshot.

Frightened at what lay ahead of him, Jim merely held up his bloodied left arm. Behind the MO an orderly was swabbing down a metal table. Before long, he found himself on it, a pad of something under his head, and the orderly was removing his dressings. From where he lay, he could not see the state of his injury, which was perhaps just as well, so he stared up at the ceiling of the dug-out that was reinforced with beams. He could just see the MO washing his hands with carbolic soap in a bowl of water, after which he plunged them into a bowl of what must have been a carbolic solution.

"I can remove some shrapnel here, if it's easy to get out,' the MO said. "Otherwise we leave it until you get to the casualty clearing station. Our dilemma is that infection will set in quickly if it's left in."

"Yes, sir."

Without drying his hands, the doctor came over to the table. "Let's take a look," he said.

The orderly put something between Jim's lips, a flat piece of wood. "Bite on that," he said, "when you need to." Then he began to cut away the blood-soaked dressings.

"I'm afraid that our supplies of morphine are very low, so we must keep it for the severely wounded and for those who must have limbs amputated," the MO said, leaning over him. "I have no other alternative to keep the pain away, other than the rum you've had."

He then began to probe about in the wounds, of which there were several. The pain was excruciating and Jim felt sweat on his forehead and upper lip, his face draining of blood, nausea and dizziness swamping him. He bit down hard on the thin piece of wood, so that his teeth met.

"I'm afraid," the MO said, "you have shrapnel lodged in here, several bits, from what I can make out. Those will have to be removed because they'll certainly become infected. I have to irrigate the wound. Even so, it looks surprisingly clean. You're lucky there."

The MO turned to the orderly and said: "Hold this retractor and pass me a pair of the toothed dissecting forceps, would you."

"Yes, sir."

They probed and pushed into the exposed flesh, while the MO grunted with satisfaction when he lifted out one of the small lead balls of shrapnel, before allowing it to fall noisily into a metal bowl.

Lifting up his good hand, Jim took the piece of wood out of his mouth and began to swear as the pain intensified and blood ran round the side of his arm.

"Good man," the MO said. "That's right, have a good swear." More lead balls dropped into the metal bowl. "We're getting somewhere."

Jim struggled up. "I'm going to spew," he said. Another orderly supported his head and shoulders while he vomited into a bowl, bringing up the tea and rum, together with bits of sandwich.

In that hellish place, in the flickering light of the hurricane lanterns, Jim moved in and out of consciousness, with the smell of blood in his nostrils and the groans of other men in his ears.

"I've almost finished," he heard the MO say, as though from afar. "I just have to irrigate the wounds, put in a rubber drain or two to allow the fluid to escape, sew up some of the larger gashes, then we'll put on a dressing. You'll have a sling, so you'll feel more comfortable. We'll give you an injection against lockjaw."

When it was over, they got him to sit up on the table so that they could apply a supporting sling to the arm. Then they helped him off the table. They held him when he buckled at the knees, supporting him to the other chamber where he could rest. What served as a bed was a shelf dug out of the side of the dirt wall, with wooden planks on it so that he was not actually lying on dirt.

"Try to sleep,'" the orderly said. "We'll be back later with some tea and food."

In spite of the terrible throbbing in his arm, he did sleep, hearing only movement and noise around him on the edges of oblivion. When he rose to the surface of consciousness, there was the same lantern-light from somewhere behind him, the same smell of smoke from it and the odour of paraffin. Time was of no importance; he did not know whether it was night or day, whether he had been there for days or hours only. It did not matter. For now, he was alive; he was out of it.

Later, they brought him tea and another very small measure of rum. Then there was a stew, of better quality than the usual, with bread. He ate it from his lap, sitting on his plank bed, his feet on the dirt floor.

⚜ Chapter 9

Later still, they came under fire, the explosions sounding distant, but he could tell they were close. As he lay on his good side, on the wooden planks, he felt distanced from that firing, as though it now had nothing to do with him. From time to time he looked down at his haversack on the floor beside him, that he had, against all odds, managed to keep with him. That kit was the only thing that linked him to the life he had had in England, when they were pretending to fight a war. In a way, the sight of it helped him to anchor a small sense of sanity, because it told him who he was.

A different MO came on duty, on what Jim assumed was the following day, to do rounds of the wounded. "Good," he said, looking at the dressings on Jim's arm very carefully and sniffing at them like a bloodhound. "There's no outward sign of infection. The dressings can be changed when you get to the casualty clearing station."

"Yes, sir. Thank you, sir."

⚜ At dusk, a convoy of ambulances prepared to move out from the dressing station, waiting for dark. Some of the walking wounded were to make their way through trenches to get to the edge of Vermelles, where they were to meet up with ambulances that would take them to Béthune.

Twelve of them set out on foot in reserve trenches that linked up with communication trenches, with a bearer who was going back behind the lines for a brief rest. They had food and water.

Before they left, Jim asked an orderly: "Has a Private Boakes been through here, do you know?"

Although the orderly looked at him as though he were mad, his answer was civil enough. "Boakes ... Boakes, it does sound a bit familiar, but I can't say. Ask at the clearing station. Things are a bit quieter there."

If Frank had died here at the advanced dressing station, he was not going to say so.

As they moved along the trenches in semi-darkness, weakened from their wounds, they were nonetheless buoyed up by the knowledge that they had survived, that with each laboured step they were moving away from the Front. They could still come under fire, but somehow they thought it could not compare to what they had tolerated. The stretcher-bearer in front carried a well-shaded hurricane lantern.

"You're better off walking," the bearer told them. "You have a better chance of getting away. Those ambulances can be stuck in traffic jams for hours, and come under shell fire, as I expect you know."

They came out of the ground at the side of Vermelles, then walked beyond it to a place of relative safety while they waited for the ambulances to come through. "We'll rest here and have some grub," the bearer said.

They passed other soldiers going up the line, who gave them items of food and cigarettes.

The devastated village, from what they could see in the darkness, looked the same as when they had passed through going the other way.

By the light of the lantern, they moved back behind Vermelles, back from the road. The men got into a grassy dip, drank from their water bottles, and fell asleep As Jim approached sleep, he knew himself to be in a peculiar state of mind, numbed and shocked. It is not a good state of affairs to know that you have been gullible, that you have been a sacrificial lamb. For what? For the redemption of old men? To fulfill the ambitions of others, in which your life counts for nothing? As a child he had been taught in the church that eventually good would triumph over evil, that right would prevail over wrong, if you did your bit to make it so. It was a doctrine that seeped into your very being, pervaded your life. Doubts came now.

The enemy, who were, they had been told, evil, thought that also. In the hands of old soldiers he had seen captured belt buckles which said: "Gott Mitt Uns." As those young men lay dying, did they know that they had been duped?

Eventually they heard the ambulances trundling through, the horse-drawn ones and the motor ambulances. All twelve men found places on the vehicles. "Good luck," the stretcher-bearer said to them. "After Béthune, I think you'll be going on towards the coast. If you get a blighty, I expect you'll end up in Boulogne, in one of the military hospitals."

"Thank you," they said to him. "And good luck to you and all." In two or three days, that man would be back in the hell of the firing line.

~ The Casualty Clearing Station was in a church in Béthune, where Jim and the others had their dressings changed. A Medical Officer there expressed satisfaction that Jim's wounds were not infected, but was of the opinion that his shattered wrist would never be able to bend. The bones needed time to knit together, at which point they would be fixed in one position, and the tendons of the wrist had been so damaged that they could not be repaired.

Private Frank Boakes was not there.

Jim and some of the others went on to a place called Lillers, after two days, a small place that was west and a little north of the route that had taken them down to Chocques from Isbergues on the way up the line to the battle front. They were told there that their destination was a military hospital in Étaples, on the coast, where they would be assessed, then would go on to Boulogne. They would eventually return to their regiments in the line, wherever that might be, or else be sent back to England as unfit for further military service. Étaples was more or less due west from Lillers.

Days later, they were moved in army vehicles farther west to a place where there was a field hospital, of tents and huts, and other commandeered buildings, swarming with wounded men. For the first time, Jim saw two female nurses. Mostly, they were tended by orderlies and the medical officers.

He was given a camp bed in a large tent, which was an open ward, divided into some sections for offices and treatment areas.

They could get baths and clean clothes. When he was settled in, with his kit stowed under his bed, cleaner than he had been for a long time, he went in search of men from his section and platoon, in areas that sheltered the more seriously wounded.

Walking between the rows of camp beds in another tent, without asking permission from anybody, he looked at each man he came to, this way and that. They stared back at him, as though expecting a visit from a long lost relative, expectantly, but without hope.

Eventually, he found Frank. He was lying on a camp bed, with his eyes closed, near a table where a medical orderly was standing up writing notes.

Squatting down beside the bed, Jim looked at the changed face of his mate, which was thin and yellowish, the eyes deep in their sockets, the hair plastered down with sweat.

A metal cage was over the lower part of Frank's body, with a rough blanket over it, signifying to Jim that he had had a leg amputated, perhaps two. Sick with apprehension that followed hard on his sense of relief, his eyes went over his friend from head to toe. Well, Frank was alive, but not too good. Around him was a smell that he knew as that of gangrene, but unable to tell whether it came from Frank.

As though aware of being watched, Frank opened his eyes, focussing slowly. "Jim! Well ... blow me!" His eyes glittered unnaturally.

"Just got here. How are you, mate?"

Frank licked dry lips, having difficulty forming words. "Don't rightly know. Lost a leg, below the knee, and got a shrapnel wound in the arm. Can't believe it's you, Jim. I thought you'd copped it."

"It's good to see you, Frank. I've been looking for you. How did you get back?"

"Well, I wasn't too far out when a shell hit. I was lucky. Someone came out and pulled me in. Lost a lot of blood."

Jim nodded.

"What about you, Jim? What about you?"

"Shrapnel wounds. I got up near the wire, where they were shelling from Hulluch. Most of our battalion dead, and the officers."

They contemplated those facts in silence. "Will you get a blighty, Jim?"

"I expect so, because I won't be able to hold a rifle properly," he said. "The wrist's shattered."

"What a flaming mess. I didn't think it would be like this. To tell the truth, I didn't have much idea of anything. I was like a babe in its mother's arms."

"No one did. Do they let you smoke in here?"

"Yeah. I could do with a puff or two, even though it sometimes makes me feel sick."

"Half a mo'." Carefully, so that Frank could not witness the shaking of his one good hand, he fumbled out a packet of fags and a box of matches from his breast pocket, both seriously depleted.

He placed one of the flattened fags between Frank's pale lips, getting a whiff of putrefying flesh as he leaned forward. Wedging the box of matches between his knees as he squatted beside the cot, he managed to light a match at the third attempt.

The flame wavered at the end of Frank's fag, then he lit his own. All around them was the steady coming and going of the wounded and the orderlies moving among them. Through the flap of the tent he could see the motorized ambulances pulling up, unloading more of the wounded to add to the rows of men already lying on the ground, waiting to be sorted out into categories according to their chances of survival.

"If you get a blighty, Jim, would you do something for me?"

"Yes."

"Would you go to see my mother? I know I asked you before to write to her. Now you'll be able to go to see her. I don't want her to get one of them letters, see? Not first off. I want someone to see her face to face, to tell her they saw me ... you know ... that I wasn't lying in some trench, like."

"Yes. I'll write down the address, Frank. I think you're going to be all right. You'll get home."

"Just in case."

"It's a good thing I've still got my right hand," Jim said, fumbling in another pocket for a small note pad and the stub of a pencil. The pad had blood stains on it. No matter, he wouldn't be sending that to Frank's mother. "Give me the address, Frank."

"It's Horsemonden, Lower Paddock Farm, on the Tunbridge Wells road. Her name's Mildred. She likes to be called Milly."

"Right you are." Jim made much of licking the pencil before writing out each word with difficulty, conscious that his lips as well as his hand were trembling. Several men nearby were moaning with pain; some were retching into bowls, distracting him. Orderlies were changing dressings, or walking between the cots with urine bottles. All around was the reek of sickness and mutilation.

Having imparted the information, Frank lay back and closed his eyes, as though the effort to recall his home had exhausted him. "What I would give to be there now," he said. "To see her and the old dog ... all the others ... to walk in the beech woods."

"You'll be there again, Frank. You have to believe that you will." Who was he, himself, Jim thought, to talk cheerfully of belief and hope for a future, when his own shock and desperation were only a little way beneath the surface of his apparent calm?

"I don't know, Jim."

"Are you in pain?"

"Not much. They gave me something. Could you get me a drink of water?"

Having observed that men were getting water from a large enamelled jug on the nearby table, Jim took Frank's beaker and filled it.

"What happened to the rest of our section?" Frank asked, after taking a drink, with Jim holding the beaker.

"I didn't see," Jim lied. "Roy was up near the wire with me, then I lost sight of him. If anyone could get through, it would be Roy." Images of Harry and Lieutenant Barton came to him.

"Sergeant Dawson's here, you know, Jim. He's in a bad way. Lost both legs." Frank's Adam's apple moved up and down several times in his thin neck as he swallowed, as he fought to control his emotions. They had all liked and respected Jack Dawson.

"You seen him?"

"No, but I heard. They say he's unconscious."

"Perhaps it's just as well that he is," Jim said, easing himself down onto the ground from a squatting position. "You'd better try to sleep, Frank. It's good for you. I'll sit here for a bit to keep you company."

"Thanks, Jim."

Later, when Frank was asleep, Jim got up and cornered an orderly. "Could you tell me when Private Frank Boakes is likely to be moved out?"

The orderly took a few seconds to recall the name. "Well, he's in no condition to be moved, because he's still on morphine and his wound's infected, so I can't say."

"If it's possible, I would like to wait here and go with him. He's my best mate, and I could do something to look after him."

"If he rallies in the next two days, perhaps he'll be all right. Men can go either way very quickly," the orderly said. He had a thin, exhausted face. "I'll see what I can do to delay your release to go back down the line, but I can't promise anything. It's the MO, as you know, who makes the final decisions. Give me your name and number."

"Yes. Thank you."

Reluctant to leave Frank, Jim sat with him for a while longer, looking at the changed face and the thin hands with their uncut finger nails rimmed with black dirt that lay on top of the rough blanket. Now and again, Frank muttered something, moaning, his face contorting into grimaces while he had his eyes closed and apparently slept.

With his mind going this way and that over the events of the past few days, Jim thought he might have killed one man. He was not sure. Neither was he sure how he felt about it, if it were so. There seemed no point to it.

❧ Chapter 10

All night long in the fitful darkness and within sound of the guns at the front, rumbling like freight trains, the convoys of the wounded and those who had died on the journey came in to the casualty clearing station.

The men who were already there in tents dozed on canvas beds or on stretchers on the ground, while the ceaseless traffic moved and shifted around them in flickering light. The motorized ambulances struggled on rutted and muddy tracks, as did others that were pulled by horses and mules that snorted and whinnied in the bleak, cold night.

Jim lay under canvas on a makeshift bed that kept him off the ground, wrapped against the cold by two rough blankets that sheltered lice. Knowing horses, he listened to their fear outside his thin shelter. Alternately he dozed or lay on his back and smoked, while the pain in his wounds burned and throbbed without respite. Sleep, when it came now and then for a few moments, was like a deadness, the oblivion of the exhausted for whom there were no greater depths this side of death.

Jerked awake frequently by the shouts and cries of men around him, shell-shocked and fearful, with pain more gross than his own, he sensed their terror as they discovered the extent of their mutilation in their moments of consciousness.

Sometimes he thought of his mother, but did not allow his thoughts to dwell there for long. She was a widow now, his father having died in 1911. Not what you could really call an old man at the age of sixty-one, his father, William, had died suddenly of pneumonia from being exposed once too often to the cold elements of his work. The real cause of death was overwork, decades of relentless work from an early age, the premature running down of the body. Born in 1851, the rudiments of his father's schooling had left him barely literate, yet he had been an intelligent man with a keen sense of justice for the working man and an awareness of politics that moved him to work for unions for farm labourers, the exploited of the rural landscape.

Jim remembered being ten years old, seeing his mother weep when his father had come home from work one day and announced "We're moving, mother!" having had a verbal altercation with his employer, who owned the tied cottage in which they lived. It had not been clear to him at the time whether his father had been sacked or had, in a few moments of self-assertion that were rare to the working man, declared that he was giving up the job. William Langridge had been a proud man, a man of self-esteem in spite of the circumstances of a life that conspired against such self regard.

What would William have thought of all this now? Of this war? It was likely that he would not approve of his being here, when there were battles of another nature to be fought at home.

Jim forced himself to settle down again into the restless doze that he had inhabited previously, while his most persistent thoughts and memories broke through and moved this way and that over the thirty years of his life. When he fell deeper into that doze, he was visited by dreams containing images of fire and madness, of faces, of staring eyes and mouths open in silent screams, of trenches that became deeper and deeper until he could not see the night sky with its stars.

As he drifted up and down he heard a man near him praying, in the voice of a child: "Now I lay me down to sleep , and pray the Lord my soul to keep."

Bugger it. Bugger.

The man began again: "Gentle Jesus, meek and mild."

Alert again, he called out in response to the cries of those around him. "You're all right, mate. We're behind the lines." That bitter humour, that had no mirth in it, was never far away. What did "all right" really mean? It just meant that you were not dead. In the deceptively simple letters that he sent to his mother, he told her that he was all right, and she would know how to interpret them.

The tent was illuminated in pale tints by shaded lanterns outside and by the glow of fags in the hands of the sleepless within, who could discern what was happening outside by the stamping and snorting of the horses and the groans of the wounded being shifted.

Jim knew that some of those wounded would be placed on the ground, to be sorted through by the medical officers. The casualty clearing station was a few miles only from the front, too close. He also understood that, if the enemy broke through the lines, and the wounded had to be moved out quickly, the seriously wounded who might not be expected to live or survive a further journey would be left outside on the ground when the tents were taken down, would be left to die.

The rescue operations were tenuous, stretched to their limit and beyond, the grey-faced medical officers and orderlies doing their best with insufficient supplies and sleep.

The scene was to him unreal, figures moving within it in the jerky, stylized movements of a Punch and Judy show at the seaside, cruel, meant to represent reality, yet bizarrely divorced from it. Here he was, in the scene, like one of the puppets himself, acting within the play that was a parody of life. And it was of his own making and the pain in his arm attested to his own stupidity. Only the men around him, a few inches away, anchored him.

Oddly, he was so much in the present moment that the past, his own personal past, was suspended in a life that he dare not yet take up lest it be taken away from him in a stroke of fate. The future did not exist beyond the hour. Only the throbbing of his wound attested to the reality of himself.

An obsessive thought came to him again, something that had been in his mind in the front line trench, in the firing line: if I don't do my bit, if I don't do my duty, someone else, one of my mates, could die because of my lack. Had he done his duty? He could not see that he could have done other than what he had done. Nonetheless, the obsession plagued him.

It would take him weeks, months, or an unknown time, to calm down, for he had geared himself up mentally as best he could for death. As a result, he had felt his sanity shifting, as though he were already dead while he breathed and moved, his mind merging with the minds of the men of his section. Now that their whereabouts were largely unknown to him, he felt lost, required to take up the remains of himself. Perhaps he never would again achieve that unthinking nonchalance of youth, for he had felt the remnants of his boyhood slip from him as he had approached the battle front.

☙ Now and again, two orderlies came into the tent silently with a folded stretcher, dark, unidentifiable figures, to take a man out who had died. They did it expertly, to cause the minimum amount of disruption. Jim turned his head away and closed his eyes when they came, trying to force his mind back to home, to a path through woods where he had walked frequently in his earlier youth. There, clumps of violets had grown, the minute flowers both white and purple that had the most intense scent, not the large dog-violets that had no scent. Sometimes he had knelt down and thrust his face into the clump to inhale. There had been bluebells in masses under the green beech trees of early summer, wild daffodils, primroses and cowslips.

The praying man had started up again: "And if I die before I wake, I pray the Lord my soul to take."

"Shut up," someone beseeched the suppliant. "Put a sock in it, do."

"Got a light, Jim?" the man next to him, less than two feet away, whispered.

"Yeah." He handed over his box of matches. "Here, let me hold the box while you strike the match, since we're both one-handed."

"Thanks."

Earlier, before lying down to doze, they had exchanged names. The other, a boy of nineteen, with shrapnel wounds in the leg and arm, was Stanley of the East Surrey Regiment that had gone over the top with his lot. Stanley had told him, in few words, how he had managed to crawl back out of no-man's-land to the safety of a trench where there was no wire. With him Jim felt almost fatherly, being more than ten years older, glad that the boy had survived. "Are you in much pain?" he had asked then.

"I would bloody say so," the boy had replied.

Jim swung his legs over the edge of the narrow cot and sat up. Stanley was more or less immobile.

An orderly came by, shielding a torch in his hand, threading his way slowly and quietly between the cots that were packed in close together. "You blokes all right?" he whispered, bending down.

"I've got a lot of pain," the boy admitted. "Don't want to complain, I know there's worse off than me."

"I'll see what I can get my hands on," the orderly said. "I take it a tot of rum wouldn't go amiss?"

"You're right there," Stanley said. Jim could hear a tentative hope in the boy's voice, lightening his desolation, the chance of temporary respite resurrecting his fledgling manhood.

As they lay back to smoke, they watched the orderly going about his rounds.

"I'm lying here wondering if I'm going to get a blighty with these wounds, or whether they'll try to patch me up and send me back," Stanley whispered.

"We're all wondering the same thing, I reckon. You should be out of it, mate. I don't know about myself."

Jim's thoughts went to those who died at the casualty clearing station, and those who were already dead when unloaded from the ambulances. They had gone to the "rest camp." That's what the soldiers called the makeshift cemetery behind the clearing station. He had seen it in his movements around the camp, where there were far too many mounds, with simple wooden crosses. If Fritz over-ran this place, it would not be a final resting place for those men.

From time to time, in odd quiet moments, he had heard the intonations of a padre as some of those men had been put to rest. He knew the words well: "I am the resurrection and the life, saith the Lord; he that believeth in me, though he were dead, yet shall he live."

Conscious that he could be there himself if his wounds became infected, or if they were already so, with gas gangrene, or the other form of gangrene, or if the hospital camp were bombarded or overrun by the enemy advance, he did not take for granted what he now felt was a tenuous hold on life. Obsessively, he sniffed at the dressings on his arm several times a day for the scent of rot, of a sign that his body was rotting away while he yet inhabited it.

He knew himself to be deeply and profoundly shocked, tremulous to the core by what had happened to him, to the others in his section and his platoon. Not knowing where they were, his mates, other than Frank and those he had seen dead, the ignorance of their fate continued to torment and haunt him as he pined for them. Then there was the image of Roy Carter crawling away from him towards the enemy barbed wire, the last he had seen of him.

∽ All night long the convoys came down the line from the plains of Loos, bringing the wounded, maimed, and dying. No doubt others would be going up the line towards it, wearily marching as he had done, along the muddy congested roads, making way for the ambulances coming the other way. Like him, they would be caught up in that confusion, chaos, and weariness beyond description.

Jim had grown his thumbnails long so that he could hold a fag between them to draw in the last bit of smoke, to make the fag burn up into nothingness. Now he could not do that. Nonetheless, he savoured as much of it as he could before it burnt his fingers.

The orderly came back, gliding ghost-like in the semi-darkness.

"Here's the bloody lady with the lamp," Stanley said.

The man carried two tin mugs. "Here you are, boys," he said quietly. "Make the most of it."

They could smell the rum before he handed them the mugs. "Much obliged," Jim said.

"I reckon you'll be moved out later today," the orderly said in a whisper, bending down to them. "Anyone who can be moved will have to go. There are too many other poor sods coming in."

"What's the news?" Stanley said.

"Not good. A slaughter."

"Where will they take us?" Jim asked, leaning sideways on his good elbow.

"You'll go by ambulance to the rail head. That's not far. Then you'll go by train to Camiers, I expect, near Étaples, to a stationary hospital. That's not far from Boulogne. There's a proper hospital in Boulogne. If you get a blighty, you'll go on there, then get the ship home from there."

"Where to?" Stanley asked.

"I reckon they'll take you to Folkestone or Dover, then on to a hospital by train, perhaps to London. Or perhaps you'll go somewhere else, I don't know."

When the orderly moved off, Jim sipped the liquid, holding it in his mouth before swallowing. His lips trembled as they pursed to grip the edge of the tin mug, as did his hand that held it. His thoughts shot back to the front, to the darkness perforated by flashing lights, overarched by crashing sound that no human ear should have to be assaulted by; then in the daylight, the tac, tac, tac of machine guns.

Roy, where the bloody hell are you?

With the rum came the welcoming dizziness and distancing, the warm, burning sensation as it went down his gullet.

"That was good of him," Stanley said, moving his head closer to Jim over the space between them, so that they were almost touching, conscious of men around them snoring, many in a deep sleep from which they would not awake. "I've heard of that Eat-apples place. A lot of people die there, so I've heard."

"You can die anywhere, mate. I'll be glad to get on that train."

"If one comes. I wouldn't be surprised if they make us walk."

They slept then, on and off, lulled by the unfamiliar alcohol. When a grey light of pre-dawn penetrated the canvas of the tent, a padre made his rounds, carrying a shielded hurricane lantern, looking for soldiers who were awake. Some pretended sleep, for the sight of the man of God seemed to presage their own death.

"Would you like communion, my son?" the padre asked Jim, who lay with his good arm behind his head, eyes open. The padre wore a dog collar with his army uniform, the only thing that distinguished him. On his cap was a regimental badge that was unknown to Jim.

"Yes, father," Jim mumbled. "Thank you." A lazy man's profession, his own father had said of priests, a remark that had made him wary of them, and even more so of the ones who avoided being within shelling distance of the Front. Yet he had seen one or two in the front line trenches. A willingness to change his mind, a need for words to take away the sick feeling of grief that held him, propelled him once again to swing his aching legs over the side of the cot.

"Yes, please, sir," Stanley acquiesced. "Thank you, sir."

Stanley was a short, thin, and weedy lad with a prematurely old face, pale and creased in lines of worry, his eyes serious and watchful as though he had never laughed much in the nineteen years of his life. It was not often, Jim speculated as he watched the lad struggle to lie on his good side to face the padre, that anyone paid Stanley much personal attention. On his face now was a certain light of expectation. His hair, light brown, short back and sides, had an extra long forelock that hung well down over his forehead, adding a boyishness to that old-young face. Being older than Stanley, Jim recognized the vestiges of the boy's innocence in that expectant face and hoped to God that Stanley was out of it for good. He could have wept.

"I will kneel," the padre said, getting down awkwardly in the narrow space between the two cots. "You stay where you're most comfortable, lads." He was one of the oldest people that Jim had seen in the army, at the Front or close to it, a pale, grey man whose weariness appeared like a mental wound.

Gently the padre placed a hand on the head of each soldier, from his kneeling position. Reverently they bowed their heads as best they could. "Almighty, everliving God, maker of mankind, who dost correct those whom thou dost love, and chastise everyone whom thou dost receive; we beseech thee to have mercy on this thy servant visited with thine hand, and grant that he may take his sickness patiently, and recover his bodily health — if it be thy gracious will — and whensoever his soul shall depart from the body, it may be without spot presented unto thee; through Jesus Christ our Lord. Amen."

"Amen," they murmured, subdued. This was a little too much like the absolution before death.

"Hebrews 12:5," the padre whispered. "My son, despise not thou the chastening of the Lord, nor faint when thou art rebuked by him. For whom the Lord loveth he chasteneth; and scourgeth every son whom he receiveth. St. John 5:24: verily, verily, I say unto you, he that heareth my word, and believeth on him that sent me, hath everlasting life, and shall not come into condemnation; but is passed from death unto life."

In spite of himself, his scepticism, Jim felt a peace come over him mentally, rather like the effect that the rum was having on his physical body; it came over him like a warm wave, and he welcomed it.

Then the padre gave them the sacrament, murmuring "The body of Christ, who died for you," after which he struggled to his feet. "Will you lads be moving out today?" he asked.

"We expect so, padre," Private Stanley Watts said.

"This place is becoming very full, more than can be coped with ... so many in the night," the padre said. "Anyone who's capable of being moved will have to go today. So good luck, lads, if I do not see you again. The Lord be with you."

"Padre, have you seen Private Frank Boakes, in number one tent? He's my mate, rather seriously ill with an infected wound." Jim found the courage to ask, the padre being of the officer class.

The man obligingly consulted a ragged note book, which he held close to the lantern as he squatted down again. "Ah, yes. Private Boakes. I have made a note that he seems to have improved somewhat during the night, he's drinking more water, which is a good sign."

"I want to wait until I can move out with him, if I can," Jim said. "To help him, like."

"Well, in my opinion, he too will be moved out today, because we have too many wounded men lying outside with no cover. He will be well enough to take his chances with the journey, I think."

"Thank you, sir. Can you tell us where Étaples is?' They were like lost children in a dark place, with no landmarks.

"It's in more or less a straight line west from here," the padre said. "On the coast. Not really very far when you're going by train."

When he had gone, an orderly came round collecting full urine bottles. Jim closed his eyes, thinking about what the padre had said about Frank, whether he had been telling him the truth, or was trying to spare him. His inclination was to believe him, that Frank would be moving out with him during the coming day. In the chaos of the move out it should not be too difficult for him to accompany Frank, to keep an eye on him. Until they were on the move, the terrible fear would not leave him.

Soon he would get up to go to the latrines. Still he had his kit with him intact, and he had retrieved his greatcoat from behind the front lines, after leaving the dressing station, where his platoon had been required to leave them on the safer side of Vermelles. There was a damp cold now, and rain, which seemed to go through into his bones, making the coat a cherished object, in spite of the lice harboured in its seams.

He remembered that, on his way back down the line, shambling with the other filthy wounded, they had passed a dead horse, one of several, beside a track that lead into Vermelles. This one drew his attention as they had to skirt around it, together with other debris of shattered wagons, broken ammunition limbers, and the like. The belly of the horse was bloated, its legs stiff like sticks, and he had looked at it quickly, a pity transcending his own miserable state. From early boyhood he had loved horses, the gentle shires that pulled the hay wagons, the ploughs, and the threshing machines, loved their clean scent, their willingness to work patiently, obediently. Here they were in the battlefields, sweet, voiceless creatures who could not give their consent, nor withhold it.

Then, before he could avert his eyes from the dead horse, a rat, sleek and obscenely gorged, had come into view behind the horse's head and looked at him, as though it had been waiting for just that moment to meet his eyes with its own. Like him, he had thought then, this creature must be marvelling at the unseemly excess that it saw around it, this terrible, unnatural glut.

&. Chapter 11

In the comings and goings around him, inside and outside the tent, his mind ranged again over all that had happened to him in the space of a few hours, as though everything that had gone before in his life had been condensed down into that.

What had shocked him most at first, as they had come within range of the heavy artillery on the way up the line, was the destruction of the buildings. In his life he had never seen anything that resembled it. Good, solid, public buildings that must have stood for generations, and peoples' homes with the simple accoutrements of their everyday lives, were turned into rubbish and rubble. The orderliness and symmetry that gave some meaning to human life, the evidence of benign human endeavour, had been taken away. The speed with which it had happened was something that he could not take in.

Likewise, the army tries to take away your self, he thought; it intends that you should die. But after the battle, when you find yourself still alive, you come back to the self; there is nothing but the self. Ideology is dead, a lie. Innocence has gone, and what is in its place is a kind of madness as one struggles to return to the self, to reclaim it.

&. He got up and made his way out of the tent into the sharp, cold air. His wounded arm in its sling throbbed and burned, yet he could tell by the quality of the pain that it was not infected with the gangrene that he feared, or with anything else. There were mercies in this hellish place, and that was no small mercy.

There was a faint mauve and pink glow amid the grey in the eastern sky. Out there somewhere were the other men of his platoon, the mates of his section, whatever condition they might be in, alive or dead. Bert Tomsitt, Bill King, Roy, and those others whose bodies he had not seen in no-man's-land or at the dressing station. The fact of Frank's presence in another tent held him together, and as soon as he could he must make his way there to assure himself that Frank's place was not empty.

Guided by the stench, he made his way in the near darkness to the latrines, a stumbling journey that took him past the "rest camp." In his pocket he had a safety razor and a piece of soap in a tobacco tin. Near the latrines was an ablutions tent, with a stove where one could get a bit of hot water for shaving. There he could take off his puttees and boots to wash his feet. Like gangrene, he feared "trench foot," in which the skin would peel off the feet and rot would eventually set in, from constant wet.

As he walked, wounded men groaned and called for help when he picked his way among them, those who had been forced to bivvy on the ground because there was no room for them in the tents. He passed a cook tent where food was being prepared in field kitchens.

The dark, simple crosses of the cemetery drew his eyes as he walked past. After he had relieved himself and shaved, he would go in there and look at the names, by the aid of the torch that he had in his pocket.

Others were before him in the ablutions tent, in various states of undress, with evidence of all types of wounds. With them was the familiar aura of unwashed bodies and clothes. All were lit up by the burning stub of one candle in a bottle.

"Whatche'r, cock," someone said to him as he passed through the flap of the tent. "There's hot water on the stove in that dixie. Help yourself."

"Thanks, mate." There were a few enamelled bowls by the stove, with tall jugs of cold water. Empty ammunition boxes served as tables and stools.

It was a luxury to pour hot water into one of the bowls from the dixie on the makeshift stove, which was a tin box with a chimney, set up on stones. In a corner where there were two boxes, he eased the tin with the soap and razor out of his pocket, clumsily with his shaking hand.

The first thing was to soak the hand in the water, then put water and soap on his face, on the stubble of his incipient beard, an indulgence that brought with it a sense of guilt with the pleasure. While others were lying dead, by the thousands, he could splash warm, clean water over his closed eyes, could ease off the caked mud from his forehead, and feel the delicious caress of the liquid through his spread fingers. The humble scent of the plain soap could override for a few seconds the scent of dissolution that permeated everything about them and on them.

As he spread lather over his face with his hand, he found cuts that he did not know had been there; they stung as the soap penetrated. By touch alone, he lathered and shaved. There were no mirrors.

After that, he plunged his head into the warm water, ran the soap awkwardly over his filthy hair. Bits of towelling hung from nails attached to posts. Like the others, he sat on a box to unwind his puttees and wash his feet, ignoring the lice that crawled on him.

"You with the West Kents?" the nearest man-boy next to him asked.

"Yeah. You?"

"The 'Buffs.' What a bloody cock-up that was back there. I reckon three quarters of the boys didn't get out."

"You're right there,' Jim said, noticing as though observing another, that his own voice shook and he was not ashamed of it.

The boy talking to him had several nervous tics — the rapid blinking of his eyes, the repeated compressing of the lips, and the jerking of the good hand that he was using to unwind his puttees, while he glanced around quickly and constantly, from side to side, as he spoke.

"We're the lucky ones," the boy said.

"I wish I felt lucky."

"You will," the boy said, with the wisdom of the ages.

"Shrapnel wounds?" Jim asked.

"No, machine gun bullets. Lucky to be alive, I am."

As they eased off their boots and peeled off rotting socks, the foul stench of their feet added to the general odour in the tent. "Here," the boy said, looking quickly all around him and pulling something out from inside his shirt. "Socks. I saw some in a sack and pinched a few. Have a pair."

"Thanks." In exchange, he gave the boy a couple of fags. "I reckon they'll burn all our uniforms when we get back down the line to a proper hospital."

"That's all it's good for." They lowered their raw, blistered feet into the bowls of warm water. "Pitiful, ain't it, that we've come to this? All I care about now is this — getting a wash, getting a bit of grub, and getting away from here."

∾ It was a fraction lighter when Jim entered the cemetery area that was sheltered by a few bare trees, yet not light enough that he could read the names that had been painted on the crosses, without the aid of his torch. It was a wonderful thing to see trees that had not been shattered by shells.

Slowly he walked between the mounds, peering at names. There were several from his regiment; none that he recognized.

"Gippo!" he heard someone calling. It would be one of the cooks bawling for the walking wounded to fall-in for their breakfast.

A cold, keen wind blew through the cemetery and seemed to whistle right through him as though he were no more substantial than they who lay in the soil. Others were searching through the names also, moving like shadows among them.

Walking away, Jim knew that it was by chance only that he had escaped, that he stood there with wounds that, had they been a few more inches to the right, could have killed him. The shrapnel and shell fragments could have pierced his heart or the vulnerable arteries and veins of his neck.

Where was God in all this? Many times the question had come to him. The poignancy and the pity in the actuality of these mounds, these young men forever to be in alien soil, signified to him that God, if he existed, took no part directly in human affairs. When you're dead, you're dead; that came to him too, as much as he wanted to think otherwise.

At this moment, in farm fields, in gardens, in villages and towns, the families of these lads were going about their business, waking to a new day of hope, in all ignorance. Soon their lives would be altered. Like their dead boys, they would enter a place from where there was no going back.

He leaned against a tree, nausea and dizziness, the ever present throbbing pain, sliding over him as though claiming him away from life. Death then seemed like a friend, when it would be so easy to sink down to the ground and not get up, to sleep and not wake. The guns had started up to the east. If only he could shut his ears so that he never had to hear the sound again.

"Come and get some grub, mate." Someone put a hand on his shoulder, one of the shadowy living who had emerged with him from the cemetery. "That'll set you up all right. Come on."

Together they moved forward, Jim stepping lightly as though in a dream, towards the cook tent to join a loose line of the walking wounded outside, a motley crew that milled about. It was understood that once they had eaten they would help to serve those who could not walk, who were capable of eating, those lying on the ground.

Dreamily he took a mug of tea that was handed to him and a mess tin of what looked like porridge, with a hunk of bread on the side. "Bacon and eggs when you get up to the stationary hospital," the cook orderly said.

With the collective sense of relief at being behind the lines, there was also a holding in of grief, the need to weep, to let go of the mask of bravery that each man had put up as best he could. Jim sensed it all around him as men silently took their food, the usual jokes missing or half-heartedly given so that few laughed. It was too soon to let go.

"This way, mate." His companion guided him over to a corner of the tent where they could eat, shielded from the wind, squatting down, with the earth as their table.

"This is a drop of good," the other bloke said, slapping his lips together after a swallow of tea. "See anyone you know in there?" He jerked his head back towards the "rest camp."

"No," Jim said, his teeth chattering. The other man was older, a corporal, with a weathered face, one half of which was bandaged, and an arm in a sling. From his cap badge, Jim could identify him as being with the East Surreys, who had been with them at Loos. It was a bond between them, almost as though they were brothers in this waste land, each drawing a bleak kind of comfort from the other.

"No more did I. All my section gone, as far as I know. Get that tea inside you, mate, you don't want to get pneumonia."

The tea was good, hot and sweet. They drank it as they ate the bread, leaving the porridge to last. Somewhere in his tunic Jim had a spoon and he fumbled for it.

"It's not knowing where they are that destroys you," the corporal said. The slight difference in their rank was forgotten at that moment, in the way that it could never be forgotten with an officer, one an ordinary bloke from Sussex, the other of the same background from Surrey.

"Fall-in, all volunteers for grub duty!" a cook sergeant called out.

Jim moved into line with the others, to volunteer. Inside himself a deep shivering informed him that he was ill, other than any sickness from the wound, any infection. Men died like flies from influenza, pneumonia and bronchitis, so he had heard. Just as many, if not more, than from wounds. There was nowhere to go that was really warm, nowhere to get away from the elements.

Those with one good hand could carry three tin mugs of tea to the wounded that lay on the ground. Pale hands reached up out of cocoons of blankets and ground sheets in the greyness of dawn to receive the tea, while murmurs of thanks drifted over the dark sea of men. Cold came up from the soil like a threat. Back and forth the servers went, carrying bread and porridge, while the guns pounded to the east.

∽ Although the padre had said that Frank's condition had improved during the night, Jim was both reluctant and anxious to see him, dreading that he would enter the tent, look over to where Frank had been yesterday and see that another man was in his place.

Yet there he was, turned sideways on his cot as Jim made his way towards him among the closely packed men. He was sipping from a mess tin, bent over.

"Jim!" Frank's waxy-looking face lit up. His eyes were a little less glazed, it seemed to Jim as he eased forward, watching him. "Help me eat this skilly, mate. Haven't got the strength."

Relief came to Jim, when he thought he was incapable of feeling anything positive. There was a smell of carbolic in the tent, disguising inadequately the odours of vomit and human excrement. He squatted down beside Frank and took the mess tin of watery porridge from him. "The padre said you'd improved," he said. "He reckons we'll both be moved out today." As he spoke, he looked around him, trying not to breathe too deeply.

"I think I can make the journey," Frank said. "I want to get out of here. It's too close to the Front by half."

As he spooned porridge into Frank's mouth, Jim knew that events were too great for them, that they had been reduced by circumstances — most of them man-made — into this pageant of the one-handed man feeding the other whose flesh was rotting on his living body. This was what they had been brought to, by some strange and evil design; they had been made to run the gauntlet. A steady, depressing anger had lodged within him, making him vow to fight for his own survival with every effort of which he was capable. With that anger and bitterness he would keep faith with Frank; he would do everything that he could to help Frank get back.

They, of the working classes, had been deemed expendable. For every Lieutenant Barton, there had been dozens, perhaps hundreds, of his own kind, the so-called common man, of those who must work for a living. From now on he would be mindful of the fate that had spared him, would be respectful of it, even though he feared that it was blind and arbitrary.

"I'm becoming ill," he said to Frank. "I think it's pneumonia. I'll be with you on the same train."

∽ The ambulances came up shortly after breakfast, as soon as they could all see what they were doing, ready to move out the ones that could be moved. Orders came to prepare one's kit for departure. Officers came round with lists of men's names, ticking them off. Frank and Jim shared one last cigarette as they tried to negotiate with their orderly to be on the same vehicle. "What I don't see, I don't grieve over," he replied.

In the chaos, Jim stayed close to Frank as the stretchers moved out from under canvas, and other men moved in. "All change!" someone called out.

With full water bottles and chunks of bread in pockets, they hunkered down under the dark canvas covers of the motor ambulance as it moved forward out of the casualty clearing station. It laboured and groaned under the weight of the wounded, stacked up in tiers, heading west. Jim curled up and struggled to put his head down, his skin burning, knowing himself to be very ill.

∽ A train bore them steadily away from the front, so that they could no longer hear the guns. There were female nurses on the train, moving among the tiers of wounded men who lay in bunks and on the floor. In his feverish state, Jim wondered at first if those women were a figment of his imagination until one said to him: "What are your injuries, Private Langridge?"

"Shrapnel wounds left arm," he said his litany from his place on the floor. "And pneumonia."

A cool hand was put on his head. "You need to be in a bunk," she said. "Get up and come with me."

As he followed her, clutching his kit to his chest, the chugging of the train seemed to keep time with the pounding of blood in his head. A bunk was found for him, not far from Frank. Cold water was poured into his mouth from a china cup with a spout on it, and he closed his eyes and swallowed until it stopped coming. "Try to sleep," the nurse said. With the clattering of the train drowning out other sounds, he slipped into a welcome darkness.

∽ When he surfaced, there was the sound of metal wheels on tracks again, as though they were chanting, we're going back, we're going back, we're going back.

All was confusion, both in his mind and on the train when it came to a halt, and his burning body felt heavy, incapable of movement. In due course he was put onto a stretcher, lifted out of the train into the open, where cold, fresh air played briefly on his face before he felt himself placed again into a vehicle. Without the energy to open his eyes, he had to assume that he was in yet another ambulance as an engine started and he was jolted from side to side. Without emotion, other than a remote kind of sadness that did not seem to be related to him, he wondered briefly if he were, after all, going to die.

Vomit rose up into his mouth and, as he did not have the strength to turn his head, spewed down the front of his tunic.

❧ Chapter 12

Someone was emptying his pockets and taking off his clothes, cutting the cloth around his injured arm with a pair of scissors. The metal was cool against his skin.

They rolled him carefully this way and that, stripping off clothes that were plastered to his body with sweat, dried blood, and mud. The movement forced him to a semblance of consciousness so that he opened eyes that seemed to have been gummed shut, and became aware of the smell of his own body.

A male orderly was deftly removing his clothes, while a woman in an unfamiliar nurse's uniform began to wash his face, dipping a cloth into a bowl of warm water. Then she put a foul smelling chemical into his hair, combing it through.

"You're in Camiers," the nurse said, in an accent he did not know, as though his question had been spoken aloud. "In a military hospital. You poor boys, you poor, dear boys. You're safe here. You might be going on to Étaples in a day or two. It's close by. Or they might send you directly to Boulogne."

Jim moved his eyes in her direction, to fix on a face that was young and fresh. He could see that they were in a wooden hut, with screens around the bed on which he lay. To save his life, he could not have spoken a word because fatigue weighed him down, as though he had an actual weight on his chest. Breathing was painful and his skin burned with fever. Every part of his body ached.

His mind drifted away to when he had taken care of farm horses at age fourteen, learning from others about their sicknesses, how you gave them Spirits of Nitre to make them sweat when they were ill with fever. Perhaps that was what he needed now. Nitre ... night ... blackness ...

Is this what it was to die? This distancing of the self, this drifting away?

While the orderly started on removing his puttees and boots, pulling him back to a sharper awareness, the nurse washed his ears and neck, bending down over him, moving quickly and efficiently. She wore a triangular white starched cap that came down beyond her shoulders, and a starched white apron over her dark dress. It was difficult to think that all this was real, that he could be now well behind the lines, so much did it seem to be a scene that had been conjured up by his brain.

"We're the Newfoundlanders," the nurse said, in response to his bewilderment. "We've been here since nineteen fourteen. I'm from Newfoundland."

When they had removed his filthy clothing, washed his body and hair, they started on his wounded arm, carefully removing the dressings. "We're going to swab these wounds out with Lysol."

He turned his head away so that he would not see how he was mutilated, and held his breath initially so that he would not inhale any scent of putrefaction. Please, God, let me not have gangrene. His hand, the left one, was fixed and bent down towards his arm, from the shattering of the wrist bones and the tendons. Forever it would be like that, he sensed. As he was in mourning for his friends, so he mourned the mutilation of his own body, while understanding came to him that this wound had, and would, save his life, for he doubted that he would ever be able to hold a rifle again with this claw of a hand.

"It looks clean," the nurse said. "Can you move your wrist?"

"No." Now he could breathe easy. The scent of antiseptics filled his nostrils as they swabbed his wounds, the pain of it bringing him back to his surroundings, to the groans of others, the comings and goings all around, like an unfamiliar, complicated dance.

A medical officer came to him later to ask him questions that he was barely able to answer, to listen to his heart and lungs. "I'm afraid," the man said, "it looks like you have rheumatic fever. That's my considered opinion. On the other hand, your wounds show no sign of infection. Remarkable."

They kept the screens round his bed, so that he thought he was marked for death, that they could more easily spirit his body away in the night. But then the nurse came back with a bowl every hour. "You're to have a tepid sponge every hour," she said to him the first time. "With water and surgical spirit, to keep your temperature down. You're to stay in bed and drink plenty of water. If your chest hurts, you must let me know and we'll put warm poultices on it to loosen any phlegm. I'm going to bring you some warm milk sweetened with honey. My name's Nurse MacDonnell. My first name's Milly, but keep that quiet."

"Am I going to die?" he said.

"No."

Darkness had come down and oil lamps had been lit when Nurse MacDonnell returned for the last time that day and folded back the screens, wheeling them to stand against the wall behind his bed. "I'm going off duty now," she said. "There will be a night nurse looking after you. She'll give you something to help you sleep. Private Frank Boakes was asking after you. He's down at the end of the hut, and he said to tell you he's all right."

Jim nodded his thanks, closing his eyes against tears. He felt as weak as a kitten.

Food was brought on a tray by an orderly, thick soup and a plate of mashed potatoes and small chunks of greyish looking meat. Nurses hurried about from man to man, helping each one eat when he required it, those who had no hands available, and those whose hands shook so much that they could not hold a spoon. Jim leaned on his side, observing all this through eyes that burned, while he tried to spoon mashed potatoes into his mouth, with little appetite. A nurse gave him a spoonful of the soup when she stopped by his bed. His senses of smell and taste had been blunted by the illness, so that the food tasted of nothing much. All through his childhood he had been taught never to waste food, so the sight of the food he could not eat brought regret to add to his other emotions.

There was little talking or smoking in the hut, Jim noted, as he looked briefly around him. It hurt to raise his head far from the pillow. Like him, they were too ill to smoke.

"How are you, Private Langridge?" the new nurse asked, sitting on a stool by his bed, taking up the spoon.

"I don't rightly know," he said. "Better than when I came in, but still pretty bad. It's a relief to be here ... can't help thinking about my mates, the men of my section, not knowing where they are. I feel I ought to be with them, back there."

"All the men say that when they come in here," she said, putting more soup into his mouth. "It's understandable that you want to know what happened to them, that you want to see them if you can." She stood up and moved around him, shaking up his pillow, straightening the blankets, before stooping down to give him more food. "I can see you can't manage too much of this, because you're not well, in addition to having the wounds. Just do what you can. You see, you must take care of yourself, as well as worry about your friends, because a lot of it is up to you now. Back there, you couldn't do much for yourself, you had to follow orders, but here you have to fight to make yourself well."

Jim looked at her fresh, open face, that was a little studious, made more so by her glasses, and thought how sweet she was. About his own age, her face held all the signs of chronic fatigue that he knew well himself. "You're very kind," he said, falling back exhausted onto the pillow. "I appreciate it. It's a miracle that you're here to take care of us."

"Don't forget, your friends will be wondering where you are, too," she said. "And here you are safe. So you must think about yourself now."

"Are we safe here?" he said wearily.

"There have been air-raids," she said. "Even though we have large red crosses painted on the roof of each hut, and on the tents. They don't care. If there is a raid, you get under the bed. I know I don't really have to tell you that. I'll be back soon with a sleeping draught for you and some fresh water."

"You're a very long way from home," he said.

The nurse smiled and looked down, shielding her expression from him. Any leave she had would not be spent at home.

So even here they were still very much in the army, still under observation by the enemy. What a diabolical thing, to bomb mutilated men, some of whom would no doubt die anyway and others who would never be a threat again, if they ever were in the first place. The nurse was right, of course; if he did not think of himself, he might not survive, might just give up. To be free of lice, to feel cotton sheets beneath his body, to have clean night clothes on, were pleasures that he would savour in the moment. To add to that, Frank was safe, in this building, very close. Certainly he was luckier than some; at least one of his mates had survived.

∽ In spite of the sleeping draught which had knocked him out for the first few hours of the night, he woke several times after to find the bed and his night clothes wet with his sweat. At least once he must have cried out, for he was suddenly awake and aware of a sound dying in his ears and a nurse came hurrying up to him, her starched uniform making a sighing noise as she moved.

"Private Langridge, what is it?" She took his hand, while she placed her other hand on his forehead. "You're burning up. You're safe here, Jim. Don't fret. I'm going to sponge you down again with cool water."

He drank from the spouted cup that she put to his lips, the water moving painfully down his burning throat as he swallowed.

"You'll be moving out of here to Boulogne soon," the nurse whispered to him. "As soon as you're fit to be moved. There are too many other poor boys coming in here from the Front."

When she sponged him down he felt better, reminding him of the times he had wiped down horses, had talked to them, cajoled them, gentled them.

After that, he slipped in and out of disturbed sleep. In the moments of wakefulness, disjointed pieces of rhymes and hymns came to him that he had known since early childhood: "Not last night but the night before, two Tom cats came knocking at my door. I went downstairs to let them in, they knocked me down with a rolling pin." "Abide with me. Fast falls the eventide, Lord with me abide."

The rhymes faded out of his mind as quickly as they had entered it and he could not force himself to remember the next line of any of them. Likewise, images of the Sussex and Kent countryside came to his inner vision, places where he had walked as a boy — meadows of tall grass that would be hay when mown, clear, swift streams where he had sometimes fished in the shallows, using a stick, a piece of string and a bent pin. The images were out of his control, coming and going.

Again he wondered whether he was dying. The brain did miraculous and strange things, he suspected, to shield the inner consciousness from the knowledge of one's own death. "Time like an ever rolling stream, bears all its sons away, they fly forgotten as a dream dies at the opening day."

Ghosts came up out of his mind, grey figures retreating across the plains of Loos, some bending down to pick up wounded comrades. They moved slowly, labouring, fading away.

In lucid moments he considered the enemy bombing from the air, from those flimsy planes, deliberately targeting the red crosses on the roofs. Yet they had allowed him to walk away in those few moments of pity, perhaps sickened by what they saw in the dried grass before them under the domed sky. Where did the depravity come from that allowed such things? No answers came to him in the fretful night.

For the remainder of his life — if he were to live — he would be aware of that chasm of meaninglessness, and then the gesture that had allowed him to live. Surely they had felt it too, those Germans who had had him clearly in their sights. They had not finished with him yet; until he got back over to England he was not safe. If he did not get a "blighty," if an as-yet-unknown MO somewhere in Boulogne decided he was fit, that he could indeed hold a rifle, he would be back at the front.

Somewhere back there the decimated ranks of the 8th Battalion of the Royal West Kents were behind the lines, waiting for orders to be sent forward. He pined for them, the living and the dead, with a sharpness that he had never known before, beyond the limits of thought or word. They would be sent to the Front again and again until not one man was left standing.

❧ In the morning the tall, thin Medical Officer did his rounds of the supine ranks of men. Some MOs were detached in manner; some were bluff and hearty but nonetheless aware of differences in rank; some met the men on what they considered to be the infantry man's level. Others were seemingly classless, displaying no sense of rank, only a quiet compassion. This MO, of an apparently melancholy persona, was of the latter ilk, with neither overt optimism nor pessimism, talking man-to-man. He wore a white coat over white surgical smock and trousers.

"This disease that you have, Private Langridge," he said, sitting down on the bed so that it groaned as though it would collapse, "the rheumatic fever, can cause damage to the valves of the heart, which is why I have ordered complete bed rest, because it is not inevitable. If it should happen, you may not feel the effects of it until you are much older. You must take care of yourself, and we shall take care of you too as best we can under these circumstances. When the fever is down, you will be transferred to a better place. You understand?"

"Yes, sir. Thank you, sir."

"I shall recommend that you return to England permanently. But it will ultimately be the decision of the MO at our General Hospital in Boulogne."

"Thank you, sir." A sense of tentative peace came over him.

∾ Opposite Jim were three men with broken legs, the affected limbs raised up in traction, with metal splints attached to ropes and pulleys, the ropes weighed with small bags of sand to pull on the limbs. Jim amused himself with speculating on how it all worked to align the broken bones. From where he lay he could not see the faces of the men, only now and then the plumes of smoke from their fags. Somewhere, Stanley Watts would be in a similar contraption, if his leg had been saved.

"Are Frank Boakes and Stanley Watts all right?" he asked the nurse when she came to him.

"Yes, both all right. Private Boakes is down that end, and Private Watts at the other. Do you want to send a note?"

"Not now, thank you, nurse. Would you tell them I was asking?" Again he speculated, with the grim humour that came to him in thoughtful moments, on the term "all right" that was used so widely and meant that one wasn't actually dying, but could still be in a bad way as far as long term prospects went. Perhaps if someone were actually dying, the nurse would inform others that the patient was "not so cheerful today."

"I would like to write a letter to my mother, if I can manage it," he said.

"If you can't, I'll write it for you," she said. "I'll get you some paper, pen and ink."

Their kindness, their willingness to do everything for you, contrasted so strongly with the chaos and madness of the battle front that he constantly wanted to weep.

There was a special writing box with an ink-well in it, with a lid to prevent spillage. Jim's hand shook as he dipped the nib of the pen into the ink and as it hovered over the paper. He sat propped up in bed, glad that the men opposite were obscured from him by their broken legs pulled up in the air by their traction, that the two men on either side of him were snoring. It was not that he suspected their censure; it was more that he was not used to displaying weakness in other than a private place. No, they would not judge him, any more than he would judge them, yet it was ingrained in him to bear up under hardship.

"Dear Mother," he wrote slowly, "I am in a military hospital at the coast of France, having a slight wound in my left arm from a bit of shrapnel. I am all right, am being looked after well. The food is good here. Try not to worry about me and bear up." He decided not to say anything about the rheumatic fever, because she would most likely know people who had died from it. "I hope to be back in England before long. You can write to me at the General Military Hospital, Boulogne, so long as you've got my rank and number. I hope this finds you well. Love to all. Your Loving Son, Jim."

He thought of his two brothers, Harry and John, too old to be in the army, and his four sisters, all married bar young Harriet who had gone to work in a munitions factory, glad to be out of domestic service. So he was the only one his mother had to worry about.

The writing was so poor that he wasn't sure she'd be able to read all of it. But, at least, she would know it was from him. He had printed the name of the hospital. Just knowing that he was back behind the lines would allay her fears, and no doubt a letter would get to her faster from here than the ten or eleven days that one took to get to and from the Front.

The nurse addressed the envelope for him, to Penshurst, Kent. The effort of writing left him trembling and exhausted.

∾ That night he refused the sleeping draught, for he feared now the drawing down of a drugged sleep, lest it drag him down deeper into death. During the day he was all right, mostly, his fear lessening.

∾ It was five o'clock in the morning and he had not been able to sleep properly. A light was coming up outside, mean and drab, as though unwilling to show the world as it was in another day. With the coming of the light, the nurses and orderlies dimmed still further the few lights inside, to save oil.

Birds were chirping in the trees outside the few windows of the hut, unaware that there was a war on. Had they known the danger, Jim thought, they would surely have been somewhere else. Their sound, that taken-for-granted loveliness, was something to hang on to from a world of life, of the normal — if indeed anything would ever really seem normal again. He had seen behind the façade of what people called civilization, had seen how quickly it could be destroyed.

Jim swung his legs over the edge of the low bed, fighting dizziness and the heavy exhaustion of the insomniac. He liked to piss standing up. There was an enamelled urine bottle in the narrow wooden locker beside the bed.

Leaving the full bottle on the floor under the bed, he got down on the floor in the semi darkness and crawled the short distance, close to the ends of the beds, to Frank's bed. "Whatch'er, cock."

"Jim! What the hell are you doing out of bed? They told me you had to stay in bed, mate." Frank was smoking, lying on his side, facing the end wall of the hut, as Jim crawled up beside him and sat down on the rough floor.

"Wanted to see you, make sure you were in the pink, as they say." They spoke in whispers.

"You all right, Jim?"

"No, not what you'd call really all right." Having a severe fever, from which you could die, was in a different category from a war wound from which you could die. The latter you expected to get, even looked forward to it if it got you home. "Got rheumatic fever. Don't worry, it's not catching, as far as I know. They said it could damage my heart."

"Hell, you should be lying down, but it's nice to see you, Jim. I expect to be going on to Boulogne in a day or two. Listen to this, they've put maggots in my leg, deliberately. The bloody maggots eat the bits that are rotten but don't touch the healthy flesh. Have you ever heard of that?"

"Can't say I have. Makes sense." The image came to Jim of the maggots on the slimy, rotting cheese that he had seen in the German dugout with the CSM, how they had been starving and had eaten it. Now he felt sick at the thought of those teeming creatures in the stinking, gangrenous wounds in the stump of Frank's leg.

"I've got to have an operation when I get to Boulogne, to clean the leg up when the maggots have finished with it," Frank whispered. "They must be doing some good, because I feel all right."

"You stink, all right," Jim remarked, from his perch on the floor close to the leg in question.

When Frank smiled, Jim knew that he had improved from the time he had first seen him in the tent at the casualty clearing station, on the brink of death. "That's why they put me down here at the end of the hut, I expect. Strictly speaking, it's only a stump, but I think of it as a whole leg. Want a puff, Jim? It's me last fag, so we might as well share it." Frank extended the cigarette.

"No, thanks. Don't feel like it."

"It comes to something when you don't feel like smoking a fag. Listen, send me word if you know you're getting out of here before me, and I'll do the same."

"I will. Cheerio, mate. Better get back."

Jim crawled back, intercepted by an orderly before he got to his bed. "What are you doing out of bed?"

"Needed some exercise. Went to see a mate."

"You silly bastard. Don't you know you got heart trouble?"

Chastened and a bit frightened, he allowed the orderly to tumble him into bed and pull the blankets up over his shoulders. He lay with his eyes closed until breakfast came, his head swimming with dizziness and the sound of his heart beats pounding through it like the banging of a drum.

❧ Chapter 13

Two days later, he and Frank, Stanley Watts, and a few others from his hut were put on a hospital train bound for Boulogne. As they were carried out on stretchers, Jim looked up at the grey sky, the blustery clouds, enjoying the wind on his face.

Each stage in this journey on the soil of France was a step closer to the ship that would take him home. In the weeks that he had been in France, all sense of idealism had been whittled away so that only a basic striving for physical and mental survival was left now that he was less than whole.

"The MO told me I'm almost certain to get a blighty." Stanley imparted the news to Jim as they were put down in their stretchers side by side on a platform beside the train. "What about you, Jim?"

Jim put out his good hand to Stanley. "Don't know yet," he said. "Don't want to take it for granted in case it doesn't happen."

∽ The military General Hospital in Boulogne proved to be a former monastery, a solid, large, majestic red brick building situated part way up a hill, surrounded by trees.

Things are looking up, Jim thought, as he was carried into a spacious, light and airy open ward, where several nurses came to meet them. The medical orderlies transferred him to a bed near the door, then handed his papers to a nurse. "Don't forget to address the nurses as 'sister'," the orderly instructed him quietly. "They are all trained here."

"How are you, Private Langridge?" the nurse asked him.

"Not too bad, sister."

"This is a medical ward," she said. "The doctors are concerned about your fever, even though you also have a wound. You'll get more rest here, not so many comings and goings as on a surgical ward."

She was very pretty, tall and stately, rather "posh," he thought. "Thank you, sister."

"One of the MOs will be along to see you soon, and I'll be changing your dressings then so that he can see the wounds at the same time. A belated lunch for you first, I think, my man."

This was paradise. It had been a long time since anyone had called him "my man." It was a proper bed, more than a few inches off the ground, with pristine sheets. Beside it was a locker of his own, into which the orderly had shoved his filthy kit, and there was a tall window across from him through which he could see evergreen trees. Someone had put a few flowers in a vase on his locker, with a small card: "Merci, cher soldat."

It occurred to him that he must certainly be in a bad way mentally, for those three simple words, which he understood, brought such a cascade of emotion that it took all his powers of control to keep his face from falling into that mask of grief of which he knew himself to be capable. Other men were all around him; there were comings and goings. He did not doubt that beneath their calm exteriors they were as affected as he was himself, their emotions battened down, near the surface, ready to erupt.

The pretty nurse came back with a tray, with covered plates on it. When she saw his shaking hand reaching for the tray, she smiled and said: "Let me do it. I'll get you started." With a flourish, she took the metal cover off the largest plate and placed it on his locker.

"Voilà!" she said.

Looking at the food, a vast improvement on anything edible he had seen for a long time, he felt again the urge to weep. "Très bon," he said, instead.

∽ Seeing that Jim was not allowed to get out of bed, other soldiers came to sit beside him over the next few days, to share a fag, to talk, including one man from the opposite bed, from whom he accepted a cigarette.

"Private Jesse Walters," the other said, holding out a hand in which dirt was ingrained, and the nails bitten down. In the chair beside the bed he eased his splinted leg out in front of him.

"Where from?"

"London. Hackney ... the east end. I was pleased to get out of bloody Hackney, I can tell you, mate'" He spoke quickly, nervously, with a Cockney accent, so that Jim could barely understand what he was saying. "I think I'd like the army in peacetime ... it just about suits me. Know what I mean?"

"Yeah. Haven't smoked for days," Jim said. "Didn't feel like it. That's what having a temperature does for you. How old are you?" The man-boy was stunted and gaunt, pale in the way that Frank was pale, from years of malnutrition, no doubt. It was a wonder that he had got into the army. It would take years of good food to get him to look any different. When he grinned, he showed yellow, rotten looking teeth.

"Twenty two," Private Jesse Walters answered. "On my records it says twenty six."

Gradually, tentatively, their stories came out, gaining momentum with the telling.

"I'm a gunner — was a gunner, perhaps I should say," Private Jesse Walters said. "My brother, Tom, in a different section, was a gunner and all ... killed in a direct hit at the gun emplacement ... blown to pieces ... without trace, they said. I had to write to my poor old Dad and tell him ... and he can't read or write ... then he was to break the news to my mother. Cor ... it must have just about killed him ... Tom was his favourite, you see, though he tried not to have favourites, we all knew it. Doted on Tom, he did, the poor old sod. I told him to bear up, not to give way. There were twelve of us kids, but I reckon they'll still miss Tom."

"It's very hard," Jim said. "There are no words. It all stays inside."

"I told them the usual ... that he didn't suffer. Well, perhaps he didn't."

"You did what you could."

"They'll never be the same, me Mum and Dad. From now on, they'll just be marking time, I reckon. They carried on something awful when he said he was joining the army."

"They'll have you ... your Mum and Dad. We won't be the same, either."

"Me!" He laughed. "I was the black sheep. Anyway, I'll do my damnedest to get a blighty. I've had dysentery and pneumonia, as well as bits of shell in my leg. It's funny ... half of me wants to get away, even if I had to lose the leg for it, and the other half wants to get back there and have another go at bloody Fritz. I want to pass the shells, to load them, to fire the guns ... for Tom and all the other Toms. I want it all to be over, not just for me."

"I know what you mean,' Jim said, contemplating the other man from his own perch in the bed, propped up by pillows. "Most of the mates of my section ... I don't know where they are."

"To know where anyone is ... well, that's a luxury, mate. It's all right if you know where you are yourself."

"Perhaps you're right there." Jim savoured the pleasure of his cigarette, pondering on the wisdom of others. "Being one of twelve kids, you couldn't have had much attention, growing up. I thought being one of seven was bad enough."

"Attention! I don't know what the word means, mate. Perhaps that's why I like the army. Standing to attention is more my line. If I make myself useful, they might keep me on in a nice cushy job back at the barracks."

"Pretend you can cook. That's all it takes."

They smoked and laughed at their own pathetic jokes, disguises for something else that had no name that they knew of.

⁓ One morning a boy from the other end of the long ward came to sit beside him, shyly, with respect, like a child meeting a revered father that he did not see often. "Heard you had heart trouble," he said, opening the conversation quietly. "How are you feeling?"

"I'm in the pink," Jim said, smiling. "You can't be more than fourteen." The face that smiled at him was fresh and babyish, the eyes a clear blue, yet showing signs of recent illness.

"I'm seventeen. Told them I was eighteen and they didn't question it. Got bronchitis and pleurisy on the ship coming over. Never got anywhere near the Front."

"Don't be in too much of a hurry. You won't miss anything. It won't be over by Christmas."

"Call me Alf," the boy said, bringing a tin of tobacco out of a pocket and proceeding to roll a cigarette. "Have you got any advice for me when I do get there?"

The finished fag, with bits of tobacco hanging out from either end, he handed to Jim without asking him if he wanted it, and struck a match.

Jim allowed himself time to think, deciding not to let the boy know how short a time he had actually spent at the front himself. "Well ... keep your head down when you're supposed to keep it down ... try to think for yourself even though they don't want you to ... look out for your mates ... try to get a blighty ... write home frequently ... eat everything you can lay your hands on ... and get drunk every chance you get."

"You are a one," Alf said. "Anything else?"

"Try not to get lost. They could shoot you for it ... your own side, that is. For cowardice and desertion."

In silence they smoked for a while. After an orderly came round with mugs of tea, the boy continued to sit there while they drank it. "Try to latch on to someone you like and respect," Jim said, "and do what he does. Try to learn from him."

"What's it really like there?"

"It beggars description. Nothing can really prepare you for it, so don't try. You live in each moment as it comes along."

∽ They kept him there well into November, in the old monastery that seemed like a stately home, when gradually all obvious traces of the fever subsided, the headaches lessened, the throat became less raw.

The tendons and muscles of his wounded arm tightened, contracted, and froze as they healed, deforming him still further. Various MOs looked at him thoughtfully, without much comment, while the nurses gently changed the dressings after swabbing the wounds with solutions of lime, potassium permanganate, Lysol, iodine, whatever had been ordered.

During that time he made friends with soldiers and nurses from various parts of the world, as well as his own part. Their presence seemed like a miracle, that they were all there for the same cause, that some had journeyed there across oceans, far away from childhood places.

Several letters came, including two from Anne Jefferson, that sweet, fair-haired girl who was "in service," training to be a cook at a big house. In those letters she told him how relieved she was that he was alive, how she had prayed for him — something she seldom did at other times, how she missed him.

He kept those letters in his pyjama pocket, next to his damaged heart.

∾ In the sleepless hours of each night Jim thought about what he would do if he got home. Part of him wanted to rejoin his regiment, the remnants of the 8th Battalion, if only to find out who was left. Loneliness in the early hours of the morning was like an abandonment, such as a young child might feel having lost sight of its mother. It was a no-man's-land of the soul, a yearning for the men who had become closer than brothers, for they had been forced into a commonality even closer than that of a real brother, held there by the fear of brutal death.

In that time that was neither night nor day, he thought about home, what sort of job he would get with the handicap that he now had. The army could only keep wounded soldiers on for a further six months after they became unfit to fight, unless they had some special skill that was in short supply. He had heard about mutilated former soldiers begging on the streets.

∾ Frank came to see him from another ward, pushed in a wheelchair by a nurse, the tall, stately one whose name was Henrietta, who had told them to call her Etta.

These days, the drawn, grey look of pre-death was going from Frank's face, Jim noticed, as they greeted each other. The maggots had done their job well, those lowly, repulsive creatures, brought into the service of man when it was convenient for man to let them live. Not unlike the situation of the private soldier of the infantry. How typical that was of the arrogance of man.

Would he himself, lowly on the scale of the caste system, be allowed to live? It came to him then, looking at Frank, that he would not ask anyone's permission to be able to live. Like his own father — a courageous man in a humble life, who had found the gift of rhetoric in himself to speak out for a farm labourers' union, to speak up for himself also, "We're moving, Mother!" — he, Jim, would quietly take back his life. Although he might pull a forelock, and say "Very good, sir," from time to time, inside himself he would be free.

The surgeons at the hospital had cleaned, trimmed, and sewn Frank's amputated leg into a neater stump, so he told Jim, and proudly displayed the item in question. He also disclosed that he did this with alacrity if anyone showed even the slightest interest or curiosity about his leg. "I'm going home, Jim. Day after tomorrow," he said, his face alight. "They're taking me to Folkestone first off, so I've been told, then on to the hospital near Shornecliffe camp in Kent ... perhaps on to London later, when I'm stronger."

"I'm happy for you, mate," Jim said, shaking his hand. "I'll miss you here."

"Likewise, Jim. Have you had word yet about your blighty?"

"Not yet."

"They can't send you back up the line, not with an arm like that, not with the fever damage."

"Remains to be seen. My chest feels raw inside sometimes."

"If you like, boys," Nurse Etta said, leaning down from her great height like a conspirator, speaking in her breathless, posh voice, "I'll arrange for you, Private Langridge, to be taken down to the docks in a wheelchair to see Private Boakes off on the ship to England. I'll push you myself. I have two hours off duty that day, just when needed. Would you like that?"

"Not half," Frank said.

Nurse Etta left them there to talk in private. "They say she's the daughter of an Earl," Frank confided. "She told me she applied to go to the Front, but they wouldn't let her ... said she had to get some experience here first."

"Mmm. Perhaps her Dad's protecting her."

"I reckon she'll get there ... she's very strong and determined, if you ask me."

"They don't let women right up to the front. It would come to something if our women got killed off."

Jim had visions of the beautiful Etta snuffed out prematurely near the battle front, her body placed in one of the "rest camps" in alien soil with the others, tragedy upon tragedy, those who had once been comely and sound of limb likewise. The army only took those who were sound.

∽ It was a dry, cold day when Frank, with others, prepared to leave the hospital. Nurse Etta came striding up the ward. "The MO has given me permission to take you out, Private Langridge, provided that you're bundled up warmly. Beastly cold day." She announced that to Jim at his bedside, with the air of one who had achieved a profound fait accompli, and he felt certain that anyone would give her permission to do anything.

"Are you up to it? That's the main thing," she said. "Of course, you don't actually have to do anything, I'll do the pushing."

"If you're willing to do that, sister, then I'm willing to just sit there. I'm grateful."

"Right you are, then. It's as good as done."

"Thank you, sister. Perhaps you could arrange for me to get a blighty as soon as possible, too," he joked.

When she laughed it was a lovely sound that echoed down the long ward, and men's eyes, without exception, looked towards her. Even the white uniform, designed to hide the feminine shape, was worn by her with panache. Tufts of wavy auburn hair peeped out from around the tight fitting cap. She wore white shoes with a two inch heel that added unnecessarily to her majestic comportment.

"Oh, you'll get one, Private Langridge," she said, smiling. "Never fear."

When no one was listening, she called him Jimmy, and demanded that he call her Etta. Far out of his social caste as she was, it did not occur to him to turn the full blast of his longing upon her. Grateful for her sincere attention, he met her on her own terms.

"We must start out at least half an hour earlier than the ambulances," she said, "since I shall be on foot, if we are to get to the docks before Private Boakes."

When the time came for him to be bundled up for the outside, Nurse Etta raised an arm imperiously for an orderly to bring up a wheelchair. Blankets were put around him and over his head, while she tied a scarf loosely over his nose and mouth. "That's so you don't breathe in the beastly cold air," she said. The scarf was hers, he suspected, for it was of a soft, fine wool that held a delicate scent of violets. It was one of those unexpected things that made him want to weep, together with her gesture as she tied it round him with a flourish.

She herself wore a thick black cloak that came down to her ankles, plus a black uniform hat with a badge on it. "Here we go," she said, when they were outside. "It's downhill all the way."

Soon they could see the smoke stacks of two ships at the docks, then the ships themselves, waiting like living things, patiently to take the boys home. "It's not a very big dock, as you can see," Etta said. "The ships usually have to back in."

A pain of longing lodged in Jim's chest as he looked at the ships and at the choppy grey sea beyond. It was peculiar how you experienced emotion in your chest like a physical pain. Although he did not have anything specific to go back for, except to be reunited with those he loved, he found that he longed for the country itself, the way it looked, the rolling green fields, nature, the song of the thrush in spring, the peculiar scent of wild current that grew in secluded places, things like that. There would be the anxiety of finding work, once out of the army.

There was a troop ship waiting out in the water, as there was no room for it in the docks, bringing fresh fighting men into France. Many people were milling around on the quay when he and Etta arrived there, in both uniform and civilian clothing. English and French were being spoken all around them.

"I know just where to go to be sheltered from the wind while we wait for our boys to come down," Etta informed him, pushing him briskly along the quay in what was now a damp cold coming off the water. "I can see our ambulances coming now."

Red Cross stretcher bearers unloaded the men. When Frank and Stanley appeared, Etta moved Jim forward to walk beside them as they were carried to the gangplank, then pushed him boldly forward so that he could take Frank's outstretched hand. Impressed by a self-assurance that was in no way arrogant, he could have laughed out loud with glee as she manoeuvred him here and there deftly, taking it for granted that they had an absolute right to be there in the melee. Clearly, she had done this before.

"Cheerio, mate! See you over home, God willing," Jim shouted. "Don't go to too many dances until you get that wooden leg."

Frank, tearful, his lips trembling, could say nothing. His grip was strong until he was carried away out of reach.

"Cheerio, Stanley. Good luck."

"Cheerio, boy."

Calls were coming all around for Etta, which she accepted graciously. "Cheerio, sister! Thanks for everything."

Etta waved like royalty, imposing and lovely in her long black cloak, her head held high. Jim, getting to know her, was beginning to admire her as a great actress with an amazing ability to compose her features according to the situation, yet not without absolute sincerity, hiding sadness. "Good luck, boys!" she called out, again and again. "Bon chance et bon voyage!"

He wanted to take her hand and kiss it, as a humble suppliant, but of course he couldn't. For one thing, she was holding the handle of the wheelchair, or waving, so neither of her hands came within grasping distance. Etta had too much breeding, he knew, to be embarrassed by such a gesture, had he succeeded.

There was an air of joyfulness, tinged with so many other emotions. Someone shouted out: "Give my wife a kiss from me!" To which someone else added: "Give her one from me, and all!"

The last Jim saw of Frank was his pale face, swathed in grey blankets, and his hand waving before he disappeared on deck.

They were quiet, he and Etta, as they began the return journey up the zig zag incline of a paved path. Jim was glad of the scarf over his face, that she was behind him pushing.

They stopped at a wooden bench overlooking the harbour. "I wish I could get out and walk," he said.

"Don't even think of it," she said, breathless.

"Do you wish you were on that ship, sister?"

"No. This is where I want to be, here in France," she said, staring back down to the sea, her eyes blank as though she were somewhere else. For the first time that Jim had witnessed with her, her habitual ebullience had left her. "This is where I ought to be, because I'm wounded inside. I've applied to go to the Front. That is, as close to the Front as they will allow me."

It was difficult for him to ask her what she meant, not his place to do so. Sensing in her a grief let loose, he knew he must wait for her to come round to telling him, if she wanted to.

"The man I wanted to marry was killed at Ypres, so you see, if I'm killed out there I'll be close to him. It's what I want."

So that was it. Perhaps he should have guessed. "You'll see things beyond belief, as well as risking death," he said, wishing again that he could take her hand. "As you must realize, almost all of the most mutilated men die before they get as far as Boulogne."

"Yes, I'm prepared for that, as far as one can be. I don't mind dying, knowing I'll be close to him. That's what I have to hold on to ... all I have. I've asked to be sent to the Ypres salient."

"You might feel differently, once you get there," he said.

"There will never be anyone else, so my life is already over ... husbandless and childless." Etta turned to Jim. "Sorry to burden you with all this ... it was seeing those men off that released it ... knowing that he will never leave."

"It's not a burden. You've done more for me than I could ever thank you for. All I can do is listen. I must say that the world would be a poorer place without you. I know that's a cliché, as they say, and I'm sorry for it."

"Cliché is the most comforting in times of dire need, did you know that?" she said earnestly. "That's why our childhood prayers stay with us, the ritual of what we knew then. I've seen it time and time again here in France, in the wards. When someone needs you to say something quickly, here in the moment ... perhaps they're dying ... you aren't going to wrack your brains for something original, you take someone's hand and you say just what is ready to come out. It comforts a man, whatever his rank. After all, what is cliché but truth repeated often. So long as it's sincere."

"I know ... I feel already the loss of you," he said, "if you don't mind me saying so."

"Don't mind. Perhaps the world will be a poorer place without me," she said, "because there are people who love me, whom one cannot discount. But in the end, one belongs to oneself."

"It's not just that, of course." Jim sought for words to fit his emotions, always aware of the shortfall in himself. "Not just about them. But we must consider those who love us, consider their grief, because when someone loves us we have an obligation to them, regardless of what we think of them, whether we love them in return."

"You're a good man."

"We must think of their grief," he repeated, carried away by the rare intimacy of the moment, trying not to be too earnest at the same time. "Whether it's someone we love ourselves, or someone we can barely tolerate."

"Yes ... yes."

"You see ... love puts that burden on us, that's what I've always thought," he said, looking at her averted face. "Men are often thought of as not as loving as women, but really men are very aware of the depth of the obligation to a women, when she loves ... so they are careful what they take on."

"And women are not?"

"Not in the same way. Women are more willing to give of themselves, if they care. Some men are willing to exploit that. Others hold back."

"I do understand," she said. "I can see that it is that way ... exactly."

"I've never said that before, to anyone. For a long time I've thought it."

"You see, for me the world is a poorer place, a dead place, without the man I love. It isn't that I feel sorry for myself, Jimmy, don't think that, when so many suffer more than I do. It's that I choose not to go on. Otherwise, one is forced into a hateful passivity."

"Are you saying you want to die there?"

Etta took his hand. "I am just very certain of what I must do, of where my duty will lead me. If it means death, then ... yes."

"I admire you," he said.

"I'm not sure I'm worthy of admiration. Cowardice is more my line, really. I always fight against it."

"Don't think that, because it can't be true."

"Why did you join up, Jimmy?"

"I don't know. At the time there was a certainty. Now, anything certain has gone ... perhaps it had something to do with the hateful passivity you mentioned."

"You're a good man," she repeated. "A brave man."

"For letting other people try to kill me, both our own side and the enemy, then managing to walk away? I don't know what to think."

"We'd better get back," she said, standing up. "Thank you for listening to me so patiently."

"Good luck to you, and God bless you," were all the further words he could get out, clichés all. In a way, he understood that it was because he was wounded and ill that she, an upper class woman, had been able to unburden herself to him, a man of the working class. Although she had revealed herself, her terrible vulnerability, to him, she still remained by virtue of her job and professional relationship to him, the wonderful lady bountiful. He was more than willing with her to assume the position of gratitude.

As they moved back slowly towards the hospital, Etta panting from the effort and their breath clouding in the cold air, a blast from the ship's siren disturbed the relative quiet.

"There they go," Etta said. "Goodbye, dear boys. God speed."

When the hospital ship had pulled out of the dock, the waiting troop ship would pull in to disgorge another load of young men for the front.

Though glad for Frank and Stanley, Jim felt utterly bereft as the sound of the siren died away, and birds that had risen up from the trees around them in clouds settled down again.

After Etta had toiled up the hill with him, resting here and there in silence with the grief strong between them, after she had helped him into bed and walked away, he turned his face into the pillow.

✏ Chapter 14

Each day seemed to blend into the next in the big ward as the days grew colder and the sea more choppy. Off-duty nurses took the men in wheelchairs down to the town, those who were capable of taking such a trip, sometimes to a tea shop by the water front, or in one of the little streets back from the quay.

The French people they met in shops and on the street were friendly, although often lugubrious and abject when speaking of the progress of the war, the latest news from the Front. "Tout les morts," many of them said, shrugging their shoulders and rolling doleful eyes, spreading their hands in gestures that expressed all they were feeling, palms upwards. "Pauvre soldat," they sometimes murmured when they caught sight of his wounded arm, particularly the women, touching him on the shoulder.

While the soldiers waited outside in their wheelchairs, the nurses went into shops for them to buy things that they had seen in the windows. Jim bought a piece of lace for his mother, some delicate embroidered handkerchiefs, and a tiny porcelain vase which had a crest on it, with the words in English: "A present from Boulogne."

How odd it seemed, buying such things. Even the mundane, normal pastime of shopping seemed strange, belonging to another world that they had left behind for ever. Even so, it would have felt even odder to go to see his mother with nothing in his hands to give her. Incongruously, there were toys in the windows for little children, and a few decorations for Christmas.

While the nurse was in the shop, Jim sat in the wheelchair in his blankets, scarf and hat, looking at the toys at close quarters. Would he ever have a child? Often he thought that he would, then at other times he dared not let himself think about it, for it seemed too far in the future for him to grasp, even though he was already thirty. The war had put a halt to normal aspirations. It hung over them like a spectre, increasing the dread it inspired with every week that passed.

Here in France, the people were right to fear that their country could be overrun by the enemy. So he thought as he looked at them, as they walked the streets, going about their business. It was in the atmosphere, that expectation, which had more to do with realism that any undue pessimism. Distances were short. Only a long line of men and guns, dug down in the soil like rats, wavering back and forth, kept them safe.

He supposed that he had joined up to help keep these people safe, and his own people who were not directly threatened yet, it seemed to him. Sometimes he thought of himself as an actor in a play, going through certain motions, mouthing his lines, as though he were not really in it himself. Things seemed unreal, like props behind the scenes, and he with them.

More sober now, in every way, than he had ever been in his life, he was not sure about anything, least of all about his own puny effort. Perhaps the most he did was to reassure these people here who touched him and called him "pauvre soldat."

When he and the nurse walked by the sea, hunched against the wind, the water was the colour of muted ink, that spoke of great depths and icy cold. England, not far away across that water, seemed to him then at an interminable distance. That other nurse, Milly, whom he had met from Newfoundland, must feel like that when she looked at the sea and knew that she could not really go home until it was all over. Grey mist shifted and formed itself into curious shapes, obscuring any view more than a hundred yards or so out to sea. A few gulls wheeled and cried near the quay, an eerie sound that broke the otherwise strange and bleak silence from nature.

The sounds came from man at war. All the time, trains of the wounded came in, disgorging their loads. Ambulances trundled back and forth, adorned with red crosses. Small boys and girls, with their parents, stood and stared at their changed town.

∽ Back in the ward, Jim put his purchases, wrapped in tissue paper, carefully in his locker, not sure yet whether he would ever be in a position to actually hand them to his mother. The medical officers and other officers responsible for deciding whether a man should be sent back to the Front or be shipped to England erred on the side of sending him back to the Front, so he had heard.

∽ "Jimmy," Nurse Etta addressed him quietly one day when he had been walking around the ward to strengthen his weak legs, "you are to go before the medical board, two MOs and two other officers, at three o'clock this afternoon. They will decide if you are to go home. The MO will tell you this officially, I'm just giving you some advanced warning. They'll want to look at your arm, so I shall take off the dressings from the scabs, put a towel round it, and put it in a sling. I'll ask one of the orderlies to get your clean uniform out of storage. You must be in full uniform, as far as your injury allows. Keep your spirits up."

"Thank you, sister." It was clear that he was still very much in the army, and must now make another mental shift back to absolute army discipline. With that shift, he could expect no mercy if he were capable of usefulness in the front line.

One of the other men sidled up to him when Etta had gone. "She's nice, isn't she?" he said.

"Very nice," he said.

"Don't be too friendly with her, mate. You could get her into trouble, and yourself too. She's not for the likes of us."

"Don't I know it," he said, moving away. "Don't waste your breath."

The brief exchange made him upset and angry. That was the army for you, always someone watching you, envious perhaps, ready to take the rise out of you. Or perhaps it just had to do with living with a group of disparate people.

Sometimes he wished he had taken the promotion to corporal that had been offered to him early on, because taking account of the rate at which men were slaughtered, he might be a sergeant by now. Had he survived Loos unscathed, he might have been even higher in the ranks of the NCOs. Perhaps it was wishful thinking on his part that he could put men like the soldier who had just spoken to him in his place, tell him to mind his own bloody business.

As he walked back to his bed he decided not to let it upset him. If someone was cussed like that, envious, it meant that he had something to be envious about. It was laughable; he had never felt less like an object of envy in his life.

∽ Even he was surprised at how bad his arm looked when all the dressings were off at once. Usually the nurses kept part of it covered up when they changed the dressings. Large reddish brown scabs covered parts that were still healing, while those that had healed were an ugly dark pink, criss-crossed by lines where the skin and underlying tissues had been stitched. The wrist was severely bent and frozen in place; he would never be able to lift it up.

When the time came, Etta escorted him to the medical board room, where there was a bench outside with three other men sitting on it. "Good luck," she said. "Wait on this bench when they've finished with you, blighty or no blighty. We don't want men walking back to the ward by themselves."

"Why?" he said. "Are they afraid we might run away?"

"Well, I'm not supposed to tell you this," she said, "but a shocked man who was ordered back to the Front ran out of here and flung himself into the sea and drowned. Since then, all men have to be escorted."

One man had already been inside, Jim guessed as he sat down beside him, judging by the strained expression on his face. "Bloody Ypres salient, I expect," he said, with bitterness, when Jim looked at him. "The rest of my lot are there, what's left of them. I've been told to report to my regimental officer here and be prepared to move up the line four days from now."

A nurse came for him then, cutting off his monologue. "Good luck, mate," Jim said. How meaningless that was. The other waiting men were silent and cowed.

There were four men in the room when it was his turn to go in, two MOs who were familiar to him, two other unknown officers, one considerably older than the other. All four of them sat in a row behind a table, and there was a single wooden chair in front of the table, some distance back from it. A sergeant at the door said to him: "Walk easy, Private Langridge. Go and stand beside that chair. Don't sit until you're told to sit."

"Very good, sergeant."

On legs that felt like putty, he walked over to the chair as instructed.

"Stand at ease, Private Langridge," the senior officer said to him, "and take the arm out of the sling, take off the wrappings."

One by one, they got up to look at his arm at close quarters. "Can you lift up the wrist?"

"No, sir." Anxiety rose in him. They were tough, he sensed, quick to bring a man down if he were swinging the lead. Accordingly, he forced himself to make his movements slow and deliberate, not to get agitated.

"Raise your arm up above your head," one officer commanded.

Slowly he raised his arm. Doing that accentuated the deformity of the wrist.

"Straighten your elbow out as far as you are able," the younger non-medical officer commanded. "Is that as far as you can do it, man?"

"Yes. It's just a bit stiff, sir, since I've had it in a sling for a long time," he said, trying to keep his voice neutral, with nothing that could be construed as "insolence" in his tone. He sensed that this officer, the less senior, would be keen to send men back to the Front. It was well known among the men that a soldier could be shot for "dumb insolence" at the Front, rather in the way that a "hanging judge" would take delight in having a man executed for a minor crime.

"Answer only the questions that are put to you, Langridge," the young officer said. "We don't need a lengthy explanation."

"Very good, sir."

They walked around him as though he were a specimen. So far, the MOs had said nothing; now one of them said: "Put your arm down, Private Langridge."

The senior officer asked him: "Is the elbow joint painful?"

"No, sir."

"Tell us about your chest, Private Langridge ... how it feels, if there's pain, and whether you feel breathless when you walk quickly."

Although the senior officer spoke with a neutral voice that was almost kindly, Jim had a strong sense that this was a trick question, perhaps that a lot hinged on it. "There's not what you could call pain," he said carefully, "although it sometimes feels raw, like, particularly when I breathe in very cold air. When I walk quickly I do sometimes feel breathless ... I reckon it comes from being in bed for such a long time." Then he remembered that he was not supposed to give an explanation.

They were back behind the table now, staring at him.

"You may sit down now. Do you notice any difference in the regularity of your heart beat, Langridge, when you walk quickly?" one of the MOs said. "By that, I don't mean the rate at which your heart beats, which normally increases when you walk quickly. I mean the rhythm of it, which should be like the rhythm of a trotting horse, which goes on and does not pause. Have you noticed any pauses? Take your time to answer."

"I can't say I have, sir," he said truthfully. "But then, I haven't walked quickly very much, I've been too weak."

The younger non-medical officer opened a drawer in the table and took out a rifle, handing it across the table towards Jim. "Take this rifle, Langridge. It isn't loaded."

Jim got to his feet so quickly to grasp the rifle with his right hand, an instinctive action, as though he had been ordered to stand-to, that he swayed slightly, a movement not unnoticed by the officers. Indeed, they were like hawks, unsmiling, watching his every move and facial expression, and no doubt drawing certain conclusions from the tone of his voice.

"Face the window, Private Langridge, present arms, and then raise the rifle to the firing position."

Automatically, with his training and experience guiding him, he did his best to present arms and then to raise the rifle quickly to his right shoulder in the firing position. The index finger of his right hand was on the trigger, and the damaged left arm awkwardly supporting the weight of the rifle.

A sharp pain shot through his left arm as he closed one eye and squinted down the barrel, trying to align the sights, noting that they wavered, in spite of his best effort.

"That's no good," he heard one of the MOs say. "The man can't hold it, let alone fire it accurately, I should imagine."

"Hold it steady!" the senior officer commanded.

Try as he might, Jim could not align the sights; his left arm trembled with weakness.

"This is a travesty," the MO said.

"Lower the rifle, Private Langridge, and hand it back to me. Take your time," the senior officer commanded him.

Taking care not to point the rifle at the officer, for that was bad form, he held it flat in his good hand and handed it back across the table. Very obviously, both his arms were shaking from the weight of it as he passed it over.

"Have a seat again, Private Langridge, and put your arm back in the sling, which I imagine is more comfortable." The senior officer allowed himself a slight smile, a mere stretching of the mouth.

The exercise of raising the gun and holding it in position had left him weak, so much so that he could feel blood leaving his face, had a sense that his lips were colourless. It would be ironic if he fainted now. There was no guarantee that it would go in his favour, he thought bitterly.

The four men were conferring quietly, looking at him from time to time, no doubt noting his pallor. In that hiatus of time, in which his fate was being decided, Jim succeeded in composing himself.

When they made a motion to the sergeant at the door, he came forward. "Stand up, Private Langridge. Stand to attention."

Back on his feet, he stiffened his body, put his shoulders back, his head up, his feet together. He stared at the wall beyond the table. He must cut a sorry figure, he though, with his arm in a sling, his uniform awry.

"We have decided, Private Langridge," the senior officer said, "that you are no longer physically fit for military service and will therefore, in due course, as the army sees fit, be honourably discharged from duty.

Your medical officers have decided that you should remain here in this hospital for another ten days, approximately, after which you will take ship for England, to a destination that will be imparted to you closer to that date, Do you have anything to say?"

"Thank you, sir. It has been an honour to serve my country, sir, and to serve with the 8th Battalion of the Royal West Kent Regiment, for whose officers and men I have the greatest respect, sir."

There was a silence for a few seconds, as though they were acutely attuned to signs of irony. "Your conduct has been exemplary, Langridge, both on the battlefield and off it," the senior officer said. "I understand that you were offered the rank of corporal early on, and refused?"

"Yes, sir."

"A pity. It only remains for us to wish you the best of luck in both your future health and in civilian life. You are now dismissed."

Jim saluted. "Thank you, sir."

"March easy," the sergeant said quietly.

It seemed a long way to the door as he moved towards it, swinging his good arm. Relief was like a warm cloak that had been thrown over him on a bitterly cold day. As of now, his body and mind no longer belonged to the army. With the relief came that peculiar pining for the men of his section; now he would never, it seemed certain, find out where the remnants were.

When he closed the door of the room behind him, other men waiting on the bench looked at him expectantly, so he raised a thumb. "What are they like?" one of them asked.

"As tough as old boots," he whispered back.

At the same time he saw Etta coming towards him along a corridor, to whom he gave the thumbs up sign as well.

"Dear boy, I knew you would be released," she said, smiling, looking splendid in her white uniform. "How could you possibly fire a gun? What a travesty to even think you might. Come on, it's tea time. Then I have a surprise for you. Well ... perhaps it had better not be a surprise ... perhaps I should prepare you."

They walked back to the ward along passages and through hallways. "What was it like in there?" she enquired.

"Pretty bad. I don't know whether to laugh or cry. It's like I've put down a burden ... it was like that saying in the bible: 'He went as a lamb to the slaughter, without blemish and without spot.' That was how I felt when I went into that room, that they would send me back to be slaughtered."

When he stopped walking, Etta waited for him, cocking her head to one side in anticipation of what he would say next, so he thought how patient and marvellous she was to listen to the drivel that he came out with. "You know, I said a lot of rot in there ... they asked me if I had anything to say, so I came out with something about it being an honour to serve my country and to be in the regiment. To tell you the truth, all I really cared about were the men in my section, and Lieutenant Barton and a few others. That's what it came down to in the end ... and now a certain pride that I came through it ... I somehow endured."

"What happened to Lieutenant Barton?"

"Killed. Shot on the battlefield. I saw him lying there. He was younger than I am."

Etta started walking again slowly. "Did you like Sergeant Dawson in your section?" she asked.

"Yes, I liked him. Why?"

"He's here. That's the surprise. A friend, another nurse, works on the ward where he is, and he was asking if there was anyone here from the West Kents."

"Blimey, Miss," he said. "Very nice bloke, he is. I've been wondering about him a lot because I heard from my mate Frank that he was in the same casualty clearing station as us, that he'd lost both legs."

"That's right, unfortunately," she said. "On the good side, he's apparently well, the wounds have healed up. The point is, would you like to see him?"

"Oh, I'd like to see him," Jim said, grinning. "So long as he wants to see me, and didn't have other people in mind."

"He would be delighted to see you, I know it," Etta said. "We'll arrange it. Now, you have to rest, I think."

"Thank you." So the Jackdaw was still alive. Well, praise be to God, and all that. Sometimes there were miracles.

⁀ As promised, Etta took him there later in the day, pushing him in a wheelchair. Sergeant Jack Dawson was sitting up in bed, writing in a note book. "Well, well ... if it isn't Private Langridge," he said, his thin face creasing into a familiar grin. "It's good to see a known face from the old days." They shook hands. It was obvious from Dawson's strained and exhausted face that the struggle for life had not been easy for him.

"Very nice to see you, Sarge." They grinned, sizing each other up swiftly, each noting the pallor, the loss of weight, the wounds, the changed manner of the other.

"Get out of that wheelchair, man. Draw up a chair. I've been writing in my diary," he said, indicating the notebook. "You know, this survived behind the lines, with my other kit. I thought I'd never see it again. I know I'm going to need this in the future to remind myself that it was all true, what we went through."

Jim pulled up a wooden chair to sit by the bed, where Jack Dawson's stumps of legs were under cover, beneath a domed metal "cradle" with a sheet and blanket over it. Such cradles were common in this surgical ward, he could see. "I was very sorry to hear that you lost both legs. I heard about you in the CCS, but didn't get a chance to find out where you were."

"Just as well. That was a madhouse, and I was in no state to see anybody ... unconscious most of the time. Tell you the truth, it's a miracle I got out of there."

They talked for a long time, about the others of their section, each tentatively seeking out what the other knew, reluctant to hear of confirmed deaths. Delighting in each other's survival, they smoked and talked eagerly.

"Roy Carter survived, you know," Jack Dawson volunteered the information. "At least, he survived the lot we were in. He stayed with me in a shell hole after both my legs were blown off ... gave me first aid, tied up the stumps, so I can rightly say he saved my life. If it wasn't for him, I would have bled to death on the spot. He helped to get me back, carried me ... then I lost sight of him. How we got back without being shot, I don't know. I reckon he joined up with the others, the few left alive from our battalion. I heard there was only one officer left standing out of the whole lot."

"Thank God Roy got out of that," Jim said. "I wonder where he is now."

"Our blokes were sent up near Ypres, so I've heard while I've been here ... south of the Menin Road. A bloody awful place ... not far from Fritz there, under fire all the time."

"It sounds as though someone wants to finish us off. Poor old Roy ... I wish I knew he was safe," Jim said.

"Here, have another fag. Don't get upset. We'll find out sometime, no doubt. You just concentrate on that blighty you're getting. I reckon you've done your bit." Jack lit their fags. "I know it takes time to shift your mind to other things. As for me, the only consolation about having no legs is that I won't have to go up before that bloody medical board."

As they talked and smoked, Jim was very aware that they each drew comfort from the familiar presence, patterns of speech, and mannerisms of the other. They were both changed, yet sufficiently unchanged that they would always understand each other perfectly, whatever age they were, wherever they met in the future, if they met at all.

"How are the wife and little kiddies?" Jim asked.

"All alive and well, thank God. I've had letters here. The thought of them was all that kept me going, once we got up to the front, then especially after I lost my legs." They parted, agreeing to meet again in the wards, and in civilian life in a certain pub in Tunbridge Wells at Whitsun.

"We'll buy each other a drink," Jack Dawson promised.

Jim walked back slowly to his ward, pushing the wheelchair. Things were looking up, there was no doubt about it.

✍ Jack Dawson opened his diary, dipped the pen in the ink pot and then wrote: "Met Jim Langridge, a man of my section. Thank God that is one more who has got away."

✍ When Jim walked to the lavatories after supper he ran into the soldier who had warned him not to become too familiar with Etta.

"Heard you got a blighty," the soldier said, standing in Jim's way as he came out of the lavatory and into the corridor. "And what did Nurse Henrietta have to do with that? I don't suppose I shall be so bloody lucky."

"What do you mean?"

"I expect she put in a word or two for you with the MOs, didn't she? You look pretty A1 to me."

"How do you know how I feel? And she wouldn't have that sort of influence."

"I bet she would. Favouritism, if you ask me," the other said belligerently

Jim moved up closer to him, stared in his face. "I don't ask you. Wound or no wound, I can still fight the likes of you. How would you like a fist in the kisser? If you say another word to me, I'll knock you into next week."

The other man, whose name Jim still did not know, backed away, going into the lavatories.

As he walked back to his bed, shaken and mystified by the other's attitude, Jim made note of the bed number of the soldier as he walked past it. "Who's that bloke in bed seven?" he asked an orderly. "Bad tempered sort of bloke."

"Oh, him," the orderly said, who was leaving jugs of water on lockers. "That's Private John Townsend. Try not to take any notice of him, he's got mental trouble ... a shell exploded near him when he was on his way up to the front ... never did get there. He was unconscious for two days, brought back down the line. He's to be pitied. It's more than likely that they'll send him back, because he isn't bad enough to go home. He's bitter, see."

Later, when he saw that Private John Townsend had got into bed, he took a new packet of Woodbines from his pocket and opened it, making up his mind. Keeping the packet of fags in the palm of his hand, he sauntered up to the other man's bed, going right up near his head so that he could speak to him without too many others hearing. "Sorry about what I said to you earlier; I got a bit carried away. The orderly told me something of what happened to you ... it must be bloody hard."

Quickly, while he had the edge of surprise on his side, he extended the open packet of Woodbines to the other man and watched him while he hesitated. "Go on," he said. "No hard feelings. You'll have to light it because I'm not much good with my hands."

By the time the two cigarettes were alight, there was a watchful truce between them. "I can understand why you might be bitter," Jim said, "after what happened to you."

"They don't give a tinker's cuss for you as a person," Private Townsend said. There were tears in his eyes. "When I have to go up before the board, they'll send me back."

It occurred to Jim that here was a man who would run out of the hospital and jump into the sea, if he could.

"Have you told the doctors that you have bad headaches, dizzy spells and blackouts? You need to build up your case long before you go to the board," he said, in a flash of what he thought was intuition.

"Of course, I've told them. What do you know about my case?"

"Nothing. But I've spent a lot of time in bed, listening to doctors and nurses talking about other cases, some like yours," he said, thinking of all that he had heard over the weeks, of men who had had head injuries, who had been subject to blast from being under heavy fire. "Establish your case for blurred vision, flashing lights, like stars, behind the eyes when you have them closed."

John Townsend looked at him, saying nothing.

"You see,' Jim went on quietly, 'they can't prove that you haven't got headaches, blurred vision, dizziness, and flashing lights. They're not stupid ... but neither are you."

"They can't prove that I have, either ... and neither can I."

"You set about finding proof," Jim said.

"Why should you help me? I don't want pity."

"Pity is not what I feel. Perhaps it's for justice ... I don't know.'

Lizzie standing beside a German bunker,
Hill 60, near Ypres, Belgium.

'Sanctuary Wood', old trenches,
near Hill 62, Ypres area, Belgium.

Lizzie at an Advanced Dressing Station,
near Essex Farm, Ypres salient , Belgium.
(Canadian doctor and poet John McRae, who wrote
'In Flanders Fields', worked as a surgeon
at this dressing station. There is a memorial
to him nearby. He died of pneumonia.)

Le Rutoire Farm, on the western edge of the battlefield,
Battle of Loos, France, September, 1915.

ENGLISH HERITAGE
EDITH
CAVELL
1865 ~ 1915
Pioneer of Modern Nursing
in Belgium and
Heroine of the Great War
trained and worked here
1896 ~ 1901

Memorial plaque for English nurse Edith Cavell
at The London Hospital, Whitechapel Road, London, U.K.
She was executed by the Germans in 1915 in Brussels.

Wild poppies at Essex Farm, Belgium.

*Part of no-man's-land of the Battle of Loos, September 1915,
looking south to the slag heaps at the coal—mining towns
of Loos and Lens, Pas de Calais, France.*

*'Pool of Peace', a British mine crater, which undermined
enemy lines, in the Ypres salient, Belgium.*

British military cemetery on the site of the St. Mary's Advanced Dressing Station, Battle of Loos, near the British front lines.

The British medal of valour awarded to James Langridge.
The Medal was awarded to soldiers
who fought in 1914 and 1915.

May Wigley in the uniform of the Royal Flying Corps,
part of the British Army. This was taken in 1917
when she was nineteen.

ᕙ Chapter 15

The 28th of November. That's when he would be put on a ship for England, so a medical officer told him. "You'll be going to Dover, we think, and then up to London by train. When you're completely well, you'll report to barracks, until the army decides to discharge you."

"Very good, sir."

When Nurse Etta came to see him, he told her that he would miss her. "Will you see me off, Miss?" he asked, reverting to civilian address.

"Of course I will," she said, sitting in a chair beside his. "I'll come alone; I won't be pushing anyone in a wheelchair." She had luminous eyes, large and beautiful, of a deep blue, almost the colour of violets. Her dark, wavy hair, of a chestnut brown, had a touch of auburn in it, which contrasted well with her pale skin.

Always aware that he stared at her a little too long each time he spoke to her close up, Jim looked down. "I'll never forget you," he said, conscious that every soldier in her wards had said that on leaving, or would be saying it to her.

"I won't forget you either, Jimmy. They've given me a posting ... they're sending me to a CCS near the Ypres salient, and I shall be there before Christmas."

A presentiment of doom came over him as he looked at her again. The Front was no place for her; it was no place for anyone. If there was a hell on earth, it was Ypres. "I could weep for you," he said, looking down at the floor.

"But it's what I want, dear boy." She spoke gently. "Those boys there need me. I shall feel that I'm doing my utmost."

"You've no idea what it's like. When you get there," he said, looking at her closely, trying to discern her real feelings, for she was a superb actress, "try to live, because you're needed by the living, as you just said. You have a lot to offer the world. When I get back home, I shall remember you as you are now ... I don't want to think of you any other way."

"You're such a sweet boy," she said. "If anything happens to me, if I'm killed, it will be in the papers." She said that without any sort of pride, any sort of "side," a simple fact.

"I shan't want to see it."

"When I'm on the train up to the front, then on the ambulances, I'll think about you and the conversations we've had, Jimmy, and while I have time to contemplate, I'll decide how to conduct myself."

How weary he was of goodbyes to people he had come to love, the involuntary goodbye of death and other partings, to those he would most likely never see again. So weary of pain.

Over the next few days he walked around the wards saying his goodbyes to those he had come to know, who would not be leaving on the same day. Jack Dawson would be leaving a week later. John Townsend had yet to go before the board.

Obeying orders, he began to prepare his uniform and kit for departure.

༄ Etta, keeping her word, was on the quay in the cold misty drizzle on the 28th to see him off, and other men she had nursed, walking among them, shaking hands and wishing them luck.

They allowed him to walk on; someone was standing near the gangplank shouting out names of the ambulant men.

"Goodbye, Jimmy," Etta held out her hand. "It's been an absolute pleasure to know you. May you have a good and happy life. And when we both leave this world, may the Lord say to us: 'Well done, thou good and faithful servant.' It's something to work for. That, and love ... what else is there?"

"Nothing," he said, tearful, holding on to her hand. Although he tried to force the words out, he could not bring himself to wish her a good and happy life, for the presentiment was upon him again. "Thank you, from the bottom of my heart, for all you have done for me, in all the ways."

"Thank you, too," she said. "You've given me strength ... you and all the other boys, but especially you here at this place."

"Come on, lads, get a move on! We haven't got all day and all night as well," someone bawled, and Jim was jostled away from Etta, his boots meeting the gangplank, his feet moving as of their own accord to take him away from France. At the top, he was not the only one shouting. "Goodbye, Etta! God bless!"

As he turned for one last look at her standing on the quay, her arms inside her long cloak, her head tilted back to look up at them, a wispy cloud of mist came down over her and obscured her for a moment so that she looked like a grey ghost. Gulls wheeled and called, their cries echoing.

Not fanciful usually, he felt cold and frightened. With others, he pushed and shoved for a space at the railing of the lower deck. There she was still, stepping back, to get out of the way of the teeming men pushing forward. Supplies were being loaded at the same time. Stretcher bearers were shifting men out of ambulances.

Jim waved again and called out. Once again she raised an arm to them, then when he was forced to take his eyes off her for a few seconds in the crush of men, both on foot and on stretchers, she was gone, swallowed up in the grey-white gloom of early winter. It was as though she had been a figment of his imagination, had never really existed in the flesh.

"Etta!"

He was jostled and pushed away from the railing.

"All ambulant men, find your berths!" The order came. "Get below deck, make room!"

Numb and disorientated, he clattered down steps, where there were men with lists. "Regiment, name, rank, and number!" They were directed to berths, each man to his own, where their kit could be stowed. Here and there, mugs of tea were being handed out. Jim sat on his bunk to drink it, surrounded by unknown soldiers. Those close to him exchanged names quickly, so eager to connect with someone.

"I won't feel safe until we're more than half way across," one man said, articulating their thoughts. They all knew that the Germans had submarines capable of sinking ships. No matter that they were hospital ships.

Having drunk his tea quickly, Jim stumbled towards the exit again from the large cabin that held fifteen bunks, against orders, to go up to a deck, making note of the number of his bunk and of the cabin. Already the boat was shifting and creaking in the uncalm sea. It would be a rough crossing.

He made his way back to the lower deck railing, to a place away from a gangplank. The ships did not linger at the docks; it was safer to get away quickly. Before long the ship's engine took on a different note and the mooring ropes were released.

When the siren blasted and the ship began to creep away from the foggy dock, Jim knew that Etta would be standing at the top of the hill on the zig zag path by the last wooden bench under the trees. "Goodbye, dear boys," she would be shouting out into the mist, alone and anonymous. "Bon voyage!"

"Cheerio, Etta," he said.

He had been in France for three months. It would be with him forever. In that hiatus he had changed, would never regain his old self. In less time than that, other men had gone mad, and he had felt his sanity shifting onto perilous ground.

Slowly the ship moved out of the confined dock, then into the open water of the channel. A precipitous darkness was coming down, swallowing them up on the choppy sea. The other men around Jim were mostly silent as they watched, against orders, France recede from them until it disappeared into the whiteness of fog, leaving them in a limbo of creaking metal and wood.

"Goodbye, France," someone said. That was what it had come down to, those two words. Thoughts were something different, images and thoughts; they churned and fought for attention as the vessel carried them away. It was a kind of spell that held them.

"Must be time for grub. Come on, boys."

∽ Jim felt ill at ease in the berth below deck, unable to get his mind away from the possibility of attack. Of all the ways to die, being trapped and drowned must be among the worst. With the precious greatcoat on, he made his way surreptitiously to a sheltered place on a lower deck, where other men crouched and lay.

As he lay on his side, curled up, he tried to project ahead. It was as though part of his mind was trapped back in the trenches of Loos, where he had last seen all his mates alive. To add to that, images of the wards of Boulogne, the people he had met there, joined in the other dance of shadows.

Would England have changed much? It was unlikely; why should it? There were those whose vested interests resisted change, those at the top of the heap who were capable of holding back the tide. If the war went on and on, perhaps even they would lose their hold. Food was more expensive, women were doing men's work, making munitions, doing things that they had never done before, so he had been told in letters from home.

Sixteen months of war were not enough to make the country change appreciably, he thought, insulated as it was from the reality of the Front, where generals were safely far behind the lines. Private grief united people, a grief that swamped the country, but grief turned you in on yourself also; it did not provide an impetus, not initially, for any sort of change. Perhaps that would come later, when grief turned to disgust.

Neither were those sixteen months enough to change the entrenched habits of the upper classes, their attitudes to those who worked for them. It would not have softened them enough to give the poor a living wage. It was remotely possible, he thought, that if the war went on for a long time, if servants became scarce, that something would have to change.

As for the change in himself, what he had perceived as a child and as a younger man had now hardened into certainty, the only certainty that he felt he had left — that if you wanted something for yourself, your family, and your class, you had to get it yourself. Ways and means had to be planned, then implemented. There would be no one else but him, and them, to lift them out of the abyss of poverty. The opposition, he knew, would be terrible, even from those of his own kind who feared change while desiring it at the same time. A few of the liberal minded of the upper classes would help, as they always had, yet there were never enough of those.

Now he had another strike against him, being handicapped, and living in fear of increasing breathlessness. All the more reason why he must use his remaining youth to fight for change through the unions that his father had advocated and fought for. If it did not come in his lifetime, perhaps his children, if he had any, would come into that inheritance of greater equality.

Nonetheless, he would have references from the army, where his conduct had been considered "very good." The word "sober" would come up a lot in those references, because he had never been drunk on duty, as some had, even though he liked a pint as much as the next man. The cheap French wine they had drunk in villages near the Front had never compared favourably with the beer he was used to.

As the ship pitched and heaved, carrying him closer to the life he had left, that life seemed to be coming to meet him with all its uncertainties. Was that hoped-for transformation what he had been fighting for? Perhaps, all the time, he had joined up for that, a new Britain, a new order? It was funny how you didn't know yourself; you were a mystery, gradually revealed, if at all. Killing Germans might not bring any sort of new order: he did not see how it could.

They shared out cigarettes, pooling resources, the few men who lay near each other on the rolling deck. Already there were the sounds of retching and muted groans from various directions.

In the pockets of his greatcoat Jim had letters from Anne Jefferson, from his mother, and from Frank, who was still in a hospital near Folkestone but would soon be going up to London, and one or two others. Every so often he put his hand on them. These were the things that held him together, that told him who he was, these flimsy bits of paper with words on them.

Soon, perhaps, he would receive a letter from Etta; she had said she would write to the hospital in London. Then his two worlds would come together, the ends would join and become complete, a circle, which would do something to ease the turmoil and the threatened madness of his mind. This is who I am, that circle would say ... for now.

∽ "There are the white cliffs," someone whispered. "We're home."

"That's fog," someone else said.

"No it's not, it's cliffs."

"Don't speak too soon, we ain't docked yet, mate."

≪ Chapter 16

Whitsun falls fifty days after Easter, when the meadows burgeon with wild flowers and grasses, when woods resound with the calls of birds, when the sun has warmth and the sky is soft blue in southeast England.

On such a day, Jack Dawson, formerly Sergeant Dawson, waited in a wheelchair at the Duke of York pub with his wife, Lilly, for Jim Langridge to arrive. The stumps of his legs were covered up with a light blanket.

Then they saw him coming, along the Pantiles, the arcade, that was at the lower end of Tunbridge Wells, wearing his Sunday best of a black suit, white shirt with a fine stripe, and a thin tie, and black leather boots of a more delicate mould than the ones a man would wear to work.

It was odd to see a man known to you from the army, out of uniform, as it was yourself to be out of it. The head especially felt naked without the uniform cap, bearing the cap badge of the rearing horse that belonged to the regiment.

Jim saw them there waiting for him, the man in the wheelchair and the wife, plump and maternal, sitting on a bench beside him with a hand on the handle of the chair. The sight of him brought a pang of regret, to add to all the other regrets pertaining to the changes in their lives. On the other hand, if it had not been for the war and the army, he would never have met Jack or any of the others who had enlarged his life.

Along the Pantiles he could see a brass band setting up to play in the bandstand, this being a holiday. As he walked he swung his arms as though marching to orders, his crooked, mutilated arm encased in the

165

black sleeve of his civilian jacket. It would be a long time before he could saunter along, unaware of how he put one foot in front of the other. They were a breed apart, the silent, dispersed army of men, moving about in civilian life as though in a dream where only their shadowy thoughts were real.

"Hello, Jim. How did you get here?"

"I walked a good part of the way, then got the train."

"Jim, this is my wife, Lilly. She's going to leave us here and go into that church over there for the service, while we have our beer."

"Hello, Lilly." Jim took her hand, thinking how charming she looked in her soft black hat with a feather in it, and the grey wool coat. There was a chronic tiredness about her that all women had now. "Very pleased to meet you."

"Jack's told me a lot about you," she said.

"I bet he has," he said, grinning at her.

She left them to go to the church that they could see on the corner nearby.

"I'll go in and get the beer," Jim said. "How have you been, mate?" Rank did not matter now.

"Not too bad," Jack said.

There was something subdued about him, Jim sensed, as he went into the cool public bar of the pub.

They sat in the sunshine under a tree, where there were tables and benches. "I got a job, Jim, with a saddler, working with leather. It's something to bring in a bit of money until I get the artificial legs. I've been fitted for them. Then we'll see if I'm capable of anything else. It'll be strange, learning to walk again. You still with the gardening?"

"Yes, I reckon I'll stick with that, I want to be outside in the air, growing things."

"We're lucky to get work. I've seen old soldiers begging here, selling matches, things like that."

Bright sunlight filtered through the big plane trees near the public house where they sat. The beer was good, the peace profound. Horses and carts clopped by at the end of the pedestrian precinct, yet still one remained alert for the sound of gunfire, for the need to flatten oneself on the ground. It was not so much a nervousness as a hyper alertness. They both glanced around continuously, catching each other's eye when they were aware of themselves doing it. "Plenty of hiding places for snipers here," Jim said, and they smiled.

Through the open windows of the church they heard the music of the organ.

"Are you all right, Jack?" Jim asked. "You seem ... quiet."

Jack brought a folded newspaper from under the blanket that covered his legs. "Before you came, I found this paper on the bench. It's *The Times* ... it was open at the obituary columns. Didn't want to say anything to the wife, she's seen enough of death. It's a bit of a shock."

As Jack handed over the folded paper, Jim could see a photograph of a woman's face, a pale, oval face, with a cloud of soft-looking dark hair framing it, which looked like a copy of a formal portrait. The eyes were large, expressive, under arched brows, the mouth generous and finely shaped. For a second or two his heart stopped beating.

Under the photograph was the obituary: "Lady Henrietta Blanche Beasley," he read, "of the Queen Alexandra's Imperial Military Nursing Service, beloved daughter of _____ ' He looked up at Jack enquiringly, who merely nodded, '_____ killed in the line of duty near Ypres, Belgium on 4th May, 1916, when the casualty clearing station where she was on active service came under fire. Lady Henrietta lost her fiancé, Captain Charles Henry Winthrop, killed in action at Ypres, in 1915. Well done, thou good and faithful servant. May her soul rest in peace."

They sat there in the dappled sunlight, two soldiers who had known Henrietta Blanche Beasley.

From the church, a hymn started up, faintly: "Breathe on me, breath of God, Fill me with life anew ..."

"Ironic, ain't it," Jack said, angry, "that here we are, maimed but alive, and she's back there ... dead. Not that I wanted to die."

"Don't try to find any sense in it, because there isn't any," Jim said. "It doesn't matter how clever you are, how deserving to live ... if you stay out there long enough you're going to cop it, one way or another." He looked down at the photograph. "I could weep."

"Breathe on me, breath of God, Until my heart is pure, Until with thee I will one will, To do and to endure." The singing filled the quiet air, until the brass band started tuning up, as though the clamour of now was trying to drown out that which had been in the so recent past, a past that filled the whole being and refused to be obliterated.

Jim wanted to pick up a stone and throw it at the church window, to quiet the sanctimonious noise.

Still the guns blasted in France while they, two men among the crowd, who had known the nurse whose obituary confronted them, kept her alive in thought. The contrast between what they had known and the peaceful, uncaring scene before them brought one to the edge of madness; Jim sensed in himself a shifting of emotion that was out of hand. Mourning for Etta blended in with the loss of those others of his section. In madness the eyes see but they do not take in; the inner vision compels the senses to other things.

∽ Jack Dawson lived in Tunbridge Wells, not far from where they were sitting. Lilly would come out of the church soon and push him home. "I worked for a carrier before this war started," Jack said, talking quickly in an effort to dampen their grief for Etta. "Had my own delivery routes. Perhaps that's why they made me a sergeant ... that, and my age."

They were on their second pint of beer. "Now everything's uncertain again. The wife does cleaning in the big houses, but with me like this, her having to push me about, and the four kiddies, she can't do much. As it is, she's exhausted. Thank God I've still got some money coming in from the army. They get me to do a few things at the barracks from time to time, because technically I'm not discharged yet ... just so I can stay on as long as possible."

"I was discharged in the middle of March," Jim said. "The end of an era. Will you get a pension, Jack?"

"They've told me I will. I'll believe it when I see it. What about you?"

"I've applied for one."

In spite of their chat, the death of Etta hung heavy between them. "Difficult to believe she's dead," Jim said. "Could I keep this paper?"

"Take it."

"My girl Anne's meeting me here a little later on," Jim said. "She's got a half-day off. She's in service as a cook. We're going to listen to the band." The mental image he had of Anne was so different from that of Etta that the image of the former blotted out the latter momentarily.

It wasn't that he had been in love with Etta, for she was of a class forbidden to him; it was that he had adored her as though from afar, even though their relationship had been an extraordinary and close one, more so than it would have been between a nurse and her patient in civilian life. She had put herself in harm's way for them. She had attended to his wounds as a mother or a sister might, without a drawing back or disgust.

A man of his class would never assume, would never even day-dream of the impossible, yet they had loved each other in their way, a mysterious empathy and compassion holding them together, that transcended social class. It came out of the understanding and the mourning, of all that they had witnessed and experienced. If they had been able to meet after the war they would have been friends, he wanted to believe that.

Now he wondered about Captain Charles Henry Winthrop, whom she had loved, so much so that she had been reckless with her life, perhaps. In war, all was arbitrary; how could he know what she had decided towards the end.

"Are you going to marry your Anne?" Jack asked.

"To tell you the truth, I'm nervous to ask her now I'm like this." He held up his left arm. "She might be disgusted. I'd like to ask her."

"If she cared about that arm, she wouldn't be meeting you here today, I reckon ... coming all the way from Penshurst, when she could be doing other things. You just ask her. Do it today, mate. Don't think about it too much. Sometimes you can do too much thinking, and it's not good for you."

Jim gave a salute, sitting down. "Yes, Sarge," he said, and they both laughed

"I'm serious, mind."

"Want another pint, Jack?"

"No, thanks, Jim. The wife will be here any minute, and two are all I can manage these days. We'll meet again soon, if we can. I usually come here once a week. I shall want to show off my legs to you. Walking on them is a different matter."

∾ After Lilly had pushed Jack away, Jim looked again at the picture of Etta as he waited, making his pint last.

"Jim!"

Anne was walking towards him, waving, looking adorable in a light summer coat of a pale beige colour, that came down almost to her ankles over her long skirt. On her piled hair she had on a flat straw hat trimmed with artificial flowers.

"You look lovely," he said, holding her arms, kissing her on the cheek.

"Phew!" she said. "It's quite hot when you're walking far."

"Come and sit down. I'll get you some lemonade," he said, his heart lifting with his love of her, coupled with a kind of gratitude that she would care for him when they had been parted for so long. Through their letters they had come to know each other better, the presence of mortality releasing reticence. "Is that what you would like?"

"Yes, please, Jimmy." Her eyes were a pale green-grey. "Is this someone you know?" she asked, looking at the picture of Etta staring up at them from the folded newspaper on the bench.

"Yes. She was a nurse that both Jack and I knew in Boulogne."

As he went into the dim, cool interior of the public house, with its calming scent of old beer and smoke, he saw Anne pick up the newspaper to read it.

"This is tragic," she said, looking up at him when he came out with the lemonade. "How old was she?"

"Close to thirty, I expect," he said. "But of course I don't know. A very good nurse, she was."

"We've been seeing soldiers on the streets," Anne said, "with limbs gone. Some people stare at them as though they didn't know there's a war on. I can't understand it. They say that train-loads of the wounded are coming into London every day, that if we go on like this there won't be any young men left in this country."

"They will go on," he said. "What are we to do? We're in it now ... no one seems to know how to get out. It makes my blood boil."

Anne had taken off her coat and hat, as the heat of the sun had increased since he had arrived there, and her soft pale hair hung down in tendrils around her face where it had escaped from the "bun" in which she had secured it.

"Let me carry your coat," he offered, when they were ready to stroll along the Pantiles to where the band was playing and an audience was gathering to sit on the flimsy wooden chairs in front of it.

They held hands as they walked slowly along in the warm sunlight, over the large, dusty square paving stones that gave the area its name, past the shops selling both luxury goods and simple food alike. They moved through the throng of pedestrians in holiday spirit.

When Jim failed to concentrate on what he was doing, France was with him, the walk on the Vermelles to Hulluch road, coming up to the Front ...

There were flower-sellers sitting down surrounded by their wares. On them he concentrated, letting the scent and the peace come into him.

"A rose for your lapel, mister? A bouquet for the lady? Forget-me-nots, lilies, anything you could ask for."

There were a few men here and there in uniform, officers mostly, home on leave. Jim averted his eyes from them, lest the ingrained servile urge to salute came over him to the point where he would go through the motion.

Sometimes women would look at him, obviously questioning why he was not in uniform at his age, so he would shift his arm so that they could clearly see his deformity and the vivid scars. It was tempting to take off his jacket and roll up his shirt sleeves, which he would have done if Anne had not been with him. Then they would have been repelled, no doubt, those sanctimonious women, who were not themselves in the nursing corps or in the munitions factories.

He felt himself growing angry. Only the company of Anne compelled him to restrain himself. He had heard that some women, of the middle classes, gave out white feathers to men on the street who were not in uniform, the feathers of cowardice.

He contemplated buying Anne a bouquet of roses, then in a quiet place going down on one knee and asking her to marry him. That was better than going down on one knee to fire a rifle. Nervousness prevented him from making a quick decision, then they were past the flower-seller.

Then, as though from nowhere, in front of them was an old lady selling bunches of violets from a tray balanced on her chest, held by a ribbon round her neck, a lady who reminded Jim of his mother. On top of her neat grey hair that was scraped back into a bun, she wore a lace cap.

"Sweet violets," she said softly, "sweet violets for a bonnie girl. Tuppence a bunch, dearie."

Jim's good hand moved to take the small bunch that she offered him, to give them to Anne, to extract the pennies from his jacket pocket. "This is your lucky day," the lady said to him. "You're an old soldier, I can see, though not old in years. I have the gift of prophecy, dearie, and the flowers will bring you luck."

They moved forward with the crowd in front of the band-stand, to find two chairs at the far side of the back row, the only two remaining empty. Anne held the violets to her face when they were both settled on the chairs, side by side. "They smell wonderful," she said.

She held the tiny bouquet of mixed purple and white blooms up to his nose so that he could inhale their exquisite scent, something he had dreamed about in the tent at the CCS when other gross scents had assailed him.

Without having to think, he put up his hand to cover her hand that held the flowers. "Will you marry me, Anne?" he said.

When she blushed, he smiled. "Jimmy ... yes," she said.

ॐ Chapter 17

A letter came from Frank Boakes, when summer was more established and swallows flitted and wheeled under the eaves of cottages and over the meadows of Kent and Sussex. It came to Jim in his lodgings at Penshurst, where he lived close to his work and not far from his mother.

"I am getting married, Jim," the letter said. "I would very much like you to come to my wedding and bring your girl. Would you be my Best Man? You remember I told you about Grace. Well, she is the one I am marrying, and we have found a house in the village, where I am working with the blacksmith." It went on, giving the details of where the wedding was to be, in Grace's village near Horsemonden, in the ancient parish church.

Well, dear old Frank, Jim said to himself, smiling as he held the letter, he has beat me to it. He was flattered and pleased, unexpectedly humbled, by being asked to be Best Man. The great import of what Frank — and he himself very soon — was about to undertake brought a sense of sobriety, almost of awe. One entered into a marriage with a faith that one was doing the right thing, for it was a momentous step that once taken could not be undone. In the last letter he had received from Frank, his mate was getting used to walking with an artificial leg.

The memory of how they had sat together in the casualty clearing station near the Front in France was so clear in his mind, as though it had happened last month. He could recall the scent of rotting flesh that had hung between them and all around them in the chaos, mingled with the smells of cigarette smoke and carbolic, making an evocative mix that one could never forget. Then Frank's sunken-eyed, ghastly yellowish face, where the skin had been tight over his bones like old parchment, showing the skeleton beneath, had impressed itself on his mind so vividly that it could not yet be successfully superimposed upon by more recent images.

Twice Jim had visited Frank at his mother's home after his release from hospital. "Frank's told me a lot about you, Jim," Frank's mother, tired and grey like his own mother, had said to him when they had both gone out to her cottage garden, leaving Frank inside. "It seems to me you're the reason he was able to pull through. He was so down, he thought that all of his lot had been killed … so he told me. Then he saw you, Jim, and that gave him the will to live again. Otherwise, I think he would just have let himself go. I have you to thank."

"Oh … I don't know," he had said, moved close to tears. "I was looking for him … was so glad when I found him alive."

Yes, he would go to the wedding, would take Anne, if she could arrange for a free day.

That evening in his lodgings he wrote a reply to Frank, accepting the invitation and the request that he be Best Man. His own writing was spidery and rather bad, compared with Frank's large, open and rounded lettering. Taking extra care to make himself legible, he conveyed his congratulations in the face of Frank's happiness. They had both come out of the maw of death, had both found girls who could love them. A peace of sorts enveloped him as he laboriously wrote the reply.

The bells of the old church rang out over the countryside, summoning people on that glorious summer day when Frank was to marry Grace. Tall grasses, littered with white daisies, buttercups, and Queen Anne's lace, waved in the warm breeze along the roadsides that led up to the church, and there was the scent of mown hay in the air. Cows and sheep grazed in the rolling fields around the church as far as they could see, for they were up on a slight hill.

The wedding party had arrived at the church, where they stood about outside in their Sunday best, next to the graveyard, talking quietly in a dignified manner that befitted the occasion, yet smiling in the collective thrill that a wedding brought forth. They were waiting for the bride, who was to come with her father in a decorated hay wain, pulled by one of the shire horses that her father worked with, loaned for the occasion by his employer. Thus, the people of the wedding party watched the road from where she would come.

Frank and Jim stood a little apart from the others, as befitted their special status. Anne stood nearby with Frank's two sisters. He thought how lovely she looked in a pale blue cotton dress and a straw hat decorated with flowers. Seeing him watching her, she came over to stand by his side, and he took her hand. They watched for the bride and her father, whose proximity would signal that they must take up their positions in front of the altar, before the bride alighted and before the organ struck up with "Here Comes the Bride." They stood beside some ancient graves, where the occupants had been interred for several hundred years. They all blended in together, those who had gone before, and the living, the old, the middle-aged, and the young.

"You're looking very smart, Frank," Jim said, eyeing the dark grey suit that Frank wore, which made him appear handsome and mature beyond his years. In the button holes of their jackets, at the lapels, they both wore cream-coloured roses that had been plucked for them by Frank's mother from her garden.

"So do you, Jim," Frank said, looking Jim over, wearing a very similar suit, a white shirt and dark tie. "I didn't realize you were so handsome. I'd better make sure Grace goes for me and not for you."

They laughed. "Get away with you," Jim said.

"She doesn't mind about the leg," Frank said quietly, after a moment. "I suppose that's obvious; otherwise she wouldn't be marrying me. But you know, Jim, as well as I do, that we'll never be free from what happened to us; we'll never get it out of our minds. I've come to the conclusion that I won't let it get me down, that I'm going to live in spite of it, that I'm going to enjoy what I have left."

"That's all we can do."

On first seeing Frank, Jim had been struck by how well he looked, how his usual pale face had a touch of the sun, as well as how happy. There was a light now in his eyes, those blue eyes that had been dull with pain so much in the recent past. In order to walk on the artificial leg he had learned to kick the leg slightly forward, to put his weight on it, in not exactly a limp but a slightly rolling gait. "You've mastered that leg really well, Frank."

Frank laughed as he squinted over the green fields towards the road, waiting for his bride. "Yes, it's not too bad. I just hope it doesn't let me down when I'm walking back down the aisle with Grace. You'd better be close, Jim, in case I need you to catch me."

"I will."

"I had a letter from Roy the other day."

"You did! Well, I never! Good old Roy. Where is he?"

"He's still in France, still all right. Well ... he was, like. The remains of our lot were sent up just south of Ypres, so he said, then they gradually moved south. He thinks something's up. Part of what he said was blacked out ... censored, like."

"Will you let me know how I can get in touch with him?"

"Yes, I will, because he asked after you ... said he's lost your address."

Jim found himself scanning the open countryside, as though searching for trenches, for snipers, for any sign of the enemy. It would be a long time before he could drop that constant alertness ... if ever.

"Here she comes!" someone shouted. "Here comes the bride!"

The bell ringers, who had stopped for a rest, started up again, as all turned towards the amazing apparition of a transformed hay wagon that had emerged from the lane of a farm, several hundred yards down the road that ran beside the church.

"Hooray!" one of the party shouted. "Hip, hip, hip, hooray!" Three cheers rang out over the church yard, bringing out the vicar in his flowing white and purple robes to view the progress.

"You must go inside before she gets close," one of the women said to Frank. "It's bad luck for the groom to see the bride up close before she enters the church."

Frank nodded, grinning, ready to comply with any old tradition. Not used to being the centre of attention, he was enjoying himself. When he and Jim took a last look at the approaching bride, seated beside her father in the middle of the hay wagon, they could see that it was driven by another man wearing a suit and a bowler hat. The chestnut coloured shire had its mane plaited into tight braids, its harness decorated with shining brasses and flowers woven around it. Its coat shone in the sunlight. The wain, similarly decorated, had three arches of wood over it, entwined with roses and ivy.

"Oooh!" A collective murmur of admiration rose up among the watchers.

The vicar, old and grey, came over to Frank and Jim. "Time to go inside, Mr. Boakes, and you, Mr. Langridge."

"Right you are, Reverend." Frank looked sideways at Jim with a happy and nervous smile, as he kicked his artificial leg forward. "Stay with me, Jim."

"Never fear, mate." Jim squeezed Anne's hand and let it go.

"I'll do the same for you when the time comes," Frank said, winking at Anne.

"You'll be sitting at the front next to me," Jim said softly to Anne.

As they entered through the main doors of the church the joyous clamouring of the bells was almost deafening. Carefully they made their way up the aisle, where Frank and Jim came to a halt to stand in front of the altar, in the spotlight. Jim felt his nervousness grow, as he exchanged commiserating glances with Frank who, it seemed to him, had become silent and intense. The vicar, after ushering every one inside, came to stand in front of them, his back to the altar. Then the mother of the bride, resplendent in a new hat and a flowing dress, came to sit in the front pew.

There was a breathless hush that lasted for a few minutes, then the organ started up with "Here Comes the Bride," and Frank turned to face the congregation and to receive his bride from her father. Looking at him, Jim saw an expression of love, humility and pride, and that his eyes had tears in them. Neither of them ever thought, in those recent dark days, that they would be in a situation like this.

"Steady on, mate," Jim whispered, standing close beside Frank, their arms touching slightly. For the umpteenth time he put his hand in his pocket to feel the ring that he had put there.

Grace, small, pretty, dark haired, wearing a flowing white dress and veil, came down the aisle on her father's arm. The father, Jim noted, looked suitably proud, although shy of the attention, as though he had engineered all this himself. At the altar they moved into position, with Grace next to Frank, Jim next to him, and Grace's father beside her.

The bells halted and the solemnity of the moment came down on all of them in the sudden quiet. "Dearly beloved, we are gathered together here in the sight of God, and in the face of this congregation, to join together this Man and this Woman in Holy Matrimony."

Jim stood with head bowed, thinking that he must handle the ring carefully so that he did not drop it as he handed it to the curate to place on the holy book.

Roy Carter came into his mind then, clear and sharp, as though he could see his face in actuality. Somewhere in northern France, Roy was under fire and waiting for orders, if he had not already received them, most likely waiting to go into battle. There was a strong presentiment in Jim that Roy was still alive. Keep Roy safe, he prayed then, taking advantage of the fact that he was in a holy place, when he was so seldom in one.

Thank God, he thought then, that we have come through, Frank and I ... that we have come to this. Thank God.

War is something absurd, useless, that nothing can justify. Nothing.
— Louis de Cazenave, World War One veteran

☙ Chapter 18

May's Story, 1915

"Listen to this! They've shot a nurse. They shot an English nurse. She came from Norfolk."

Edward Wigley, gamekeeper on the Calborne estate, Sussex looked down at the newspaper that he had spread on the kitchen table of his cottage, amid the breakfast things, on a Sunday morning. His wife, Harriet, with a tea towel slung over her shoulder, drew back from the cast iron stove where she was cooking. The children stopped talking.

"Who has?" Harriet said, turning from the stove to look at him. It was a cold day and the whole family, the six children, were crammed into the warm kitchen. Outside, rain and wind battered against the small window that was above the sink and the wooden draining board.

"The Germans ... they executed an English nurse ... put her in front of a firing squad,' he said, looking up at them, around at his children. By the seriousness of his demeanour, they took their cues from him.

There was no sound now other than the sizzling of bacon in the large frying pan on the stove, and the sound of the wind. Harriet came to stand behind him, to look over his shoulder at the newspaper, as did his daughter May, seventeen. "Where?" Harriet asked.

"In Brussels, on October the 12th." The disbelief in his voice was mirrored in their expressions, his wife and children, as they looked at him. Except for the baby, Reg, three years old, who banged a spoon on the table, the children understood what he had said. After May, there was Mildred, fifteen, then Cedric, eleven, William, eight, Frank, six.

"They shot a woman?" May said. "It seems impossible. Whatever for?" She and Mildred crowded in to look at the small print.

"There she is," their father said, pointing at a photograph in the newspaper. "Her name's Edith Cavell. It says here that she helped English soldiers and others to escape, after she'd cared for them in hospital, after she'd nursed them, and the Germans didn't like that."

"They shot her for that?" his wife said. "What is this world coming to? It's all madness."

"The Germans are occupying Brussels, see. And they allowed her and other nurses to stay there to nurse the wounded, because she'd already been working there for years," Edward Wigley informed his family. "There were plenty of wounded from Ypres, and after the retreat from Mons of our boys."

They all stood near to look at the photograph. "That's terrible," Mildred said, her voice trembling. "She looks lovely. It says they shot her at dawn." Then she began to cry, causing the younger children to look at each other and at their mother in consternation and worry.

"How could they do such a thing?" May whispered, tears gathering in her eyes.

"Because they're Germans," her mother said. "That's why we're fighting them. They've taken over Belgium, which they have no right to do."

"I can't bear it," Mildred sobbed.

Their mother returned to cooking the bacon, angrily turning the rashers this way and that. "If we lose this war, there's no knowing what sort of world we'll live in," she said. "I dread to think of it."

When breakfast had been eaten and Edward Wigley had gone outside to feed his dogs that were in kennels at the back of the rear garden and May and Mildred had finished the washing up, May took the folded newspaper from the table. She went out to the passage by the back door, put on her coat, hat and scarf, and quietly let herself out to the blustery morning.

It seemed that the war was not going well for them, considering the many thousands of their boys who were being killed and wounded. Every day her parents talked about it, speculating on how and when it might end, and they agreed that the news was worse than they, part of the general public, were allowed to know. It was possible, she thought, that the newspapers were reporting the death of the nurse in order to stir public opinion to support the war. If that were the case, it had succeeded with her.

There was a sense of heightened awareness of terrible danger that she could never get out of her mind. That fear brought a restlessness with it, so that she felt like an animal in a cage, designated to pace up and down looking for a way out and not finding one. They were better off in the country, being able to grow some of their own food, at least.

She made for a bench that was near the house, sheltered by dense juniper trees, where she could be alone to read the paper. With cold hands she opened the pages. Nurse Edith Cavell had a beautiful face, a high forehead with hair swept back from it, a direct, calm gaze, well defined brows. How was it possible that she had been shot? For such a little thing? It did not seem real. May hunched over, shivering.

Miss Cavell, she read, had been born in Norfolk in 1865, had trained to be a nurse in London. Two years before her own birthday, May could see, Miss Cavell had started her nursing training. London was not far away, yet then it seemed far because she did not know it. This brave nurse was old enough to be her mother. That made it seem all the worse somehow, that this dignified woman, after a youth of hard work and personal sacrifice, should be put in prison, then ignominiously shot for doing what she must have considered her duty. The deliberate, calculated inhumanity of that execution was impossible to understand.

May brooded on the fact that it was late autumn now, and more than six months to her eighteenth birthday. Perhaps when that time came her father would let her do war work, as she wanted to do, when emotions were still high, as there was plenty of war work for girls and young women. They would not forget the execution of the nurse. When she had broached the subject with him and her mother recently, they had both firmly denied her request, even though she had assured them that she would almost certainly not be going overseas. That time, her birthday, seemed so far in the future, when she wanted to take action immediately.

Likewise, her father had not wanted her to train as a nurse, which she so desperately wanted to do; he would not pay the fees. It was not that he could not afford to do so; it was that he had told her it would be hard and a terrible life, that she would see things that would upset her.

May sobbed quietly, hunched over the photograph, not wanting her father to hear her. If only she could serve, if only she could do something in some small way to make up for the death of the nurse whose face stared out at her calmly from the newspaper.

Surely she could do something here in her own country, if she were allowed to do so. As the eldest child, it was up to her, the only one old enough to serve. Before her eighteenth birthday she must tackle her father.

Back inside the house, she cut out the article and the photograph to paste them in a scrap book that she kept of people and events that interested her. In this case, she pasted them beside articles she had about Emmeline Pankhurst and others who had campaigned before the war for votes for women. Even in this country the authorities were capable of great cruelty, she knew that. They had ordered those suffragettes in prison on hunger strike to be force-fed, had subjected them to other humiliations.

∞ Months went by, restlessly, as she worked at jobs in the town of Tunbridge Wells, doing work that junior men would have done before the war.

Then, to her delight, she found out that the women's armies had appeared on the scene, the Land Army, then the Women's Royal Naval Service, with its punning motto "Never at Sea." She read about them avidly as the weeks went by, as she scoured the newspapers for reports of the war effort. Women, she read, were doing work for which they had to be sworn in under the Official Secrets Act, as well as more humble work as cooks, housemaids and waitresses in the Navy Headquarters and at ports. These "Wrens," as they were nicknamed, were causing consternation, apparently, among some male officers in the service. Secretly, May found out as much as she could about the services.

Weeks became months, as she bided her time to choose the moment. Conscious always of watching and waiting, although not waiting

on God as one was sometimes exhorted to do, she saw at last one day
that a Women's Army Auxiliary Corps had been formed. It was Febru-
ary, 1917. The Corps came out of the Women's Legion, an organization
that did war work, May read, and knew by some kind of instinct that
this was for her, this was her calling.

In the first instance, she read, one had to apply to the Labour Bureau, then go before a Selection Board and a Medical Board. Women
were already employed in the Legion as drivers in the Motor Transport
Section, and women had already taken over from men as cooks. No one
under twenty would be accepted for overseas work.

Over the next days, May waited with a secret, inward joy for the
right moment to confront her parents. All the information she had
discovered about the WAAC, and the attached Royal Flying Corps, she
obtained from a recruiting office at the Labour Bureau, going about it
all with a quiet determination. The RFC, she discovered, wanted
women for clerks and cooks, among other things, to take the places of
men who had gone on to fight and where there were not enough other
men to take their places.

If she were accepted into the RFC, they would give her a capacious
peaked cap to wear, with a badge on the front of it, a serge skirt that
came down to a few inches above her ankles, an unflattering, double-
breasted long tunic with a loose belt that hid her feminine shape. She
did not care; she would tuck her handkerchief into the tunic where it
over-lapped her forbidden bosom.

A door had opened to her and she planned to go through it. In
some small way she, and thousands like her, would make up for the
death of Edith Cavell, for those lost young men whose names appeared
in long lists every day in newspapers across the country. Already that
shadowy sisterhood was taking shape, of which she would be a part,
coming into focus in her mind. She would leave behind her scrap book
of Emmeline Pankhurst, Anna Pavlova, and Edith Cavell, to enter a
new reality. As winter moved into spring of 1917 her spirits soared.

∞ Her parents gave in when the time came, as May had sensed they
would, when they were presented with a near fait accompli, with her

new maturity and confidence. They capitulated when she assured her mother that she would not yet be sent overseas, if ever. Surely the war would end soon, before it came to that.

Their uncertainty was tempered by a pride in her that she could see, veiled, in their eyes as they looked at her searchingly, when they all stood in the sitting room by the fireplace, the other children elsewhere. It would not do for her to see that pride overtly, because that emotion really did go before a fall; it could lead to an overweening pride in the self, a false confidence, that would not do, would especially be unseemly in a young woman. One was kept safe by common sense, a certain humility in the face of difficult circumstances. Later, perhaps, when she came through, they would tell her. All that she knew, as she hugged them compulsively.

She knew that they too would be thinking of the massive losses in France and Belgium, of the train-loads of wounded and maimed soldiers that came into London every day. Women were making munitions, were doing many jobs that they had not been allowed to do before, not considered physically or mentally fit to do.

∞ As she packed to go away, May felt the final lifting of that terrible paralysis that comes over one when the way to action is unclear. Sometimes in quiet moments her own assurance frightened her, because she had few skills, not much to offer other than her youth, energy, and the willingness to work hard at whatever might be assigned to her. At other times, she sensed that would be enough.

They had taken her in the Royal Flying Corps, had assigned her to an aerodrome in Yorkshire, near Tadcaster, at a place called Bramham Moor. There she would be working in the officers' mess and in the kitchens. It was a long way from home, and to get there she would have to take a train up to London, to Charing Cross, then cross London to a station where trains were bound for the north, would eventually get off at Tadcaster. There would be others with her; she would never be alone to make her own way.

Visions of Yorkshire came to her frequently: heather covered moors, green vistas as far as the horizon, dotted with sheep, very old towns and villages, cathedrals, ancient precincts, all places where she could walk in her days off, to draw her mind away from war and loss.

When the day of departure came, she dressed in her new uniform, finishing with the sensible laced shoes with a two inch heel and the squashy peaked cap with a RFC badge on the front. Most of all, she was proud of that cap and badge as she looked at herself in the mirror of the dressing table in the small bedroom that she shared with Mildred. Her soft, dark, curly hair peeped out becomingly from around the edges of the cap, which made up for the serviceable other parts of the uniform. There would be no time for vanity at the Yorkshire airfield, she sensed.

"I wish I was going," Mildred said enviously, as she leaned against the wall of their bedroom, watching May adjust the cap.

"Your turn will come, I expect."

"Fat chance."

"You'll have this room to yourself now."

"You'll come home on leave, won't you?"

"Don't know yet."

"Come on, May!" her father called up the stairs. "You'll miss the train."

"That's Dad," Mildred said, "always worrying about missing things. He'll get you there half an hour too early."

They clattered down the stairs, where her mother and brothers were waiting at the bottom to get a look at her in the uniform. Gratifyingly, they stood in awe, parting ranks to let her pass.

"Cor, you look smashing!" her brother Will said.

May could see that her mother had been crying, and now Harriet started again, dabbing her eyes with a handkerchief as May came forward. "Don't cry, Mum. I'll be all right. It's not as though I'm going out of the country, and I'll write at least twice a week, I promise."

When her mother put her arms around her and whispered in her ear the forbidden words: "I'm proud of you," her own eyes filled with tears.

Edward Wigley had hired a pony and trap, with a driver, to take his daughter to the station from where she could get a train all the way up to London. Before the appearance of the conveyance, he carried May's luggage out to the lane in front of the cottage so that he could load it onto the trap at the earliest opportunity. May took last looks at the cottage, conjuring up in her mind the images of the surrounding vast woods, almost a forest, of quiet and solitude, that started where the gardens ended, criss-crossed with lanes and paths. There was only one other house nearby, just along the lane.

She looked at her father as he waited, knowing she would miss him, his common sense, his understanding of fairness. He was short and wiry, and now stood first on one foot, then on the other, seldom on both at the same time.

May and her entourage followed him outside as the pony and trap came into view.

"Whoa!" The horse, wearing blinkers, stopped obediently in front of the thatched cottage where the garden was burgeoning with flowers of spring. Sunshine bathed everything in a delicate yellow light.

All at once, May found herself looking around her at the scene that she saw every day and took entirely for granted, as though now she was to leave it she could step outside herself and see it as a stranger might, with its surface charm and beauty which hid the sustained work that went to maintaining it.

May looked at her mother, who was wearing a long, navy-blue dress with lace collar and cuffs for the occasion, seeing her weariness. Now Mildred must step forward more often to be a second mother to the younger children.

"Good morning, Mrs. Wigley, Mr. Wigley. Good morning, all. And a fine day it is for a young lady to be going off to the wars," the owner of the trap, a Mr. Parsons, addressed them as he and Edward Wigley began to load up the luggage.

Harriet dabbed afresh at her swollen eyelids. Mildred now cried unabashedly, while the boys stood in silent wonder that their sister should be dressed in uniform and going on a long journey.

Again they all embraced. Then May was handed up into the trap, to be settled on a horsehair seat. Her father was to go with her to the station.

Harriet reached up to take May's hand. "Write to me as soon as you get there," she said.

"I will."

"Gee up!" The horse moved forward on the command of Mr. Parsons, and the moments of farewell were over. The sounds of its hooves were muted on the packed clay of the lane. May, holding herself very still and controlled, heard a muted indrawing of breath on a sob from her mother.

"Bye! Bye-eee! Bye-eee!" her brothers called, moving into action as though from a stupor.

As the trap approached the turning in the lane where it went sharply to the right to get down to the road that would take them on to the village and the railway station, May turned for a last look. Her mother stood in the centre of the lane, surrounded by her remaining children, her hand to her face. The older boys waved handkerchiefs above their heads, while her little brother Frank waved his cap.

The sight of them there, as though grouped for a photograph, would be in her memory when she was in Yorkshire. As she waved for the last time, the horse turned the corner, taking them steadily a little downhill towards the road. On either side the sunlight filtered through tall trees, above banks where heather grew. She loved this lane, with the scent of pine and heather, loved its quietness other than the sounds of birds. Goodbye old home, she said to herself as she compressed her lips to prevent them from trembling. Never would she show tears to her father who, as like as not, would order the driver to take her back home again. "That's enough of all that," he might say. "You're not going anywhere, my girl."

Tactfully, perhaps, he said nothing for quite a while, as they both looked steadily forward. He was a very handsome man, her Dad, in spite of his short stature, especially so now, dressed in his Sunday best, May thought, as she felt proud to sit beside him for all to see. Women often looked at him with veiled or open admiration, which he seemed to accept with a modest reticence. She herself had inherited his dark, thick hair, his light-green eyes and pale skin.

On the paved road the horse's hooves clopped noisily. "Giddy up!" the driver called, flicking his whip a little, so that the horse pricked up its ears and speeded up. May drew the scent of horse into her nostrils, as though for the last time.

There were a few people walking on the road as the trap went by, people who recognized them instantly and the import of the journey, people who waved and called out: "Good luck, May! Good-day, Mr. Wigley!"

Edward Wigley was well known at the Wesleyan chapel, where he preached often as a lay-preacher. At those moments May felt like Queen Mary waving to the public from her carriage.

As they both waved back to those people from the village and surrounding countryside, her father broke his silence. "You make sure you write to your mother," he said. "She would die if anything happened to you."

"Oh, I will," she said. "I shall be quite safe."

As Mildred had said, they were much too early for the train, so her father paid the driver of the trap at the station and declared that he would walk home. "Very good, Mr. Wigley. Good luck, Miss May. We'll be thinking of you, all of us in the village, and praying for you, as we do for all the others."

"Thank you, Mr. Parsons," May said.

The two men heaved her luggage onto the platform after she had shown her special pass that would allow her to travel without charge. There were two young men in army uniform waiting for the same train, who stared at her and smiled, those smiles drawing her into a special fraternity. Self consciously she stood straight, beside her luggage, as people looked at her, drawing all eyes.

"Where are you going, dear?" a woman asked her.

"Yorkshire."

"Well, that's a long way from home. Good luck, dear."

"Thank you." It's not as far away as France, she wanted to say, although perhaps it was from where they stood now.

When they heard the train chugging in the near distance, her father put his arms round her. "Now then," he said, "you be a good girl. Don't take any risks."

"Oh, I won't, Dad."

The two young soldiers heaved her bags onto the train before her Dad could do it, so they stood side by side, father and daughter, amid the smoke and steam and the general business of porters moving luggage and boxes into a baggage compartment.

"We'll get a seat for her, Mister," one of the soldiers said to Edward Wigley.

"Much obliged," he said.

How young they looked, May thought, as she watched them. About fifteen, she would have guessed.

Edward Wigley kissed his daughter on the cheek. "We'll miss you, May. Watch out for all those young men; they'll be after you like moths round a flame."

May laughed. "I'll be all right, Dad."

From inside the train she leaned out the window above the door, taking her Dad's hand. "Goodbye, Dad. Thanks for coming with me."

"Stand clear, please!"

The train's whistle blew and its engine chuffed loudly as it began to move forward.

"Cheerio!"

Her Dad, together with mothers seeing off sons, and others, receded into the smoke as the train speeded up out of the station.

The train was packed with soldiers and civilians, so that May could scarcely move in the melee until one of the young men who had helped her before pushed towards her. "This way, Miss," he said, taking her arm. "We've kept a seat for you."

Moving forward with him into the crowd prevented her from giving way to the tears that she had held back, saddened by the sight of her father standing in the smoke. He had not wanted her to go, she knew that; it had taken a certain magnanimity and trust on his part to let her go.

"This way, love. Excuse me!"

Pushing and shoving, as politely as possible, May found herself propelled into a seat by a window, through which the Sussex countryside was speeding by.

"Are you going to France? Just joined up?" May asked the two soldiers, one of whom sat opposite her and the other beside her. Cigarette smoke wafted around them, together with the noise of shouted conversations.

"Yes, we're going to France. No, we haven't just joined up, we've been home on leave."

"What's it like out there?" she asked.

"Better not to know, Miss," the one opposite her said, leaning forward so that she could hear him over the din of the engine.

"It's hell," the one beside her said.

Even though the train stopped at many stations, the journey seemed short. In May's mind the images of her grouped family standing in the sunshine outside her home, of her father wreathed in the smoke from the train, became less distinct as other immediate images superimposed themselves. There was a sharpness to this scene in which she found herself, obliterating all others, something that she had never experienced before, a state that made her forget herself and how she was moving around in the world. Somehow she was able to project herself forward so that she felt part of a larger world, of a whole. She had been caught up in something that was carrying her away at great speed, and it was not just the train.

A porter stuck his head into the carriage that she was in, calling out: "Next stop Charing Cross! Make sure you take all your luggage. End of the line!"

"We'll help you, May," one of the young soldiers offered. In the interim, they had exchanged names and addresses, May finding out that they were Walter and Arthur, who were with the Royal Sussex Regiment. Matter-of-factly they had informed her, when she asked, that they had been in several battles in France, were lucky to have got out alive. "We think we're due to go somewhere else, but we don't know for certain. Something's up. They don't tell us anything, the higher-ups. A lot of the time they don't know themselves what's really supposed to be going on. Everything gets mixed up pretty quick when the guns start firing. We go on rumours."

Charing Cross station was solid with people, mostly in uniform, as the three of them got off the train, shoved from behind and crowded in front. May felt a few moments of panic when she looked out at the mass of people, all seeming to know where they were going. "Don't leave me yet, boys," she said.

"We won't," Arthur said. "You'll have to report to your Commanding Officer. He'll be hanging about here, don't you worry. We'll find him for you."

"It could be a 'she'."

With bags on shoulders and under arms, they shepherded her unerringly in a certain direction, weaving through the crowd, until they were confronted by a large sign, one among many, which said Royal Flying Corps, Tadcaster, Yorkshire, where an elderly male officer in army uniform was checking names off on a list.

"There you are, ducky," Walter said to her, urging her forward. "That's his nibs. Don't be shy."

"And who are you, Miss?" the officer asked her. "Full name, please, and destination. And give me your chitty."

"May Harriet Wigley, Sir," she said timidly. "Going to Yorkshire."

"Right you are, Miss," he said, ticking her off on his list. "This is your travel pass. Wait over there with the others, please." Up to then she had felt more or less invisible in the milling station.

The two young soldiers heaved her luggage over to the designated spot and dumped it down. "Well, cheerio, May," Arthur said, extending his hand. "You take good care of yourself now."

"Don't forget to write to us," Walter added. "We live for letters and good grub."

"I won't forget. Thank you both, so much," she said, taking their hands. "Good luck, boys." Then they were gone, disappearing in the general melange of khaki and blues. When she could no longer distinguish them, she felt more lonely than she had ever felt in her life.

"The others" that the officer had mentioned proved to be a small group of women, some about her own age, a few older, all in the same uniform as her own. "I'm May," she said to the nearest person, a thin-faced, pale girl who seemed almost lost in the heavy uniform.

"I'm Alice. Were those boys your brothers?"

"Oh, no. I just met them on the train."

"Poor boys. I wonder how many of these boys here will come back. As for us, what a lark this is. Eh?"

"I'm not sure I'd call it a lark," May said honestly. "It's very ... strange."

"You said it there, duck. You going to Yorkshire?"

"Yes. Tadcaster."

"Same as me," Alice said. "We'll have some fun. You wait and see. I'm from Tunbridge Wells."

"I'm from near Fernden," May said. Already things seemed to be falling into place, that moment of loneliness dissipating now that she had a local girl standing next to her.

"Attention!" An officer instructed them that lorries were to take them to Euston station in north London, where they would get on a train for Yorkshire. "Put your luggage on the carts that the porters will bring to you, then follow the carts, proceed to the front of the station and wait for further orders."

"Stick with me, May," Alice said.

"I will." Barriers between people broke down quickly in the face of the strange urgency that gripped them, May thought, as she lifted her bags onto the porters' carts. Already she felt that she had known Alice for a long time. They were both country girls; they understood each other. It was as though part of one's individual will was harnessed and incorporated into a collective will with a common purpose, cemented by fear. The need to speak, to express emotion, caused one to gaze into the faces of strangers as one groped for words, as one asked for help when needed. Seldom was one denied or repudiated.

As they, the women of the RFC, moved en masse towards the front of the station, following the porters with their bags, May felt sick with excitement and a rare peace in knowing that at last she was doing something in her own way to help prevent the invasion of their country by the enemy. Often she had lain awake at night visualizing the enemy landing on the shores of England, swarming over the countryside, along the roads, the lanes, the railway lines, killing at random as they went, pillaging and burning, giving orders, taking away the freedom to think and do for one's self.

This, too, was for the defenseless nurse who had been shot at dawn.

∞ On the train speeding north, May sat beside Alice and shared the sandwiches that her mother had made for her and carefully packed and wrapped in a linen napkin. She poured cold tea from a cyder bottle into an enamelled tin mug. A kaleidoscope of unfamiliar suburbs, towns, villages, countryside, more cities, moved past her line of vision when she looked out. Wherever they stopped, soldiers got off and on, some looking exhausted, pale, with the mud of the trenches still on them. At the sight of these young men, May lowered her eyes, determined not to let them catch her staring, yet she was drawn to them, wanting to offer them food and too shy to do so. Their eyes seemed unfocussed.

Already a new life was reaching forward and drawing her into its grasp, as though her life up till then had been an unwitting preparation for this.

∞ Lorries took them from Tadcaster to the aerodrome out in the countryside, a place of huts for people and hangars for the aeroplanes. Most of the craft, flimsy and mysterious, stood in the fields.

∞ When May had been there for several weeks, working with Alice in the officers' mess, a small group of new pilots arrived to receive further training and May, dressed in an unbecoming mob cap and long white apron over her indoor uniform, was confronted by them as she cleaned tables after the mid-day meal for the men.

"Hey!" one of the men addressed her. "I didn't know we were going to get beautiful girls here. No one prepared us."

Straightening up to look at the speaker, from where she had been bending over, energetically washing a table top, May doubted that she looked beautiful at that moment. Her face was sweaty and flushed, her hair falling in wisps around it. What surprised her was that this young officer, in the uniform of the RFC, had an American accent, in this case, soft and charming in its unfamiliarity.

"Are you going to tell me your name?" he asked, holding out a hand, a gesture not common from most of the other officers. Unthinking, she gave him her moist hand that was rough from all the washing up and other work that she did there.

"I didn't know the Americans were in the war," she said, not sure whether she should call him "sir".

"Just got into it," he said. "About time, if you ask me. We're attached to the British army for now. I'm Frederick George Decker ... that's Fred to you ... and this guy here is Sam "Tubby" Tubbington the third. Lieutenants Decker and Tubbington, that's us, both from New Jersey." He pronounced it Loo-tenants, at which she smiled.

Then it was impossible not to laugh, for the nick-name did not suit the man, who was tall and as thin as a lathe. "I'm May," she said. "I'm from Sussex, south of London."

Lieutenant Decker was slim and tall, had fair, straight hair that flopped over his forehead in a boyish way, an angular face, and very blue eyes.

Love at first sight was a concept that May had heard about but did not believe, yet as she looked back at the man, only a year or two older than herself, perhaps, she had the uncanny premonition that here was someone she would love. And it would not just be casually, it would be profoundly. The exotic nature of his unfamiliarity drew her to him. For all his casualness, she sensed an underlying seriousness and thoughtfulness that appealed to her. In his turn, he was sizing her up, grinning, as though he did not find her wanting in any way.

It was not wise to love a pilot, especially one who was destined to go to France, an internal voice of common sense warned her.

"Pleased to meet you, May," he said, enveloping her hand with both his own, in a way she was not used to. "Hey! Come out for a drink with us tonight. We can take a truck into town."

"Well, I ..." she began, overwhelmed.

"We won't take no for an answer," he said. "Bring a couple of friends."

Usually in the evenings she was so exhausted that she only had energy to wash herself, do some laundry and fall into bed. The hours of work were long, starting at half past five in the morning.

Frederick George Decker was standing smiling at her, his presence lighting up the utilitarian room in the wooden hut that passed for the officers' mess. Then she knew that common sense would not prevail. The force of the attraction, while welcomed with a sense of joy, also frightened her. Particularly so because she sensed that it was reciprocal.

He had not taken his eyes off her. For the first time she seriously confronted her own naivety and found herself at a loss.

∞ In a pub that evening, where the presence of the Americans caused some curiosity in the local population, mainly of middle-aged and old men, May sat with Fred Decker at a small, quiet table, where they both endured stares. "I'm not used to being in a pub," she said to him, self-consciously holding a glass of lemonade. She had changed out of her uniform, wore a civilian coat and a matching hat.

Alice and another girl had come with them, three girls to six men, who were sitting at other tables, while the local men leaned against the bar in a proprietorial manner.

"I'm lucky to be in England," Fred said to her. "Some guys I know who joined the infantry have been shipped directly to France. This gives us a breathing space. Of course, I want to see some of the action, when I'm ready. I worked in a bank before we were brought into the war."

"What brought you in?" May asked. "I don't have as much time to read newspapers as I did before I came here. We hear rumours, and we don't know what to believe."

"The Germans are after our shipping, have sunk our ships bringing food and other stuff over here," he said. "We can't stand for that. Before that, no one wanted to send our boys over here."

They held hands under the table. "I expect I'll be sent to France when I'm more experienced with the kites," he said. "We can't afford to wait too long."

"No." A powerful unaccustomed happiness that had taken hold of her not long before was now laced with an apprehension of inevitability, an intimation of loss.

"We do what we can," he said. "Each to his own, according to his ability."

∞ After that, they saw each other every day, by design and in the course of their work.

"Come for a walk with me after dinner, May," he said to her one evening in the mess. "Just around the edge of the 'drome."

"All right," she said, smiling at him. "I should finish work at half-past eight."

It was almost dark when they met. The airfield at the edges was a meadow where May could put the reality of the war out of her mind for a short while as they walked through the grass. "There are cows over in the next field," she said.

"Yeah. Seems unreal, all this, at times," he said. "Which is most of the time." They put their arms around each other as they walked.

"I've been wanting to tell you, May, that I'm of German origin. It's ironic, my being here," he confided in her as they walked. "My maternal grandparents are German, both born and bred in Munich. They emigrated to America. My parents were born in America, my Dad from German stock on both sides. My grandparents sure didn't want me to come here, to join up. They see it as some kind of betrayal. Maybe if I'd joined the German army they wouldn't have minded so much. I can't really say, and maybe they couldn't either."

"Why, then?"

"I'm an American really, see?" he said. "I know who I am, and they don't. We're a free people. I'm here to fight for that freedom, for the old world and for the new. Do you think any less of me because my people are German?"

"Oh, no. You can't help where you came from. You say you're free, but what about slavery?" she asked. "Not everyone was free."

"You're right. I didn't know much about that. Can't say I agree with it."

"I went to a small village school," she said, "and I had to learn some of the American poets by heart ... Henry Wadsworth Longfellow. 'The Slaves Dream' impressed me."

"'Beside the ungathered rice he lay ...'" Fred quoted as they walked.

"'His sickle in his hand ...'" she finished for him.

"That's very impressive, May," he said, "for a village school. I can't say I memorized any English poets, and Shakespeare bored me."

"'Under the spreading chestnut tree ...'"

"'The village smithy stands ...'" he added.

"I really like that one," she said.

"So do I." They walked on, the shadowy outlines of the aircraft in the background.

"Why did you join up, May?"

"I don't know," she said. "I thought I knew at the time, but now I don't. Partly it was just that I couldn't stand the inactivity. War is a kind of madness, isn't it?"

"I suppose so."

"On the way up here to Yorkshire, on the train from London, I saw soldiers who were on leave from the Front ... they had mud on their uniforms, they were carrying their rifles and their kit ... they looked absolutely weary, pale, and ... blank, somehow. And they were so young. I knew by just looking at them that they had seen the most awful things that I couldn't even imagine. They had dead eyes. Then I wasn't sure, because it all seemed beyond us, so out of hand."

"I know what you mean. We have to defend ourselves, May, when we're threatened. Like our ships were attacked, unprovoked aggression."

"Yes ... but why do we get to this state? Why do we allow it?"

"So many questions that we don't know how to answer. I wish I knew," he said. "Sometimes it's a good thing to say we don't know, to admit it, so long as we're striving for something good. They say that God is good, God is love. Perhaps that's it. People who say they are absolutely certain about something are generally insane."

The warmth of his arm around her, his closeness, were all that she could be sure of at that moment.

"My friend Alice thought it would be such a lark, at the beginning. It's all going on so long. But it isn't a lark, is it?"

"No, it sure isn't that."

He took her in his arms and kissed her as they stood in the dew-covered grass, from where they could hear cows moving about in the next field. "You're the nicest thing that's happened to me in a very long time, May," he said. "Will you think of me when I've gone? Because I will have to go."

"I shall think about you all the time," she said. "I wish you didn't have to go."

"That's why I'm here. We wouldn't have met otherwise. I can survive if I know you're thinking about me."

The fear that was frequent with her now came back as they walked. Was it a gift of God to be able to love someone whom you would never have met in normal times, if only for a few weeks?

∞ They danced together at dances, sat next to each other at impromptu concerts, went into town. They walked endlessly when days off coincided, through heather and meadows, watched birds wheeling in the sky that seemed vast in the open spaces below, went into quiet, ancient churches. Sometimes, in there, she prayed silently that he would be safe, would come back. All the other times, he flew in the flimsy craft, becoming more proficient. May noticed that those who were good went away to France.

Once she took him home to Sussex to meet her family, where they walked through the woods and along the lanes, breathing in the scent of bracken that grew under the oak trees beside the lanes. Her brothers looked at him with awe, hung on to his arms, asked him endless questions.

"This is a great place," he said to her as they walked, hand in hand.

When they were back in Yorkshire, his training intensified so that she saw him less.

"Something's up," he said to her one day. "I have a feeling that we're going in for the kill."

To her, and to the others who worked in the mess, he seemed like a golden boy who could not be touched by death. He personified life itself to her.

"Be careful, May," Alice said to her in the kitchens one day. "They're not for us, all those lovely boys, especially the Americans. They're just passing through." May turned her face away then so that Alice could not see her fear.

"I know," she said.

∞ Once she went into Tadcaster to have her photograph taken in uniform at a professional studio, wanting to give something to Fred of herself. In the meantime she lived from moment to moment, day to day.

"I'll keep this in my pocket close to my heart when I'm flying," he said when she gave him a photograph. On the back of another copy she wrote his home address that he dictated to her, New Jersey City Heights, New Jersey, and slipped the picture inside a book in her room.

"Sometime soon I'll have to fly over to France," he said. "I'll come back as often as I can. Don't forget your promise to think of me. And you can write."

"I'll always think of you," she said. While he was still with her he was never out of her mind.

"You're the first girl I've ever loved."

"I love you too," she said, as they stood outside a back door to the kitchens of the mess, where he smoked a cigarette and seemed restless, which made her suspect that he already knew when he would be going, but did not want to tell her. "Words are cheap, and inadequate, aren't they? You know that I love you."

"Yes."

They danced together that night in the officers' mess, an event got together quickly, while an officer played the piano. They held on to each other, never looking at anyone else, sensing that it was for the last time.

∞ The day came shortly after when he and others went; it happened matter-of-factly and abruptly. Fred, wearing his full kit, came to see her in the porch behind the kitchens, where he hugged her. "It's time, May," he said, his face very pale and tired, as though he had not slept. Then the full import of what he had to do in France came to her, and fear was like a physical pain in her chest as she hugged him back. "Knowing and loving you has been the centre of my life."

"Come back," she said. "Good luck."

May and Alice stood out on the grass near the officers' mess and watched them taxi away, then fly up into the blueness of the sky; watched them go until there was no more than a vast nothingness. May locked herself into a lavatory near the kitchens and wept.

Some weeks later Lieutenant Tubbington came back and sought out May in the quietness of an afternoon, and he took her hand. "This is difficult for me to say. Fred was shot down in France," he said. "He's not dead, he's wounded. He sends his love to you, May. It looks as though he'll be sent back home."

"Not here?"

"No, not here."

"Are you telling me the truth, that he's not dead?" How odd it is that, when one wants to howl and scream, the voice comes out calm and steady.

"Yes, I am. I wouldn't have come back to tell you that he's dead, May. I wouldn't have had the guts. Here's something for you."

In a crumpled small white envelope with her name written on it was a lock of bright hair.

When she could, she got away from the airfield by herself, to walk and walk on the moors, struggling through the springy heather that was wet with rain, that gave off a delicate scent. She stumbled through streams, toiled up hills, coming down again through gullies. As though from afar, she listened to the calls of birds floating on wind under an immense sky, going on until she had exhausted herself. In some of the places that she had walked through with Fred, she imagined that he was with her. After waiting beside a road, not knowing exactly where she was, she got a lift back to Tadcaster in a lorry driven by a soldier.

◐ Chapter 19

They were married in the autumn of 1916, Jim and Anne, when the leaves were turning yellow, orange, and brown in the counties of Kent and Sussex, and the scents of the late harvest, especially of apples, were in the air. They married in the small parish church at the hamlet of Walters Green, surrounded by green fields of the rolling, fertile countryside.

Members of the wedding party threw confetti when they came out of the church into the soft autumn light, little rounds of coloured paper that floated in the gentle breeze and mingled with leaves that fell from the trees nearby. From there they were to walk to Anne's mother's cottage where they would have a reception. The day was beautiful, mellow, with a delicate misty sunlight. Anne laughed when the confetti covered them, when it clung to Jim's best grey suit and her dress of satin and lace, her long veil that was held in place by orange blossom. They held hands as the bells rang out.

"This is the happiest day of my life," Jim said, speaking close to her ear.

Frank was Best Man, there with Grace and his sisters. Before they all moved away from the church door to go along the path to the gate that lead to the village High Street, Anne threw her bouquet of pink roses towards the sisters. There was a general cheer when Frank's sister Emily caught it, and a few male voices called out: "Marry me, Em!"

Jim put an arm around his mother's shoulders and kissed her. "Six down and one to go," he said to her. There was only his sister Harriet left now to marry. "You look lovely." His mother wore a light grey straw hat, and a dress and jacket that she had made herself, of the same colour. Sixty-nine now, she relied on her children to help support her, having worked hard all her life until recent times.

"I'm glad you're back home," she said. To his recollection, she had said that at least a dozen times before.

He nodded, thinking of the stilted, censored letters that he had sent home to her from France. With Anne's hand warm in his, with his mother alive and well beside him, with Frank, he saw this occasion as the beginning of a new hope. It was more than he had expected when he had been discharged from the army in March.

As they walked, he thought of the cottage that he and Anne were to move into later that day, where all was as ready as they could make it for now. He knew he had been fortunate to get a good job in a kitchen garden and market garden, with Lord Denman, on the large estate near Penshurst, where he and Anne had been able to get a tied cottage that went with the job, with two bedrooms and as substantial a garden as he could wish for.

Already he had been there many times to clear the overgrown garden, to clean and paint the house, to have the chimneys swept, as no one had lived there for six months. He had cleaned the cast-iron cooking range in the living room, cleared the grate of cinders and clinkers left by the previous occupants, then did the same with the firebox under the copper in the kitchen where they would heat their water. He swept away evidence of mice, moved spiders outside, opened windows and cleaned the glass, mended and polished, washed floors, nailed down loose boards, made sure that the well worked, that the bucket could be wound down and up, that the water was fit to drink. He had cut and sawn wood for the fires, chopped kindling, brought in coal.

Yes, the immediate future was welcoming and he gave thanks to a nameless deity. Yet he knew he would never forget his recent history, or those mates whose fate he did not know, who seemed to have disappeared as surely as though they had never been born. It was a weight on his heart that would always be there.

He and Anne had a plan to go to the seaside for three days for their honeymoon, where they would sit on the beach, would walk and look in shops, even though the summer sun had gone.

∽ When he returned to the cottage with Anne after the honeymoon, she set to work to arrange their belongings as she wanted them. She black-leaded the range, polishing it to a sheen. "Jim, I'm going to bake bacon and onion roly-poly in this oven," she said, "with thyme and sage. We'll have treacle tart, rabbit stew and rabbit pie, toad-in-the-hole, Yorkshire pudding, and all sorts of lovely things."

"I'm ready and waiting." He picked her up under her arms and swung her round in the living room.

"I love this cottage," she said breathlessly when he had put her down. "Perhaps we could get a cat. And a dog."

"Why not. I'm going to nail a horseshoe over the door," he said. "For good luck."

There were late roses blooming in the front garden, white and pale pink, some of which he had cut to put in a vase in the sitting room, from where their scent filled the house.

∽ They settled into their life together.

"There's a dog we could have," Jim said one day, "a mongrel that looks like a cocker spaniel. Old Mr. Watts in the village just died and there's no one to take his dog. She's a nice dog, good natured, I've met her a few times, so you could say she knows me."

"We'll take her," Anne said. "It's sad about Mr. Watts. That dog's going to need a lot of love. Do you know her name?"

"He called her Loopy." They both laughed.

"We'll keep that name," Anne said.

"She's four years old. Not too old to get used to us."

In due course, Loopy came home with them. At about that time they got a kitten; Anne chose the only black one from a litter of six. "There's something very special about black cats." she said. "They seem to have a sixth sense, as well as more than nine lives. We'll call him Felix."

"Well then, you won't be too lonely with Loopy and Felix when I'm at work," Jim said.

Every morning at about half past six Jim left the cottage to walk to work through a wood, as well as over fields and paths, carrying his food in a bag for his mid-day meal, together with a bottle of cold tea. When he left to come home in the late afternoon, Anne met him half way, whatever the weather, with Loopy walking ahead, watching for him. Spotting him, the dog would race ahead to greet him.

"Hello, old girl." He made a fuss of the dog, hoping she had accepted him as a new master. Together with the dog they had inherited an old jacket that had belonged to Mr. Watts, that Loopy now slept on.

"I'm frightened to wash that jacket," Anne said, more than once. "In case the smell of Mr. Watts disappears and the dog goes into mourning. Pretty soon we won't be able to stand the smell ourselves."

"I reckon she's been mourning all right. She knows he's gone."

Every day a paper-boy from the village came to the cottage on his bicycle to deliver a newspaper, which Jim read in the evenings as he sat by the cast-iron range where the flames roared up the chimney. There were long lists of the dead and the missing in France and other places, as the war went on. There were grainy photographs of trains in London railway stations, disgorging the wounded on stretchers and the walking wounded, by the thousands.

"Is there anyone you know?" Anne asked. Jim knew that she made her voice casual, gently enquiring, as though she knew full well the dread that he would experience if his eyes lighted on a familiar name.

"Not so far," he said. "But then I know I've missed some of the lists, and it is eight months since I left the army. They went on to the Somme, my lot. Not many left."

"Any news of Roy?"

"Not recently. Frank said he had a letter from him some time ago. I hope one day I'll see him again."

⁓ One day in mid-November Anne waved to him from the other side of the meadow that he crossed to get home, the dog with her, then she slipped her hand into his when they met. "Jim, I'm expecting a baby," she said. "I went to see the new young doctor in the village today, and he thinks it's almost certain. I didn't tell you before because I wanted to wait a little to be sure."

They stopped there on the path and she went into the circle of his arms. "I'm very glad," he said. "Are you?"

"Yes, it's what I want."

Jim put his arm round her, holding her against him as they walked, his happiness tempered with a sober consideration of childbirth, a serious business with inherent dangers, perhaps especially for Anne who was small and slender. "What did you think of the new doctor?"

"He seemed good, very pleasant and respectful. His name's Dr. Bayley. He said he would talk to Mrs. Martin, the midwife, that he and she would both be at the confinement and they would both look after me in the lying-in period. My mother will come, of course."

They walked with bent heads, looking at the path where rain had left puddles. Jim did not doubt that Anne was nervous, the first baby usually resulting in the longest labour. The skill of the midwife could often mean the difference between life and death for the woman in labour, as well as for the child.

"I've heard that Mrs. Martin is the best midwife," Anne said, echoing his thoughts. "I've seen her in the village, but haven't actually spoken to her. Dr. Bayley said I must go to see her next week at her cottage."

"I'll come with you," Jim said. "I can get half a day off."

✑ Late autumn moved into winter, and their life became more settled at the cottage. Jim pruned and cut back shrubs and trees in the garden, dug the soil again in preparation for planting in the spring. There were raspberry and gooseberry bushes, black currents and red currents, apple and pear trees, a plum tree, as well as the roses and a fuschia bush in the front garden. He had planted daffodil, tulip and snowdrop bulbs to bloom in spring.

Inside the cottage the fires under the copper and in the range burned for long hours, using up fuel greedily to keep the place warm as the winter winds became colder and snow began to fall just before Christmas. He went frequently into the woods to look for downed tree branches that he could drag home and saw up for firewood. Lord Denman allowed his workers on the estate several bundles of faggots per household throughout the winter, delivered by horse and cart.

As the weeks went by, Anne prepared for her confinement, with a layette and bedding for the child. She knitted and sewed in every spare moment, made two voluminous dresses for herself as she became bigger. Still she walked to meet Jim on his way home. Jim ordered a cradle from a local carpenter, made out of oak, which would have flowers carved into it.

As the time drew near and summer reached its zenith, Jim made sure that there were buckets of water in the kitchen before he went to work. For some time now Anne had not wound the handle of the well to draw water. He made sure that there were pots and kettles of water on the range, where they would heat up slowly throughout the day and then boil when moved closer to the heat. He brought in wood and coal, banked up the fires. Every day Anne's mother and sister came from the village to see her, bringing cooked food.

"Don't you lift anything," Jim said, every time he left. As he walked away he repeatedly dredged up every bit of knowledge he had gleaned about childbirth over the years, going over it again and again, trying to separate the old wives' tales from the real.

"I think the baby's a boy," Anne's mother said to him on one occasion, "because it's big and riding high."

Not too big, I hope, he had thought. He knew something about babies too big to be born easily, most of his knowledge coming from calves, foals and lambs. He had seen ropes attached to calves to pull them out of their mother's body. He hoped and prayed that young Dr. Bayley and Mrs. Martin knew what they were doing.

They saved clean newspaper to pad the mattress above oilskin sheets on the bed where Anne would give birth. He brought fruit for her from the greenhouses of Lord Denman.

∽ One day in high summer, after the first hay-making, when grass and flowers were growing again in the hay fields, Jim walked home across the big meadow. So far he had not seen Anne, who usually came out of the small wood that bordered on the meadow at the far side, where there was a path. As he looked for her, their dog burst out from the trees and ran towards him, barking at the sight of him, reaching him out of breath. There was a frantic quality to the dog's barking, as she ran back and forth, going from him and then coming back.

Jim began to run then, shifting his dinner bag so that the strap was across his chest, following the dog that darted ahead. Something was up. He was frightened as he tried to increase his speed, running through the wood and out the other side to another open area where he could see his cottage in the distance. As he came close he saw that the door was open, that the dog ahead of him had burst through it.

Gasping for breath he came into the sitting room, to find Ann lying on the sofa, her face pale.

"Anne, Anne! For God's sake, are you all right?" Down on one knee, he took her hand, which was hot and clammy. Her face was beaded with sweat.

"It's started," she whispered. "About two hours ago."

He got to his feet, found a cloth and plunged it into a bucket of cold water, then wiped Anne's face and hands.

"Have the waters broken?" he asked. "Is there blood?"

"No ... no. I have some pain."

He poured her a glass of home-made lemonade that they had in a jug out in the cold pantry. "Drink some of this," he instructed, bending over her. "Then I'm going to run to get your mother and the midwife. Don't get up from the couch while I'm gone."

"I won't."

"I'm going to shut the door to keep the dog in. She came to get me, you know."

"I sent her to get you," Anne said weakly. "She knew what I meant; she knew something was not right."

He bent down and kissed her on the forehead. "I won't be long."

The edge of the village was not far away, no more than five hundred yards, he reckoned as he ran. First he would go for Anne's mother, who would be waiting for the call and would get Anne's sister; then he would go to Mrs. Martin's cottage, she being the more important person of the two when compared with the doctor, he calculated. Then he would go for the doctor himself. By the time he got home, at least Anne's mother would be there. All was ready at the cottage, as far as he and Anne could possibly make it.

All night Anne laboured, while he moved in and out of the cottage, sometimes standing at the bottom of the stairs to listen to her moans, tears in his eyes, sometimes walking out in the fields that were still warm from the sun, thinking of the summer previously when he and his platoon had engaged in mock battles that bore little relationship to actuality as it turned out. Now, as the women engaged in bringing forth life, he felt helpless.

One of his jobs was to keep the fire going; he brought in fuel, sawed and chopped wood in the shed, keeping himself occupied.

At five o'clock in the morning Anne's sister, Esther, called to him from the cottage garden, to his seat on a tree stump out in the field where he sat smoking. "Come in!"

"Go up to see her," she said, when he came through the door. "I'm going to make some tea."

Wordlessly he climbed the stairs. Anne was in bed, propped on pillows, looking exhausted and relieved, holding her baby wrapped in a sheet, while her mother moved things around in the room, cleaning up.

"It's a boy, Jim," Anne said, managing a smile as he went down on his knees beside the bed and looked at her and the child, his child, that appeared red-faced and crumpled, his eyes firmly closed. There was something of himself in that small face, so Jim thought, the wide, high forehead, the well defined lips.

"Are you all right?" he asked softly, feeling self-conscious with the midwife in the room, as well as Anne's mother. "And is he all right?" It looked as though Dr. Bayley had already left, as he was not in evidence.

"Yes ... both," she said. "Oh, Jim, he's so bonny."

"Yes, he is." He cried then, bowing his head, letting the tears fall unashamedly down his face. "I'm so thankful."

After waiting for two weeks, to be sure that their baby would live, they set about naming him.

"What about Will?" Anne said. "I've had that in my mind for a long time."

"So be it," Jim said. "We'll see about the baptism in a month or so."

They watched over their Will, the most precious thing they had ever had, taking their responsibilities seriously.

The war in France wore on and on.

∽ In March, 1918, which was bitterly cold when wind and sleet blew around the cottage, Will became unwell. "He feels hot," Anne said to Jim early one morning as she bent over the cradle that was beside their bed, "and his breathing is not quite right."

Will, wearing a long flannel night-gown, lay there looking up at them as they bent anxiously over him. He has beautiful blue eyes, Jim thought for the umpteenth time, that contrasted with his fine dark hair and pale skin. When he touched his son's cheek, he could tell that the boy had a fever; he sniffled when he breathed, his face was flushed.

"We must wash him down with tepid water," he said. "Cool him down when he's hot, then make sure he's warm at other times. I won't leave for work until I know he's all right."

Reluctantly he left later, leaving Anne and Will in the sitting room. "I'll come home early," he said as he left. "If he's no better, we'll take him up to Dr. Bayley."

Leaning into the wind, he made his way across the field towards the wood. He had put on an oilskin cape against the rain. Before entering the wood, he looked back towards the cottage. It looked snug and warm, with smoke coming out of the two chimneys from the fires that he had started before he left. God willing, his son would be all right. Although the sight of the warm cottage reassured him in one way, he still felt ill at ease in another, wondering if he should have stayed at home for the whole morning, then taken Will up to the doctor, or asked him to call at the house.

Anne had been given a sturdy wicker pram, second hand, by someone in the village. It had large wheels, easy to push over rough paths, and a hood with a waterproof lining, so it was easy to take Will out.

∽ After he had eaten his mid-day meal of sandwiches and cold tea, with one of the other gardeners in the potting shed where they had a coal stove, he went to the tall domed greenhouse to water the grape vines that they grew there. It was pleasantly warm in there, a little humid, a pleasure to be in on a day like this, he told himself as he pulled the hose to where he wanted it to be.

All morning his mind had been on Will, so that he went about his work automatically. He sprayed the grape roots with water, moving the nozzle of the hose back and forth.

When the door of the greenhouse opened to reveal Anne in the aperture, holding on to the wicker pram, he thought he had conjured them up out of his imagination. Then he saw the expression on her face, an abject fear that he had never seen before. That fear transferred itself to him. "What is it?" he said, walking deliberately over to the tap nearby to turn off the hose.

Anne had struggled through the door with the bulky pram. "Jim, he's not breathing properly," she said, wheeling the pram towards him. "I'm so frightened."

"Oh, God," he said, as he bent over Will, pulled back the covers to reveal his baby swaddled in a shawl. Will's face was very pale, with a blue tinge around his mouth and nose. Jim lifted him out, placed him on a bench. Far from not breathing properly, Will was not breathing at all.

Once, he had seen a doctor blow into the mouth of a baby that had stopped breathing, had resurrected him, so to speak. He did that now, blowing into his son's mouth several times. There was no response. His son's soft, plump cheeks were cold.

"He's dead," he said, his voice shaking. He picked the boy up in his shawl, held him against his chest.

Anne's cry of anguish, then her unearthly keening filled the huge greenhouse. "Oh, no, no no!"

They wept as they stood together holding their boy, cradling him between them, for a long time. It seemed to Jim that a malign fate, having failed to kill him in 1915, had taken his son instead, a being whom he loved beyond reason.

But for the pallor of Will's skin, he looked as though he were asleep, his long dark lashes resting on his cheeks. "He's so bonny," Anne whispered.

༄ Joy went out of their lives as they mourned their son in an age of mourning that touched the lives of everyone, as train-loads of the maimed, wounded and shell-shocked rolled into London, as the legions of the dead were interred in French and Belgian soil and elsewhere, as the names of the missing were recorded in their hundreds of thousands.

"It was easy to forget about the war when we had Will," Anne said. She took to obsessively walking their dog around the fields and woods as the weather warmed and spring came into full bloom, lavishing her un-used-up love onto the animal. In the evenings she sat with the cat on her lap, stroking it, staring absently into the fire. The cradle remained on the bedroom floor; they could not bring themselves to move any of the evidence of Will, as though at any moment he would need those things again.

"Was it my fault?" she asked Jim. "Was I neglectful?"

"You know you were not. We never took our eyes off him." He took her hand as she sat silently, staring at nothing.

Will was buried in the village churchyard, where Jim vowed to plant a rose bush in early summer. It was as though their lovely child had been lent to them for a short while, he thought as he and Anne stood beside the tiny grave, so that they might learn something of the profound love of a parent for a child, like no other.

༄ Jim wrote to Roy Carter in France, but received no reply. It was a distraction to him. As he scoured the newspapers in the evenings for Roy's name — for he felt that all the others he had known must have already gone, he read in May, 1918, that a mysterious illness had made an appearance in Scotland. Already it had hit the troops in the trenches in France, and had been dubbed by some as the Spanish Influenza.

"I don't want to think about that," Anne said, when he read out the reports to her. "All I can think about is Will."

Nevertheless, he continued to read the reports as they became more numerous over the next few months. The disease was spreading like a plague throughout the country, then more widely over the world, targeting young adults in their prime. Most were dead within three days of becoming ill. It could not be ignored.

"Let's go to the seaside for a few days, Jim," Anne said to him in August. "I want to get away. Then I'd like to visit my sister Liza in Croydon, if you don't mind being alone."

"You must go, it will be good for you," he said, hoping that she would come out of the deep depression that she had entered. "I'll take care of the grave, don't you worry." Every day Anne went to Will's grave, with flowers. "I'll see about getting a few days off very soon. We could go to Hastings, if you like."

"I'd like that."

They duly went to the seaside, then Anne prepared to go by train to Croydon, just south of London.

"I'll take you to the station with the hand-cart," Jim said, considering that the station, which they seldom needed to go to, must be one and a half miles from the other side of the village.

When the departure day came, he pushed her and her bag to the station. "You enjoy yourself," he said to her after they had gone through to the platform.

"I'll try," she said. "You're so good to me, Jimmy. I'll miss you."

"You look lovely," he said. She had on the blue dress and the straw hat that she had worn to Frank's wedding, her pale hair curling about her face.

Before she stepped up into the train he kissed her. "All my love," he said.

When the train moved out, he felt bereft and disturbed, watching it go.

༄ While Anne was gone he often sat outside in his garden in the evenings when the sun was warm, under an apple tree, looking at the newspaper. On cooler evenings he sat by the fire, where the dog curled up on his feet, as though beseeching him not to go away. "It's all right, girl," he reassured the dog. "I'm not going anywhere." Sometimes he wondered if the dog still missed old Mr. Watts.

Often he tried to resist the urge to read the columns of the war dead, which served to deepen his sadness, yet found that he could not help himself. At such times he felt guilty that he was not there in France, that he was not using the training and experience that he had received, at the same time knowing that his chances of having survived this long would not have been good.

On one such evening, as he sat by the fire, he had a sudden premonition that something had happened to Anne, a premonition so powerful and mysterious that he put down the newspaper on his lap and looked at the door as though he expected someone to come through it. He was alert and tense. The dog lifted her head from where it had been resting on his foot, looked at the door and gave a short, sharp bark.

Then it seemed to him that a delicate breeze passed through the room, rattling the cups and plates on the Welsh dresser. He took that to be her communication with him.

He was frightened, yet peculiarly calm at the same time, as he experienced a certainty that something had happened that would call upon him to have more courage than he had ever had to find in himself before now.

When the telegram boy came to the house very early the next morning, walking up the brick path to the front door, having left his bicycle by the gate, Jim knew what the telegram would say. Through the sitting room window he could see the boy.

He opened the door to wait for him.

"Anne died suddenly from influenza [stop] Please come [stop]," he read when the boy had gone.

As he sat alone, with the telegram in his hand, with his hands on his knees, head down, as he had sat when he had received letters in France from home, he thought of Etta because she came into his mind then. He did not question why. "My life is already over," she had said to him. "Husbandless and childless. There will be no one else for me."

Like her, he found himself entering that barren wasteland where love is withdrawn from one, that love which is one's whole existence. In his mind now the face of his wife would be ever in repose, his dear, sweet, beloved Anne, beside that of his son. The love for a child was a different kind of love from that for a woman; it held in it a tender protectiveness of a different sort, a selflessness that bordered on awe at the phenomenon of new life. As he had looked at his tiny son, he had not known before that such love was possible. With Anne he had borne that loss. As he thought about that now, he knew that he would have given his own life for both of them.

"What am I to do?" he said aloud. "Whatever am I to do?"

Upstairs in his cottage he took out the old newspaper from the bottom drawer of his chest of drawers to look at the photograph of Etta, for it now seemed that she was with him. "Courage, dear boy," she would have said. When he had been at his lowest ebb, she had been there, as had the nurse Milly, and others. Now he turned to them in memory. Later, he would walk to tell his mother.

"Well done, thou good and faithful servant." He read the words again from Etta's obituary, then propped the paper up on the chest where he could see her eyes looking at him.

Those words he would ask the vicar to read at the funeral service of his dear Anne. More than many, he had known both love and happiness.

Now the desert came to meet him and enveloped him in its barrenness.

∽ During the next day he took the train up to Croydon to accompany Anne's body home, having gone to see the vicar before heading to the station, walking like one in a dream, going about the business of what he had to do.

"She took ill so quickly, Jim," Anne's sister, Liza, said to him over a cup of tea after he had found the house in Croydon, where he had never been before. "We called the doctor to the house and he came immediately, but it was no good, there was nothing he could do. She couldn't breathe, you see. The doctor said it was the Spanish Influenza, that she had congestion of the lungs." Liza cried, twisting her hands nervously together in her lap.

"Where is she?" he asked.

"The doctor told us that she had to be taken away by ambulance to the hospital mortuary, because it's so infectious, see. She couldn't be allowed to stay in the house. We could all get it." Liza sobbed anew, into a handkerchief. "What an awful thing, Jim. Five people on this street have died of it."

"Children?" he asked.

"No. The doctor said it hasn't affected children, so far. It takes people in the prime of life."

She reached for his hand. "They want you to identify her body as soon as possible, Jim, you being her husband. I'll come with you."

"Thank you," he said, looking around the comfortable, modest room, trying to picture Anne sitting there. The house was one of a row of small, terraced houses in a quiet street, for working people, where the front doors opened right onto the street. He could see that any disease could spread very quickly there. So this was the place she had seen in the last hours of her life, rather than the countryside that she had loved. He would make it up to her, he promised himself. Every day he would bring flowers to her, from their garden, and wild ones from the fields and hedgerows.

Liza squeezed his hand. "She didn't suffer at the end, Jim, I'm convinced of that. She became unconscious and just stopped breathing, when we were all with her. The doctor was here then too. She seemed to have no resistance at all."

He nodded. "Thank you for your kindness, Liza. I'd like to see her as soon as I can."

"I've got some dinner ready for you. We'll eat that, then go up to the hospital, it's within walking distance. George will be home soon, he'll come with us."

"Much obliged," he said. "I can hardly take it in."

"Of course, you can't. Neither can we."

When the war came to an end later that year, Jim put flowers on the grave of his wife and son who were buried together. Although it was November, he had scoured the shops and gardens for violets. Not the small, sweet scented violets of early summer, for he knew he could not find those. Rather the large purple dog-violets that have no scent, which he eventually found. With them were flowers from his own garden, of his tied cottage, the ones that had survived the cold, that he had nurtured to their mature beauty, for he devoted his life to that now. He was thirty-three years old.

Later, with others, quietly, he went into a church to pray — although he did not believe in anything he could honestly call God — for those he loved … as a mark of respect … for Harry Baker, Lieutenant Barton, Roy Carter, for the unknown Captain Winthrop and all the unknowns, and for Henrietta Blanche Beasley.

When that was done, he prayed for his Anne and his son, whom they had named Will, who had not lived long enough to know his own name.

Last of all he prayed for himself … even though he did not believe.

Flags and bunting filled the streets to celebrate the end of war. Brass bands played; there were feasts in village halls, songs of praise. All the time he moved about as though in a dream.

Not long after, he received a letter from Roy Carter: "Dear Jim. It has taken me a long time to track you down."

∽ As much as he liked it, as much as he liked the garden that he and Anne had cultivated, it became impossible to stay in the cottage belonging to Lord Denman without Anne and Will. Every time he opened the door on coming home from work, he expected them to be there. The loneliness crept into his soul. One evening, as he walked the dog over the fields, he determined to look for a new job, perhaps with Lord Calborne near Fernden, a place that he liked. It would mean leaving Anne and Will in the churchyard, untended, but he would come frequently with the flowers he had promised, would plant spring bulbs there. His mother would go there; he knew that.

Yes, he would take the dog and the cat, his few pieces of furniture and his personal belongings and move into another tied cottage where he would begin anew to make a garden his own.

❧ Chapter 20

Fate or God — should there be a God — had given Jim a talent and a skill for sensing the needs of living things. As time went by he honed those skills until he knew and understood every flower, tree, shrub, and all things edible that grew in his part of his native land; he knew many more as well that came in from hotter and exotic places, and other plants that would survive only in greenhouses.

He learned about propagation, about diseases and cures.

Sometimes as he walked among his charges, he felt a quiet joy.

During those days he drew strength from knowing Frank Boakes, Roy Carter, and Jack Dawson. Roy had come home at last, with the exalted rank of Warrant Officer, about as far as a working man could go who had found himself still alive when his superiors were dead and had had to take command. They had given him medals for extraordinary bravery, those in the army who had done their best to ensure his death.

When Jim saw him again for the first time, he could see at a glance that Roy was old and mature far beyond his years, that in many ways he had been destroyed, and that only strength of character held him together. They drank beer in each other's company in pubs, while they told stories of their lives, their speech halted by silences when the telling was not easy. There was something about Roy that invited confidence in spite of his hardness, and he had a rare quality of listening. And Roy seemed to find the same in him, Jim felt.

Roy did not have a girl, he told Jim, but hoped to marry one day if luck was with him. "If any woman will have me," he said, fixing Jim with a glance from his tired eyes. "I have bad dreams, nightmares. I wouldn't be easy to live with. I've forgotten what it's like to be in civvy street."

"Frank has a sister by the name of Emily," Jim said. "A very sensible young woman. I reckon she could take you on."

Roy smiled. "Well, you can introduce me, make it look like an accident."

"I'll see what I can do."

"The army wants to keep me on for a while," Roy said, "and for want of something else to do just now, I've accepted. There's talk about making me an instructor. I reckon I'm one of the few people they've got left who have had the experience that I've had."

∽ For much of that long period of time Jim had been working for Lord Calborne, on the Calborne estate, Sussex, where the palatial gardens offered enough scope for any man who longed to grow things in abundance, to lose himself in his creations.

∽ It proved surprisingly easy for Jim to introduce Roy to Frank's sister, because it happened when he had not intended it. Frank had invited him and Roy to tea with himself and Grace at their home near the village of Waters Green on a Sunday, and Emily happened to come by.

He had taken the train a few stops to the nearest station to where Frank lived, still leaving a fair walk that took him along footpaths and lanes, over meadows and through beech woods that he knew well, where massed bluebells bloomed in late spring, as well as primroses along the sides of the paths. Roy, coming from the barracks at Maidstone, had arranged to meet him at Frank's cottage. It was a pleasant day in mid summer.

"How did you get here?" He greeted Roy as they shook hands in Frank's back garden.

"I got a train from Maidstone, changed at Tunbridge Wells, got the Fernden train, then walked the rest of the way." Roy offered Jim a cigarette and struck a match.

"That Fernden station must be a good two miles from the village of Fernden," Jim remarked, "and about the same this way." He considered that Frank's cottage was about that distance in the other direction, near a hamlet called Beech Wood Down.

"Yes, about that. I was looking out for snipers all the way, Jim." Smoke wreathed around them. "Once I jumped down into a ditch because I heard a noise."

"What was it?"

"A pheasant, I expect. It didn't sound again. It comes to something if I can't identify a pheasant."

"I know what you mean," Jim said, recalling how he moved his head from side to side when he walked through fields and woods, scanning the area.

"We'll never get over it, Jim."

"I don't suppose we will. Is your father still a gamekeeper?"

"Yes. I won't be going out with him any more. I hope never to shoot anything again — bird, animal, or man. To kill for sport, to take a life, that sickens me. It's different if you're starving. But how many of those bloody nobs on shoots are starving, or wanting for anything under the sun."

"It makes your blood boil," Jim said. "And they seldom want to pay a man a living wage for dawn to dusk labour."

Roy took a long pull on his cigarette, held the smoke in for a few seconds, then blew it out. "I could tell you a lot about the buggers who were giving us orders over there, pointless, stupid, calculated to kill men in the thousands and achieve nothing."

Roy's right hand shook as he held the fag up to his lips, Jim noted. "I've always reckoned that too much education knocks the common sense out of you," he said.

"A lot of them never had any to begin with."

I could weep now, Jim thought. I could bawl like a baby. Unexpectedly an apparition of great beauty appeared in the doorway from the kitchen to the garden, so that Jim became aware that his mouth was hanging open in surprise. That vision was Emily, in a floral dress that just skimmed her ankles, and a straw hat that was perched on her piled hair.

"Why, Emily," he said, aware then of a certain social inadequacy because his mind had been on very different things. "It's very nice to see you. This is Roy ... Roy Carter. And Roy, this is Emily, Frank's sister."

With more aplomb than he had himself, Jim noted, Roy transferred the fag he was holding from his right hand to his left, in anticipation that Emily would offer him her hand, too much of a gentleman to make the first move. She offered her hand.

"Well," she said, very calm and collected, seeming very mature, as she shook hands with Roy, "Frank and Jim have told me so much about you that I have been thinking you were too good to be true." She turned to Jim. "So lovely to see you, Jim."

"Oh, it's all true," Roy said, giving her one of his rare smiles when she fixed him with her assessing glance. "I wouldn't claim to be good, though. Now, Frank hasn't told me anything about you. I wonder why. I expect he's trying to protect you."

Emily was beautiful, Jim considered again, with blue eyes and dark hair like Frank, but taller, statuesque, with a maturity and self-possession beyond her years. "I can protect myself," she said. "And what are you going to do now that the war's over? Come into Frank's garden and tell me."

"She's a one, isn't she!" Frank said, smiling as he came out to stand beside Jim, raising his eyebrows as his sister took Roy into the depths of the garden.

"Come and see the radishes," they heard her saying.

"She can hold her own with anyone," Grace said, as she joined them. "That's what comes from working in a munitions factory. I don't think we have any radishes."

Later, Jim found Emily alone in the kitchen, while Roy was in the sitting room with Frank and Grace. "What do you think of Roy?" he asked, deciding to take the bull by the horns.

"He's an amazing person," she said. "Still waters run deep."

"He's a good bloke," Jim said, "who's had a terrible life over the last four and a half years, or so."

"I can see that, Jim. It breaks my heart to witness that. Frank told me you're with Lord Calborne now, over Frant way?"

"Yes, not far from Fernden. I didn't know you were in a munitions factory, Emily."

"I keep it quiet, unless someone asks. Some other women seem to be affronted by it, as though I am deliberately making them feel guilty for not doing the same, especially those who used to go around in the towns giving out white feathers to young men not in uniform. Of course, I sometimes let it drop when I think I need to, just to give them their come-uppance."

"Good," Jim said. "I heartily approve."

"Come out to the garden, I want to ask you something." Emily walked down towards the bottom of the deep garden, with Jim following. "Roy asked me to walk out with him. Should I?" She turned to face him. "I value your judgement. Not that I can't make up my own mind, and I know he's your friend."

Carefully Jim considered his reply. "I wouldn't say no," he said. "He'll need time to get over what has happened to him, if he ever will. You know that, I'm sure. He's the sort of person who would never let you down, wouldn't do anything shabby or underhand. At the same time, he's no angel, he would be the first to admit that, I reckon. I expect he's killed his fair share of the enemy. Perhaps that's why he survived, though I don't think so ... it's a sort of luck."

"I sensed all that in him," she said.

They sauntered back to the house. "What will you say to him?" Jim asked, trying to sound casual, knowing that the happiness he felt on Roy's behalf was a little premature.

"I think I will tell him yes, but to bear in mind that it's a woman's privilege to change her mind."

"There, you've covered yourself," he said, "in one sentence. I don't think you'll regret it."

Over the next fourteen years Jim moved about in sunshine and rain, snow, hail and sleet, in summer mists and in winter fog, mourning and remembering as he grubbed in the soil, planting, nurturing and harvesting for Lord Calborne, as well as for himself in his own garden.

He shared something vicariously of the happiness between Roy and Emily, who did indeed marry after a decent but not too long an interval from the time of their meeting. They decided to grasp that chance at happiness, as war had taught them that life could be unpredictably fragile and, like love, was something not to be taken for granted. Emily gave birth to two babies, born one year after the other, first a girl and then a boy.

It was as though she feared that the ability to bring forth life would be taken away from her if she did not hurry. As so much else had been taken away, Jim thought when he visited them at their home, witnessing the quiet pride in Roy's eyes when he looked at his wife and children. They named the girl Anne and the boy Jim.

As for himself, the future was unknown. Everything he planted grew and thrived as though, he fancied, it needed just the touch of his hand as well as the sun and the rain. Only then did he feel fully alive.

⚘ Chapter 21

May's Story, 1932

May was at home again with her parents in 1932, another employment position of nanny having come to an end when the child for whom she was responsible had reached the age of going to boarding school, when there had been tears all round and goodbyes. There was always a mutual love between her and the children, difficult to reconcile with the reality that they would most likely never meet again after her own departure from their home.

She had been back home for several weeks, with no new position in the offing because she had not applied for new employment, needing a rest. Besides, her parents were both sixty-four now; she could be of help to them, although her father still worked for Lord Calborne and remained spry and healthy. Her mother, weary from rearing her six children, seemed frail now, even though the youngest child had departed seven years before from the home to take up an apprenticeship. As much as she could, she relieved her mother's domestic burdens.

"May," her father said to her one summer day, "Bill Green has promised me some celery from the Calborne gardens, if I can go and get it. He's the Head Gardener. Well, I haven't got time. Would you take a walk up there, May?"

"Yes, all right," she said, feeling restless at the unaccustomed inactivity, having already finished work in the house. In her bedroom she changed into a summer dress, for it was uncommonly hot, and took a straw hat from her wardrobe, one with a wide brim and a pink ribbon tied round the crown.

Taking a basket, she let herself out of the house into the bright sunshine, where life seemed slow-moving and drowsy, the air busy with the sound of bees and with floating seeds of dandelions and thistles, and resplendent with the scents of flowers. The quality of light made the colours of nature brilliant. She walked slowly, through short cuts and lanes, to the gardens. The gardens were impressive, with tall, large green-houses, and cinder paths dividing the sections of land where different things grew. There was at least one spinney and what was called a pleas-ure garden, so her Dad had said. May wandered there, enchanted, daz-zled by the colours, the flitting butterflies. Scents of flowers engulfed her, the scent of Sweet William vying with the scent of roses.

When she remembered that she was there to get celery, she walked over to the vegetable gardens where she saw a man watering with a hose and, as she walked slowly along the cinder path towards him, she had time to look at him before he noticed her.

He was a slim man, muscular, and simply dressed in dark work trou-sers and a plain shirt that was open at the neck, with the sleeves rolled up. Curious to know who he was, she tried to rehearse mentally what she might say to him, other than: "I want some celery, please."

Nothing much came to mind, other than the mundane, although there was an odd presentiment that what she said to him was important, that her meeting with him was to mean something.

Since Frederick Decker, she had not automatically known what to say to men, had not always been at ease with them, because that first confidence of youth had gone from her, and she had felt dead to the stares of men, as though she were herself invisible.

When he saw her coming, the man turned off the tap to the hose and pushed back the straw hat he had on his head against the strong sun. Not tall, about five feet, six inches, he was what you could call aver-age in that regard, May noticed, surprised at herself.

"You must be May Wigley," he said, when she was near him, reliev-ing her of the necessity to speak first, "come to get the celery. Bill said you would be coming." He held out a hand to her, after he had wiped it clean on his trousers.

"Yes," May said, as she he took the hand. He had a clean-shaven, open face, with a high forehead and square jaw, one of those faces in which there was no subterfuge. He must be in his mid-forties, she thought. When he looked at her, full in the face, she noted that his eyes were very blue.

"Come over to the greenhouse and the shed," he said, jerking his head towards the nearest greenhouse that had a high, domed roof like a Gothic cathedral. "I've already cut the celery for you."

As he passed her to walk ahead, he gave off a scent of onions, celery, summer soil, and good, clean sweat. He walked, she thought, like a soldier.

In the large, cool potting shed he offered her a glass of lemonade from a generous glass jug in which pieces of sliced lemon floated. The jug had a muslin cloth over it, to prevent wasps from getting into it. "This is from the big house," he said. "Home made."

"Thank you."

"Lemons are scarce," he said. "But if you have the money, and know where to look, I suppose you can get more or less anything."

"Yes, I suppose so."

"Sit down, while I pack up the celery for you."

She sat on an old wooden chair, on which there was a flattened cushion, to sip the lemonade. "This is very refreshing," she said.

On a work bench, three large bunches of celery sat on some newspapers. "I don't think I told you my name," the man said, taking off his straw hat to reveal dark brown hair, slightly grey at the temples. It was fine hair, thinning a little on the crown of his head. "I'm Jim Langridge."

"It's nice to meet you," she said, wondering why she had not heard of him before. "I like to come to the gardens. I don't often get a chance though."

"Well, you can visit any time. No one will trouble you, and you don't need to have a reason."

"Thank you."

Sitting there, she watched him as he wrapped the celery carefully in the newspaper and tied each bunch up with string. "That should prevent it from wilting," he said. "Give me your basket."

Carefully, he packed the celery in the basket. His left wrist and lower arm, she noted, were damaged, the area livid with dark pink scars, the hand bend forward towards the arm and fixed in one position. That must be a handicap, she thought, for any man.

"Were you in the war?" she asked, unable to stop herself, even though her parents had taught her not to make personal remarks, because it was ill-mannered, and not to ask very personal questions until you knew a person well.

"Yes," he said mildly, not seeming to mind. "I went to France, in 1915. Shrapnel wound." He held up the arm for a moment.

May nodded. "Did it save your life?"

"I expect it did. What was left of my battalion — and there weren't many of them — went on to the Somme in the summer of 1916."

"What regiment were you in?"

"The Royal West Kents."

May nodded again. "Does it trouble you much, the hand?" she asked.

"It did at one time. Then I accidentally cut some of the tendons underneath with a sharp gardening knife, which served to release them a bit and give me more leeway. At the time I got the wound, they did the best they could, the MOs, but there wasn't much they could do, other than get out the shrapnel and patch me up. Some of those men were not trained as surgeons."

May could tell that he was not used to talking of these things. "I was in the Royal Flying Corps myself," she said, "from May 1917, which was when I joined up."

He looked at her with interest, as he poured himself some lemonade. "Were you! Where did they send you?"

"To Yorkshire, a place called Bramham Moor where there was an aerodrome, near Tadcaster."

"That was a long way from home," he said. What he meant, she knew, was that it was a long way from home for a young girl who had not seen much of life.

"France was a long way for you," she said, to which he smiled.

"You could say that. I was twenty-nine at the time."

"Well," she said, "at least I could get on a train and come home when I had leave, and I was not under fire. Not like you."

"There is that."

"There were a lot of Americans there, at the aerodrome," she said, not knowing why she came out with that. "There to train, before they went over to France."

He nodded, as though he knew all about it. "It took them long enough to come into the war," he said.

"Not many came back," she said, "when it was time for them to come on leave."

"You could say the same about the army," he said. "A terrible time. It's never out of my mind ... not really." He downed the lemonade in a few gulps. "Look, you stay sitting there and I'll cut you a bunch of flowers. Just for you, mind." There was something sweet and genuine about the smile that he gave her. "If you want more lemonade, you just help yourself."

"Thank you."

With pruning shears in hand, he went out.

May drank the remainder of the lemonade and poured herself another glass. It was delicious and she was so thirsty. When he came back, bearing a very large bunch of the most beautiful assortment of flowers and greenery, she said: "Oh!"

Standing, she watched him tie the stalks up with string, then put them in newspaper and tie the stalks again, then fit the bouquet into her basket. "Hope that isn't too heavy for you," he said.

"No, it won't be. Thank you so much."

"Wait a minute," he said, when it was time for her to go. Disappearing for a few minutes, he came back with something wrapped in white tissue paper. "That's for you. So don't think of giving it to anybody else."

Opening the paper, she saw that it was a peach, the largest and most perfect she had ever seen, a pale yellow with a blush of pink here and there.

He escorted her to the iron gate that let onto the path that she would take to walk home. "Don't forget," he said, "you can come here any time."

"Thank you again."

When she looked back, he was standing by the gate watching her, and he waved. Awkwardly, with the basket in one hand and the peach in the other, she waved back. Emotion welled up in her and she knew she was going to cry. Bowing her head, not looking back again, she realized that for the first time since Frederick Decker, she had lost herself for a short while in the presence of a man, that his sweet, unaffected kindness had brought her to tears.

In a wooded area she put down the basket, unwrapped the peach and bit into it, bending forward so that the juice could drip down onto the ground. It was the best peach she had ever had, warm from the sun, sweet, fresh and perfect.

When she came through the wood, into an open area of sunlight, she dug a shallow hole in the soil with the heel of her shoe, put the peach stone in there and covered it up. It was possible that it would grow into a tree, even though she knew that the summers were not usually hot enough to ripen peaches outside of a greenhouse.

Not wanting to go home yet, she sat on a convenient tree stump on the edge of a meadow. The tree had very recently been cut down, the wood still fresh, giving off a scent. The unexpected agreeable nature of her encounter with Jim Langridge had taken her unawares, so that she wanted to think about it before she went home to be engaged with the task of helping her mother prepare a late afternoon tea. The impact that he had had on her was surprising, so that now she did not know what to think of it. Almost always there was an ache in her heart for Frederick Decker, even after all this time. As she sat there, it was an extraordinary thing that she had an ache in her heart for what Jim Langridge had suffered, and an admiration for how he had compensated for his disability, how he had deftly tied the string after he had wrapped the celery and the flowers. A sadness had taken hold of her when she had looked at the crisscross of scars on his arm, his deformity.

A tortoiseshell butterfly landed on a flower near her, then a cabbage white, then a tiny blue butterfly whose name she did not know. There were buttercups, Queen Anne's lace, white daisies, cornflowers and rosebay willow herb growing near her, where little honey bees hovered.

She wondered if Jim Langridge knew anything about her, had heard any gossip about her, if indeed there was any, or if he would take any notice if there were. It had come as a surprise to her in her maturity to discover that one was very often under observation by others, one's doings taken note of, in a way that was not always benign in intent. Not a gossip herself, she usually found such interest incomprehensible. As she stared out over the meadow she wondered if he had heard anything about how she had been taken away. It was over ten years ago now.

Alone in the quiet meadow she allowed herself to think about it. Most of the time she tried to keep the memories away, as there was a certain shame in them, yet one cannot pretend for long that real things did not happen.

First of all, she had been de-mobbed, as they had called it then, in 1919, along with thousands of others. Their lives had changed within a few days, as the ones on the home front were released from duty to make their own way home, going on crowded, chaotic trains, through equally chaotic stations, lugging bags that became heavier by the minute. As she had made her way among them she had been very aware that this was the last time she had to wear her uniform, that at some point soon she would have to give it up. She particularly liked her cap with its badge of a crown above an eagle with its wings spread.

Some of those who lived in the country were lucky enough to get an army lorry to take them the last few miles to their homes, reporting first to what had been the army recruiting office in the nearest town where the train came in. She had been one of those lucky ones, dropped out in the lane in front of her home, where she had last visited with Frederick Decker, when she had been innocent and full of hope.

Her parents and family had welcomed her back into that quiet life that was the antithesis of the life at the airfield that she had become used to. The silence, welcome at first, began to weigh on her, to allow her overburdened thoughts to come to the fore.

May let herself remember how they had come to take her away, all those years ago. First, the doctor had come up the lane to her parents' house in his pony and trap, followed by the vicar.

"What is the matter, May? What is the matter, dear? Can't you tell us?"

No, she could not have said why she had started to cry and could not stop. It was early summer then, June, such a beautiful summer. Perhaps it was the way the yellow beams of the gentle summer sun had slanted through the tall oaks that lined the lane near the house, where they made shifting patterns in the yellow clay dust. That sunlight signified a promise of the fruitful season to come, of love, youth, passion, hope and the resurgence of life. It should have been her time, because she was young. Instead, there was an emptiness; all that was left was dross.

In the places where she had walked with Frederick hand in hand along the lanes, she seemed to see him there in the shadows, walking ahead, just out of reach. Perhaps it was partly the scent of bracken beneath the oaks that moved her so, with the smell of moist earth that promised life, and the barely perceptible buzz of insects.

They were mystified and frightened by her, her parents and the official delegation from the village, as she had wept and keened, rocked back and forth in her chair, not to be consoled. The fear was in their eyes as they peered at her, yet she could not help them. The grief, battened down, had come up. It was 1919.

"Can't you tell us, May?" They looked into her face, held her hands that were agitated like restless birds. "Do say something, dear."

Of course her parents had not wanted her to join the Royal Flying Corps, even though they had let her have her way. No good would come of it, they must have thought then. She was such a young girl, a country girl, like a wild fawn, used to quiet, shady places, sent far away from home to an alien life. She could see those messages in their faces. For her part, it had been a revelation to her that she could help in some way; she had wanted to get out of that stultifying life, the predictability of it, as much as she loved the country.

So her reserve had broken and she had keened for him, Frederick George Decker of New Jersey, who had flown to France and not come back. "Goodbye, May. See you soon," he had said, as though he really would see her.

See you soon, see you soon, see you soon. The words mocked her in the songs of birds, in the empty promise of the summer sun of June 1919, back home in her quiet life.

And so she had wept, on and on. Someone had come to get her and taken her away in a big black car, like a hearse, to the county asylum in the countryside where the gardens were beautiful and mocked her afresh. "Be a good girl," a nurse said to her there, "and we'll give you a sweetie."

No point in trying to tell them that she was not a child; she was a woman. No words would come.

"Tell me, my dear," one of the doctors said to her. "Tell me all about it." He had been a medical officer in the war that had just ended, so he had told her by way of a preamble.

Because he had an air of easy authority and a kindly concentration just for her, she uttered the words: "All those lovely boys."

"Ah," he said.

Eventually she had stopped crying, was left with a silent welling up of tears now and again. They did not allow her any knives or forks, only a spoon.

"Where did they send you?" the former MO asked kindly.

When she told him, he made a clicking noise with his tongue, signifying disapproval. "A long way from home," he said. "How old were you?"

"I was eighteen in May, 1916. I joined up about a year later, when the WAAC started."

"That's why your parents called you May," he said, smiling.

"Yes."

"I was in Belgium and France, you know," he said. "In the Ypres area, mainly. Bloody awful place ... a cemetery with mud. The Germans never broke through there. Somehow we managed to keep them back. At what cost, though ... at what cost." He became silent then for long moments, looking back.

She nodded, knowing something about Ypres. Now, she felt, they were friends. Very carefully she began to trust him.

When he questioned her, she talked, about how she could never get Frederick out of her mind, how she had seen him go away, up into the sky. There was a sense in her of waiting, always waiting, of holding herself in readiness for something that was never going to happen. Grief and loss had not diminished with time; they had grown like monsters that were with her day and night. And now everyone who was close to her thought she was mad.

Every day she talked to the former MO, who was in early middle-age, prematurely grey haired and exhausted. She liked to think of him as the MO, because that designation was a further link to a recent past that he did not think had gone away any more than she did. He did not think that what she said was silly. Not like her mother, whose favourite expression in the face of inexplicable behaviour was "Don't be silly!" It was a relief to be with him, not to have to wade through a fog of incomprehension.

"You poor, dear girl," he said often. Sometimes they walked out in the grounds of the hospital when the weather was good, where his gentle questioning seemed more like a conversation.

"Is it possible that your young man was married?" he asked on one such walk. "I am sorry to have to ask that, but I must. A young man from overseas ... you understand? And you've never had a word from him."

"I did think of that afterwards,'" she answered, "especially as my brother, Will, asked me the same question. But never at the time ... never. He was so young, you see."

"Nevertheless, some would have married before going overseas, a sort of hedge against not coming back, a move to permanence, you might say."

"He came home to meet my family," she said. "He said he loved me." It was difficult for her to say that, to reveal her innermost thoughts that sounded naive when she voiced them.

"I expect he did love you," the MO said. "He was leading two lives, with the second one most likely to be his last. He was not going to deny the good parts of that life. And now, we know nothing about his injuries. He could be incapable of writing a letter."

"Yes. It's not knowing ..." she said.

"Of course. I understand."

Weeks went by; she talked until there was nothing left to say.

"You can come back to see me any time," he said, when it was deemed all right for her to go home, uncured but relatively silent and tearless. "Otherwise, I want to see you in two months' time."

Privately, when the stolid nurse had not been present, he had said to her: "One day you will find someone else. You will marry and have children. It isn't that you will forget your young man; it is more that you will decide to go forward, to embrace life, because it is your duty and in your nature, and because you are young." He had not added that she would marry because she was beautiful, but she could see in his face that he thought her so.

No reply was possible to what he had said, so she had given none. Such an eventuality was incomprehensible, so she had thanked him politely on parting, as she had been taught to do from an early age.

"My advice," he said, "is that you should get a job, if you can, instead of just living at home with your parents. It will take you out of yourself, which is what you need."

Young ladies — and she was on the cusp of being "a lady," he must have thought then — did not in the normal course of things get jobs. The war had been an exception, had shown them what they were capable of, then had taken that opportunity away again. Not that it had done her much good, but you never knew; perhaps that was preferable to a stultifying narrowness. Those thoughts passed through her mind when they shook hands to say goodbye.

Although he had most likely deplored the social caste system that he would have been especially aware of in the Army, she had thought then intuitively, he had to accept for now that they were both very much a part of it simply by having been born in Britain. During some of their walks in the hospital grounds, he had expressed an opinion that it was the sergeants, the NCOs, with their bravery, maturity, and common sense, who had conducted the war in its everyday chaos. Yet in the official histories of regiments, histories of wars, these men were not mentioned by name, unless they had died, in which case they would be on a "roll of honour." Alive, maimed, driven mad, they were not mentioned by name; it was as though they had never existed. They were rendered invisible, like the ordinary soldier. These were all things they shared during their talks.

"Goodbye," he said. "I will see you in two month's time. If you feel the need, you can come to see me any time."

"Thank you." As he walked away from her, she realized that she would miss his own stories of the war, that it was those stories and insights, as much as her own stilted speech, that had helped to take her out of herself, to shift her thoughts away from herself. Indeed, he had been wise in that.

The same black car took her home, back to her parents' thatched house on the edge of the forest, along the dusty clay lane from the main road. Both the house and the forest belonged to Lord Calborne. The driver of the car was an elderly man, a volunteer, who spoke with a gentle, genteel accent of the upper classes. He was kind to her and bought her tea at a café on the way back. From time to time he pointed out beauty spots to her as they drove sedately through the charming Sussex countryside. Sometimes he would slow down to a walking pace so that he could point something out to her. "Ashdown Forest," he said once. "A beautiful place to walk in."

∽ May got up from the tree stump, lifted up the basket and began to walk back home slowly through the grass that had been mown, where new flowers were blooming close to the ground. She must get home now to place the flowers in water before they started to wilt. She would put them in a large vase to keep on her dressing table in her bedroom, where their scent would fill the room and she would see them last thing at night and first thing in the morning. They were for her personally, Jim Langridge had said. No doubt he had grown all of them himself. She would go to the gardens again soon, would wander there freely, where there were no high walls and no locks on the gates.

Chapter 22

Jim leaned on the garden gate until May had disappeared from view, she in her bright dress going in among the trees of the wood, from sunlight to shadow. From the droop of her bent head he had the sense that she was crying, and he had an urge to run after her. Most likely she needed privacy. Had his actions brought up some grief from the past? Chastened and amazed, he pondered on that.

When he could no longer see any sign of her, he had an odd sensation for a second or two that she had been a figment of his imagination, born out of his loneliness. The feeling disturbed him as he turned away to walk back along the path to the potting shed. In the coolness of the shed he saw the glass from which she had drunk the lemonade, together with his own, and the jug, almost empty, with its muslin cover.

Of course she had been real, he knew that. It was as though her presence lingered in the dim interior that held the familiar scents of onions, celery and flowers. There was the chair on which she had sat. He had sensed her suffering, had seen it in her downcast eyes and clasped hands, as he had felt moved to offer her flowers.

Once again, as it had done long ago, he felt his world shifting. He saw himself walking up the stairs of the cottage he had shared with Anne, after the telegraph boy had come, to find the newspaper that held the faded photograph of Henrietta Blanche Beasley, saw himself kneel on the floor in front of his chest of drawers to take the newspaper from the bottom drawer. He had been swept up by events far beyond his control at that time, into a vortex where he had struggled to find a footing.

Then in his mind he saw the image of Anne coming into the greenhouse where he had been working all those years ago, pushing the wicker pram that cradled the body of his dead son. He remembered how she had pushed it cumbrously through the door, an expression on her face that he had never seen before, that he knew to be dread.

Yes, in May Wigley he had sensed a grieving akin to his own, as they and myriads of others moved like spirits in a world that was both familiar and alien, not knowing quite where they belonged, as though real time for them had stood still at a very particular moment.

Tears came into his eyes. Since the war and the deaths of Will and Anne, he had never thought seriously of suicide, yet several times he had thought of death as a friend that he would not shy away from if he felt himself to be in its presence. Sometimes he doubted his sanity. Now he felt sombre and sane, as though he were coming back into the full responsibility of himself, as the present seemed to claim him.

Moving automatically, he placed the glasses into an enamel bowl that he would take up to the big house kitchens later on. He placed the jug with the lemonade on the brick floor beside the workbench where it would stay cool. He felt himself being moved forward by circumstance that he recognized more by intuition than by thought, into something more substantial. It seemed to him that he was shifting into an acute awareness that made him less a shadow that was moving wraith-like on the surface of the earth, more someone who must risk the claims and losses, the uncertainty, of everyday life.

Outside, the welcome summer sun touched his bare forearms and the skin of his chest where his shirt was open. He moved into it as in a warm sea. Such a beautiful summer, he thought, rare in its constancy. Birds twittered and called in the air that was hazy with heat and floating seeds. He would resume the tasks that had been interrupted by his encounter with May, tasks that would be distanced by her presence in his mind. From his pocket watch he could see that not much time had elapsed from the moment he had seen May walking towards him along the path, yet it felt like hours.

Once again he turned on the garden tap, directed the hose to where he wanted the flow of water. The thought came to him powerfully that he had been blessed with a renewed gift of life in 1915, that the circumstances of the 26th September had come together in such a way that he had been spared, while Harry Baker, Bert Tomsitt and the others whose exact fate he did not know had been taken. Whether his life had been spared by an impersonal fate or from a so-called gift of God, he would never be able to say. Convinced now that May Wigley had been in tears when she had left him, he again stood in wonder that he had affected her thus, that she had been vulnerable to his everyday, run-of-the-mill actions. Tears filled his own eyes as he sensed that such a lovely young woman — for she was still young — had felt so alone.

It was as though someone had tapped him on the shoulder and explained it all to him, that he was alive and that others suffered as he did, quietly in the secrets of their hearts. Of course he had known it; he had not felt it truly, as he felt it now. It was as though he had been walled off, in his own place. Now he felt ashamed standing there surrounded by beauty, while others who had no known resting places had been cut off in their sweet boyhood, fair of limb and full of youthful grace, only the best for war, as though old men had voraciously sucked the life out of them for their own sustenance. He wanted to kneel on the cinder path and ask forgiveness. Instead he moved forward with the hose, squinted up at the sun to gauge how far it was past its zenith, considering that it was not good to water plants in the full heat of the day when the sun would simply draw it up again. He could see the other gardeners in the near distance watering and hoeing, all together and each in his own world of creation at the same time. The sky was vivid, the green of the vegetables shimmered before his eyes.

When he was ready, he turned off the tap and coiled up the hose neatly. All was as it should be here, because he had made it so. He had not been able to remake himself in his entirety. As for what would come next, he must not get ahead of himself; he knew that. Time was running out for him, like the sand in an hour glass, not enough for the long courtship and waiting that he and Anne had endured, waiting for life in general to be better. Was there to be another courtship for him? He could woo May with flowers from his own garden, the chrysanthemums in autumn, the brilliant orange montbretia, roses and lavender in summer, the snowdrops and daffodils in spring, the Jerusalem cherries in pots from the greenhouse. They could talk about what had happened to them. To be presumptuous was the way of the fool, yet he knew without any doubt that he would see May Wigley again before very long.

∾ That evening, after his supper and after he had rolled himself a cigarette and sat outside in his back garden, he felt a renewed sense of inevitability about his encounter with May, as though he had been waiting for her. They were both damaged by war, he had sensed that in her, in her silences; it could bind them together if they chose to let it. Her beauty, her dark hair, her grey-green eyes and pale skin, had impressed itself on his mind, like a portrait once seen never forgotten. There had been no rings on her fingers.

Perhaps because she was different from Anne he allowed himself to dwell on her, to overcome his deep loyalty to Anne without letting go of it, which he would never do completely, he could see that now; she and the boy would forever be part of him. With her naturally wavy hair, May was more like Etta, whom Anne had known about and admired. Because of that, there had been something endearingly familiar about May, which he knew he must not take to mean that May had a character and personality like that of Etta. There would not be an instant understanding between himself and May just because she reminded him of Etta in some ways. So he cautioned himself as he ruminated.

This woman, daughter of a gamekeeper, was unknown to him. He knew her father nominally, a good, morally upright man who was also a lay preacher at the Wesleyan chapel in the village, whose words he himself had never heard. Like father, like daughter, perhaps.

In front of him, his own garden delighted him in its abundance, one part given over to vegetables — potatoes, runner-beans, broad beans, carrots, lettuces, marrows, cabbages and Brussels sprouts — and the other half to flowers, all that he had loved from the early childhood gardens that he had known, when they had drawn him in to their unconscious world of nature. He had intuitively known that he was a part of them.

Perhaps his son, Will, had he lived to be a lad of seventeen, would be in such a garden now. It was easy to picture him in the muted sunlight of a summer evening, bending, hoeing, harvesting, his skin touched by the sun, a shock of fairish hair falling over his forehead, his shirt sleeves rolled up. It was a white shirt, he imagined, the braces that held up his trousers criss-crossing the back of it, the trouser legs pulled up a little from his boots and tied with twine just below the knees, as was the country fashion, to keep the hems out of the soil.

He smiled at the image. It was good to sit there in peace, on an old chair low to the ground, a fag that he had rolled himself in his hands, to be able to afford the price of tobacco, to hear only the benign sounds of nature all around him and to watch the thrushes, blackbirds and cheeky little blue-tits that came to plunder the fruit trees. Sometimes he had a bonfire at the bottom of the garden, on which he would burn the dried brush from the shrubs he had pruned. He liked the scent of that smoke, so unlike other burning that he had known, just as he also liked the scent of a burning candle in a quiet room at night.

Beyond the garden fence was the green of fields, dotted here and there with cows and sheep, and the occasional horse. And there were trees, mostly oaks, spreading and powerful, benign and lovely, as far as the eye could see.

May Wigley would come here. She would walk with him along the narrow brick paths that he had built himself, in through the rock garden and by the tiny lily pond where he kept goldfish. She would walk under the wooden arbour that he had built for the white climbing roses, and pass by the fuchsia bushes near the back fence, and they would sit on the rustic bench that he had made from birch wood. They would drink lemonade. From there they could admire the trellises along the side fences where he had pear and apple trees espaliered over them, and the clump of pampas grass that grew near the back door, its white fronds waving in the breeze. Near the back fence the Victoria plum tree would drop its dark purple fruit at their feet. Honey-bees would buzz among the lavender as he cut her a bouquet. She would see honeysuckle, white and yellow daisies, poppies, hydrangea, black and red currants, gooseberries, and all those small flowers that grew close to the earth, that one had to kneel down to see and touch, the scented violets that he loved, and the tiny blue forget-me-nots.

"What would you like to take home?" he would say to her. "Anything you want."

And she would clasp her hands and say: "Oh! How can I possibly choose! I want it all."

❧

He and May were married at a country registry office in Ticehurst, Sussex, on the 10th of March, 1934, he being forty-eight years old and she thirty-six. They walked in his garden every day. It fed, nurtured and delighted them.

May sat often on the rustic bench when she was heavily pregnant with her first child. From there she could gaze over the exuberant sea of colour, as the present drew her in. "It is not that you will forget your young man," the hospital MO had said to her in her youth. "It is more that you will decide to go forward." The exact words were lost to her, but now she was grateful to him for his wisdom. At the time she had thought he was being coercive, had fought against it, so had said nothing to him. One could not will forgetfulness, nor forgiveness; they were not under conscious control. She would not forget. It was not just her young man, she knew that now more than ever ... it was all the others too. Yes, it was all the others.

Although she was nearing the end of her child-bearing years, she had found, with both gratitude and a measure of fear, that she was not too old to conceive and carry a child. Now she could feel that child moving within her as she sat in the garden, to be their first-born, in October, when the bronze-coloured chrysanthemums would be in bloom. They would call a girl Joanne; a boy would be James Henry. It was 1936.

❧

Lizzie was born in October, 1938, the second girl to be born to May and Jim. By that time, Joanne had already become the diminutive 'Jo'. He had never thought that he would have another child, let alone two, and he loved them with all the thwarted love that had lain dormant from the time of his son.

This tiny second girl wandered with him along the paths of his garden, when she could toddle, and in the fields, taking it all in quietly, as though she knew that she was part of nature, that she had a right to be there and to be with him. When he carried her high in his arms during her first and second summers, she could see shimmering silver birch trees in the distance, where the leaves danced in the wind. And then she felt herself to be as ancient as the earth around them, even though she could not have put it into words then ...

Unknown to her, the clouds of war were forming and darkening over the idyll of her fledgling childhood. She had been born on the cusp. Meanwhile, her father carried her over the fields of peace.

Talking came early to her, although generally only her mother and father could fully understand what she said.

One day she asked: "Can Lizzie have a garden, Dad?"

"I don't see why not," he said. "We could start with a few flowers."

∞ The bond between them grew strong as she ran to meet him, day in and day out, as soon as she could run, when he walked home from work, as she reached up to take his hand.

∞ It took her seventy-four years to tell their story.

❧ Chapter 23

Nothing in human affairs ever ends; a thing that happens reverberates and reverberates down the generations. So Lizzie thought as she stood at her hotel window in Verdun, looking down at the street. It was a thought from early years that had come to her again soon after she had come to Ypres in Belgium. It stayed with her as she had gone on to Loos in France during the previous week. It had been with her as they had moved south along the old Western frontline, through Arras and Reims, the battlefields of the Somme, and all the other places. The knowledge was strong here in Verdun also, coming back gradually like an ancient wisdom uncovered. This was the end of the line for them. They would never forget.

There had been a sense of urgency in Ypres; no time to waste, so much to cover. It was there that the Germans had tried to break through into France from early in the war. All those on the tour had felt that urgency, as though their own intensity could bring back the dead, if not in their physicality, at least in memory. Ypres had been razed, then rebuilt from its own rubble.

In all, there were only nine of them on the tour, seven from the United States, including the two tour guides, and she and James from Canada. The driver, a man from Antwerp, made the party up to ten people. Because they were few, they rode in a van rather than a bus.

They shook hands with each other when they met in Paris, individuals from vastly different backgrounds, united in a purpose of exploration within and without. Disorientated and tired, they anticipated the journey ahead, in the spirit of remembrance, trying to prepare themselves for the poignancy that their discoveries would bring. At least, that was what Lizzie had supposed, because that was what she felt herself as they had started off in the van. Some had been there before, a few many times, she discovered as they exchanged brief life stories. All had connections with this land, in some way, through war.

How different their journey was, driving comfortably east along good roads out of Paris, from that of the men of the Royal West Kents and all the others who had gone forward in cattle cars and then on foot in the long days and nights of marching up to the Front, holding themselves in readiness for their first hearing of the guns. She and James sat side by side as they moved through the suburbs, then the countryside. They looked at maps; old soldiers from other wars among them exchanged stories. No one else had had a father in the Great War, yet all were fascinated by it.

Verdun, the last base on their journey, had much in common with Ypres. Fierce and desperate fighting had held the line against the enemy, even when few remained. *They shall not pass!*

As they had approached Ypres, Lizzie fancied that she felt something of the apprehension, the anticipation that the unknown brings, the fear of death, in common with those of ninety years before. Safe in the grip of peace, it could be no more than an inkling.

They had gone to the Menin Gate Memorial to the Missing of the Ypres Salient, where they found a dominating monument spanning a road, where buglers from the fire brigade play the *Last Post* every evening at eight o'clock. Lizzie saw that many people gathered silently there, perhaps to conjure up something in themselves, she speculated, of what they did not know personally of that Great War; from grief, for respect, for gratitude. The war was there all around them; those ninety years of the interim caught in a moment as though they had not intervened.

As the bugles sounded, as the well-known poem was read, Lizzie forgot herself, forgot that she had cancer and that the numbers of her days could be few. Thousands of names carved in stone impinged upon her, of young men, boys, too young to have sired children, to have found mature love. They had loved their mothers, their fathers, brothers and sisters, and were for the most part, she hoped, loved in return.

There, at that place, she went away from herself, withdrew from too much consciousness of self, came instead into their loss, a generation gone. A man recited:

They shall not grow old,
As we who are left grow old;
Time shall not weary them,
Nor the years condemn;
At the going down of the sun,
And in the morning,
We will remember them.

She knew that neither poetry nor the clear lament of bugles would erase the crime of their murder, all those whose names were carved there in stone, the names of those whose bodies had never been found, or on the graves of those in the vast Tyne Cot cemetery nearby, a city of the dead, where they, the pilgrims, were to go the next day.

She walked around that huge domed memorial at the Menin Gate to find the men of the Royal West Kents and the Royal Sussex who were there in name. Just as they were suspended in time, cut off in the flesh, she knew herself to be cut off there also. For her it was a blessed relief that the mind was stilled, that it entered into a world that the soldiers had known all too briefly.

Words became meaningless here, in front of the etched names. Poetry, from the soul, simple, unadorned, came the closest to the enormity of loss. No exaggerated poignant word could summon up the reality of emotion, or anything else; each word that was conjured up in the confused brain became obscene in the face of a greater obscenity. That must be why old soldiers became silent when asked about war.

∾ Now in her hotel room in Verdun, looking back over the past few days, she knew that the sense of going out of her consciousness of self was complete. Moved to write her own poetry of loss, she wrote sentences in her diary as they came to her: "Give me the gift of words, O Lord/ That I may speak for the dead/ Give voice to the voiceless/ Say the unspeakable/ Not in the arrogance of the living/ Purporting to know the dead/ But in humility and compassion/ And in the infinite sadness of mourning/ Make my words mighty/ That the sword be sheathed/ And that our sons may rest in peace in life/And not in death untimely."

She wrote of how they had gone to Arras after Ypres and Loos, had visited Vimy Ridge and Beaumont Hamel. Then they went on to the Somme, where another memorial to the missing at Thiepval stood in the green and peaceful countryside. There in a quiet wood were mouldering trenches that she felt were haunted. Corn grew around a small walled cemetery in a large meadow, beyond the edge of the wood. At the towering memorial, of necessity vast to accommodate the names, Lizzie found an H. Langridge. Not a common name, an old Sussex name; she assumed he was one of hers.

There was a peacefulness about Verdun, as though the guns had only just fallen silent and the thankfulness of peace was still rushing in to fill the void. Yet there seemed to be an echo of their chattering, just beyond the reach of human senses, and phantoms inhabiting the streets between the living. She had bought postcards to send from there. What can one really say from an old battle-front to those who have not been there, from a place where guns have gone silent but the reverberations remain in the atmosphere and are reborn in the mind of the observer? One cannot stand aside. Especially, how can one say it on a piece of card that measures three by four inches. Pax, written twenty times? They would think she has finally gone mad, that Lizzie whose home was bombed when she was two years old.

Each human soul must meet its own Verdun, an American poet and journalist, Berton Braley, had written.

Yes, this is a place, she considered, where one's thoughts gyrate, never resting or resolving. As she and James had walked over cobblestone streets beside quiet canals, she saw something of what was, what is, and how one is forced to accept the fact of it. But not the raison d'être of war; never that.

So hard to write; easier to look out the window at inanimate objects that in other forms have witnessed much, raised up from rubble of former lives. You inherit your parents' lives, she thought, like something new coming out of rubble, yet it is the same. From childhood she had felt burdened by that, by the clamour of wars and the destruction of youthful sweetness that had spilled out into her own life. It is only when you are old yourself, have acquired the ability of retrospection, that you can claim your own life. What a little time of one's allotted span is left for the self.

Unsought for, the revelation comes like a flash of lightning during a night storm where the watcher from the window sees for a few seconds the brilliantly illuminated sky and landscape in all its detailed sharpness, before the dark plunges down. In that moment one gains the self.

There is a craving for a state of being, to find oneself in that state of having arrived at something, instead of living always in a condition of becoming, of striving. Mating and marrying helped, the love for one's children. Perhaps only in death is one in a state of pure being, a state of final unconscious acceptance that one could not find in life, the mind stilled, even as the body disintegrates. One hoped for an eternity of the mind, in a state of peace.

There is no line between self and them, those antecedents; it is all one, to which I add my small piece, she thought. What will my children see in me, she wondered; and how will they be burdened by incompleteness. We want to put the past right, to give back that which was taken, as though we could be outside time. Only God, someone said, is outside time and space, while we are trapped within. What we can do is offer a speck of light to the future. It may be ignored.

There would have been refugees here, she suddenly thought, coming in and going out, and all the way along the front line. "Displaced persons," DPs, they had been called. She thought about them as she looked out from her window in France. The very term was an obscenity, conjuring scenes of tramping, bleeding feet, always moving away from gardens, apple trees, roses, lavender, warm hearths, wine with dinner; carts piled with bedding when there is no place to sleep but a field or ditch; children, dogs; people squinting along dusty roads, destinations unknown.

There are young men in Verdun now, men of hope and sweetness, who wait on my table in restaurants, she thought, who smile when they bring my food and wine, try out their English and smile again when I bring forth a few sentences in the French language. One such boy had served her last night on a restaurant ship docked on a canal. It was a piece of heaven there, quiet and lovely in the haunted air. No fixed bayonets for them. It seemed like a miracle to her that they were there.

She thought of the French soldier, Jacques Péricard, whose memorial plaque she had seen in a wood in the Verdun sector: *Ici, le 6 Avril 1915, L'Adjudant Jacques Péricard, du 95ème Regiment d'Infanterie, au cours d'une violente attaque ennemie, lança a ses compagnons blessés et hors de combat, le cri memorable: "Debout les Morts!"* (Here, the 6th of April 1915, Adjutant Jacques Péricard ... the memorable cry: "Arise the Dead!")

They shall not pass!

"I think you would be taken out of yourself here," she wrote on a postcard, to someone she thought would be receptive. "It would blow your mind."

She would take the postcards down to the hotel lobby, where the concierge would find stamps for them and would mail them to far-off places. Later, she and James and a few of the others would go out to the quiet streets to find a café. There was so much to think about. She had come to find something of her young father. He was here; something of him would always be here, as surely as he belonged to the countryside of England.

Soon she would leave France. Perhaps something of her spirit would remain here, as his had remained. Now he lay in a country churchyard in Sussex where he belonged, a few miles from where he had been born, a beautiful journey between those places, a natural landscape, over fields and woods, as the crow flies. If there were a soul, perhaps his soul rested more serenely now that she had walked across the Lens-La Bassée road, deliberately, standing upright, without fear. *Mais avec tristesse, toujour la tristesse.*

Vengeance is mine, sayeth the Lord. Those words came to her. Restitution was within her own grasp in some small degree, not least by her presence there. One can vow to celebrate memory, not to forget. One can write.

co "What does it all mean?" she had asked Bob, their guide.

"There is no meaning, other than what you can see and imagine."

He might have added: "If there is, I don't know it yet."

Jo, the first-born to May and Jim, travelled in her seventy-third year to Lille in north-eastern France. The Germans had occupied Lille in 1915, a little east and north of Loos. She went with the man she loved, older and more frail than she, on a brief adventure. They went by train from Sussex in south-east England, all the way there, through the channel tunnel. They walked the streets, sat in pavement cafés, felt the freedom, slept there for two nights. Then they walked to the station to return home. The liberation of Lille had been an objective of the Allies, a victory not to be seen by Jim and those others of the 8th Battalion of the Queen's Own Royal West Kent Regiment.

Jo had not gone there consciously to find the young Jim, so she told Lizzie on her return. "I wish I had known him when he was young," she said. He had been fifty years old when Jo was born.

Lizzie wrote in her diary: "Almost a century has gone by since he took ship from Southampton, crossed the dark, choppy water to France, not knowing how much longer he had to live. That is true of all of us. Yet for the young, their lives are stolen from them by murder, an unnatural death when war is waged. It is natural for the old to contemplate their mortality."

She thought of the time when their home in Sussex had been bombed on the 11th November, 1940, when another war had come to them, this time bringing her and Jo into it in its fury. Jim had rescued his war medals from the ruins. One was for valour, a bronze star and crossed swords. And he rescued his framed "honourably discharged" certificate, which stated that he had "served with Honour and was disabled in the Great War." Its glass and frame were smashed. Only one photograph of him survived from before that day.

"I was born before my time," he had said to her, in her early youth. She had not asked him what he meant.

⟡ Acknowledgements

I would like to acknowledge my editor, E. Alex Pierce, formerly of Cape Breton University, Nova Scotia, with many thanks, whose expertise, gentle critique and much encouragement kept me engaged. She is now senior editor with the Boularderie Island Press. Also I wish to thank my mentors at the writing studio at the Banff Centre for the Arts, Alberta — Greg Hollingshead and Edna Alford — who, in 2006, gave me much encouragement to make a start on the war stories.

∞ About the Author

Elizabeth Langridge was born in 1938 in the south of England, in the county of Kent, and grew up in Kent and Sussex, surrounded by beautiful countryside. Her earliest memories are of the Second World War. She lived in a rural area about thirty-five miles directly south of the east end of London, which was very heavily bombed because of the docks on the Thames. The enemy bombers went directly over her and her family. They could see London burning on the horizon at night. Their home was bombed in November, 1940. The family escaped with their lives, but not much else.

The war was still on when, at age four, she started at the village school, where there was a bomb shelter in the playground. Those memories of war and how people dealt with it, their courage and bravery, their common sense, their humour, have remained with her.

She trained to be a nurse, although her first love was writing. In 1966 she married a Canadian who was in London working for two years. That year they came to Toronto to live. They have three children.

The story is for all those who suffered and endured during the two World Wars, which were not of their making. May they not be forgotten.